TAMING the BRIDE

Brides of Mayfair series – Book 2

MICHELLE MCMASTER

Published by Michelle Killen
ISBN-13: 978-0-9947817-3-4

Cover Art by The Killion Group, Inc.
Interior Formatting by Author E.M.S.

CHAPTER ONE

London, 1816

"There, Miss—" Dolly said as she yanked Prudence's plunging neckline quite decidedly lower, "ye looks just like a proper Drury Lane trollop. Sort o' like me when I was plyin' the trade."

"I do look most convincing, thanks to your expert touch, Dolly," Prudence replied, assessing her reflection in the mirror.

She had done this so many times, yet still the sight of herself thus dressed—or *undressed*, as it were—still surprised her, to say the least. Thanks to Dolly's ministrations, Prudence's breasts swelled enticingly over the tight, red satin bodice, like cream-puffs rising out of a pan. Her skirts were hiked up to expose a generous length of her thigh, which was clad in a scandalous striped silk stocking. Her flame-colored hair, usually held captive in a severe knot, now fell wildly about her shoulders in a tangle of curls.

She looked like a harlot.

Which was exactly what she wanted to look like.

She wondered if she would she ever get used to it. But what choice did she have?

Dolly bent down to tuck Prudence's skirts up around the red satin garter that hugged the top of her thigh. "That red hair o' yours naturally draws the eye," she pronounced, "and when they see this shapely leg—ye'll be stealin' all the gents away from the proper lightskirts, or my name ain't Dolly Simms."

Apparently satisfied with her handiwork, Dolly regarded Prudence with a serious expression. "But miss, are ye sure ye should be doin' this? A young lady like ye walkin' the streets—well, it don't seem right, it don't. Ye should be settin' at the fire with yer needlepoint, not dressin' up like a tart and lurkin' about London at night."

"I like to think of it as more of a treasure hunt," Prudence said, patting her friend's arm. "And I have Mungo with me for protection. How else am I to find more students to keep you company at the Atwater Finishing School for Young Ladies? Why, you and I would never have met if I didn't make a habit of walking the streets."

"That may be true, miss, but for ye to be puttin' yerself in danger for the likes o' us—"

"The 'likes' of who?" Prudence said, cocking an eyebrow. "There are only *ladies* at the Atwater School, Dolly—no 'likes' of anyone at all. And there is no danger. None that I can't handle, at any rate."

Dolly laughed. "If ye say so, miss."

"I do, Dolly," she confirmed. "Danger or no danger, it is our duty to help those who are not as fortunate as ourselves. That is what Papa taught me—that education is the great equalizer of society. With the Atwater Finishing School for Young Ladies, I intend to take as many unfortunate girls off the street as I can, and give them a quality education. It is what Papa would have wanted to do himself, if he had lived longer."

"Lud!" Dolly exclaimed. "What would 'e say if 'e saw ye now—lookin' like a such a lewd hussy? I daresay 'e wouldn't let ye go about town in such a manner, no matter what ye say."

Prudence felt a lump form in her throat and promptly swallowed it. "He would understand the necessity of such actions," she said, quietly. "I'm sure he would."

Dolly put an arm around Prudence's shoulder and gave a gentle squeeze. "An' so 'e would. Yer father must 'ave been quite a man indeed. Raised a right fine lady, so 'e did—and ye just a girl when yer poor mother died. She'd be proud of such a courageous daughter, I'll reckon."

Dolly smiled warmly at her. "I remember the night ye come across me, miss...rainin' as 'ard as it was, and ye tryin' t' pass ye'self off as a lightskirt. Ye looked like a drowned rat, so ye did. If ye 'adn't taken me home with ye, well it don't bear thinkin' about. I 'adn't eaten for days, and there was no work that night. Probably would o' died if it 'adn't been for ye. And now thanks to ye, I've got a real job as a housekeeper. I thank ye miss—ye and Lady Weston both."

Prudence fastened the clasps on some cheap-looking earbobs and said, "I shudder to think of our patroness's reaction to knowing I was dressed like this, out on the streets myself. Lady Weston might very well pull her support from the Atwater School, and we need her funds to stay afloat. We must strive to keep my nocturnal adventures a secret from the dear old lady."

"Not t' worry, miss," Dolly replied. "I've told a few white lies in me time. I can tell a few more."

"Thank you, Dolly. Now, be a dear and tell Mungo that I will be down in a few moments."

Dolly nodded and left Prudence alone in her bedchamber.

Prudence applied the finishing touch to her costume, fastening a custom-made garter around her thigh. It held a sheath and a sharp little dagger which Mungo assured her would do considerable damage if need be.

It was Mungo who had crafted the garter for her out of leather, and he who had shown her how to defend herself with a blade. So far, she had never had to use the skills the former pirate had taught her. Settling her skirts to conceal the weapon, she hoped she never would.

Looking at the clock, Prudence threw her cloak over her shoulders and headed downstairs. It was almost time for the theater to let out. And that was when most of the customers would come by, looking for a little more entertainment after they'd enjoyed a conventional performance. The streetwalkers would be waiting for them in their usual places. And Prudence would be waiting for the streetwalkers.

"Ah, Miss Atwater," Mungo said, stooping his towering form to bow as she entered the salon. "Ye look delightful this evening."

"Delightful?" Dolly said, quizzically. "She don't look delightful. She looks a disgrace, just as she should." She fussed with Prudence's hair and adjusted the violet silk cloak about her shoulders. "There. Every harlot should be so lucky."

"Thank you for all your help, Dolly," Prudence said, smiling at her friend. "But Mungo, we must make haste. The theater will be letting out. Have you the carriage ready?"

"Yes, Miss. And 'ave you that little dagger I give ye?"

Prudence patted her thigh. "Right here, Mungo."

"But ye won't need t' use it with ol' Mungo around," he

said, smiling a gap-toothed grin. "I still got a few pirate tricks in me yet, miss, never fear."

"What would I do without you, Mungo? And you, Dolly—" Prudence asked.

"Probably some more lady-like things than this," Dolly muttered.

Prudence chuckled and took Mungo's offered arm. "Alas, duty calls. Don't wait up."

"But ye knows I always do, miss," Dolly answered.

Mungo opened the door to the carriage and handed Prudence in. Soon they were on their way, and the clip-clop of the horse's hooves echoed down the dark cobblestone street. As she stared out the window, Prudence thought of the task that lay ahead of her this evening.

How many girls could she reach tonight? And how many would she never have the chance to help at all? It was the latter thought that sent a chill to the pit of her stomach.

Prudence had to show these unfortunate women that there was a better way...that there was hope. She had already done so successfully with almost a dozen girls. She hoped to add to their number tonight.

The carriage stopped down the lonely street where it usually did. She heard Mungo hop down from the top and then the door swung open, his big strong hand reaching in to help her out. He spoke a few words to the driver instructing him to wait. Then they headed down the dark narrow lane towards the Theater District.

"Why does ye go t' all this trouble, miss?" Mungo asked. "For a bunch o' whores? I mean, I think it's lovely, ye dressin' up an' all, but why don't I just swipe a few for ye? Save a lot o' time, it would."

"No, Mungo," she replied. "They must come to the

school of their own free will. Kidnapping these girls would do no good. They'd simply run away. One thing my father taught me was that you can't force happiness on a person. They must reach for it themselves."

Prudence motioned for them to stop behind a leafy oak. The light from a nearby gaslamp fell in a dappled pattern across Mungo's face and made him look even more terrifying than usual. Prudence wanted to laugh, for in truth Mungo Church was as gentle and faithful as an old dog, though he liked to play the roaring lion. Tonight, she would need the lion's protection as she went on the hunt.

"I see a few girls across the street, there," Prudence said. "I'll stand here for awhile and make my way over to them. You may keep watch from behind this tree, Mungo, but keep well-hidden. No one must see that you are with me. If I need help, I'll scream."

Mungo nodded and folded his arms across his chest. "I'll be beside ye before the first scream can pass yer lips, miss."

"Wish me luck," she said, turning toward the street.

"Good luck, then," he said and gave her a nod.

Prudence walked to the corner, pushing up her breasts as if they were feather pillows that needed to be fluffed. She shook her hair and arranged it over her shoulders. Then she pinched her cheeks to make them rosy, though she didn't know what good it would do in the dark.

She stood for awhile, keeping to the shadows as she watched the passersby amble down the street. A few gentlemen walked by, some looking at her with leering grins, and some ignoring her completely.

Soon a dark-haired young girl appeared on the next corner. She eyed Prudence warily from the shadows, like a frightened alley-cat looking for food. Her clothes were shabby, much shabbier than Prudence's costume, and her face looked gaunt and smudged with dirt. She couldn't have been older than sixteen.

Prudence wondered how long the girl had been coming to this corner. Weeks? Months? A sick feeling swam in her gut. But as the girl made eye contact again, Prudence felt the rush of promise in her heart. This could be the Atwater School's next student.

Prudence began to stroll toward the girl nonchalantly, as if she were simply looking for a better spot to peddle her wares.

But something made her stop.

She felt a presence near her, quite close, in fact. Whoever it was, she would have to handle it like an experienced streetwalker or risk destroying her disguise. Hadn't she done it before?

Forcing her nerves to stay calm, she turned slowly.

A man leaned back against the wrought-iron fence. He seemed to be lounging there, as if in a favorite club, with his arms folded easily across his chest and his glossy boots crossed at the ankles.

He was dressed in a fashionably cut frock coat, which looked almost black in the lamplight. His neck cloth was tied in the latest fashion and his shiny beaver hat perched at the perfect angle upon his head. Dark curly hair framed a face that could only be described as devilishly handsome.

Prudence realized that he was grinning at her. And in the shadows, his eyes—which seemed to be as black as the night around them—sparkled mischievously.

"Without appearing to be bold," the man said in a languid voice, "may I ask what it is you are doing?"

Prudence winked at him and shifted her shoulders. Trying to emulate Dolly's cockney accent, she said, "Just plyin' the trade, Guvna. And not ta worry—I likes 'em bold."

He chuckled, saying, "Do you, now? I must say I find that surprising."

"Ye shouldn't be surprised, sir," she replied. "I mean, me bein' a trollop an all."

"And yet I am," he said, smiling and standing away from the fence, "for you look about as much like a trollop as I do."

"Oh, Guvna!" Prudence exclaimed, feigning injury. "Yer hurtin' me feelin's, now. Be assured, sir, that I am a trollop. Of the first order."

With a sweeping bow, he said, "My apologies, madam. I am mistaken. I did not mean to insinuate that you were anything less than Drury Lane's most experienced, most highly regarded, most sought after trollop in recent history."

Prudence glanced over at the girl she'd been watching on the next corner. She was ambling down the street, presumably to find a better location.

Prudence would have to move fast or risk losing her.

She smiled again at the man. "So right, sir—so right. Ye've hit the nail on the 'ead. And now, I must go join me friend, there. Good evenin'."

She made to turn away, but the man's voice stopped her, though why it should, she didn't know. Perhaps it was the velvety smoothness of it, or the complete confidence of his tone that made her freeze as if suddenly rooted to the spot.

"But you have not given me a chance to ask for the pleasure of your company this evening. And I would so enjoy the pleasure of your company, little flower."

The man stepped 'round and stood directly in front of her, blocking her path. He reached out to touch a tendril of her hair, and for a reason Prudence couldn't fathom, she let him.

"You see," he continued, gently twirling the hair around his finger, "I know your secret, Lady Trollop."

Prudence swallowed. "My secret?"

He stepped closer. *Oh, where was Mungo? And why wasn't she calling for his help?*

But all Prudence could do was stare at this dark stranger who stood so close to her and curled her hair about his finger as if it was the most natural thing in the world for him to do.

"Right away, it was obvious to me that you did not belong here," he began. "And it took a few moments to understand why. But now that I do, I wish to help you."

"You do?" Prudence said, confused.

"Yes, my sweet." He touched her face lightly with the back of his knuckles. The intimate sensation of his warm skin brushing against hers was shocking, yet exquisite.

"You see, now that I know the truth," he said softly, "I've decided I would like nothing more than to oblige you by being your *first paying customer*."

CHAPTER TWO

"**M**y first *paying* customer?" Prudence stammered.

"Why yes, unless of course you would like to waive your fee," he replied.

The man was as arrogant as the day was long.

She forced a smile. "Don't believe I would, sir. Ye'll excuse me, but I must go join me friend, there, who, as ye can see, 'as been waitin' for me the entire time ye've kept me talkin'. Yoo-hoo, Sally!" She waved frantically at the girl across the street, who was not even looking her way.

He laughed out loud, saying, "Ah! I see the problem. But it is easily remedied, I assure you."

"Appreciate the concern, Guvna, but I must be off now," she said, trying to step round him and watching in vain as the girl walked farther and farther away.

"Not only is this your first night as a light-skirt," he continued, "but you are a *virgin* as well." He polished his fingernails on his sleeve, then looked back at her with a sly grin. "I would be perfect for you. Gentle as you could ever hope for, and lots of experience deflowering virgins. A skilled, considerate lover. Why, if anyone should charge a fee, it should be me."

"Is that so?" Prudence said, amazed at the man's blatant arrogance.

"You'd be wise to accept my offer," he said. "And as you can see, your friend has abandoned you."

The girl was nowhere in sight.

He braced his legs apart and folded his arms across his chest in a stance of victory. "Come, my sweet—it is a generous offer for a girl in your position."

Prudence felt her blood boil. It was men like these—pompous, unfeeling, selfish men—who provided the market where wayward girls would sell their bodies to strangers. And to top it off, he had made her lose her quarry. She felt nothing but contempt for this man.

Pausing for a moment, Prudence smiled sweetly at him. "I do thank ye for the generous offer, sir, but alas, I must decline. Y'see, I'd rather eat broken glass than sell meself to ye this evenin'—or any other evenin', for that matter."

"What's this?" he asked. "You're refusing me?"

"Ah! Ye 'ave a mind as sharp as a rapier," Prudence replied sarcastically. "Good of ye to catch on."

Instead of being offended by her words, the man seemed amused by them—by *her*. He smiled and said, "You might want to reconsider, my dear. I can assure you that you'll find me a more congenial partner than most men who will proposition you this evening."

Prudence huffed. "I must not 'ave explained meself clearly just a moment ago, so I'll try again. Y'see, sir, I'd rather slit me own throat with a wee butter knife than spend one more minute in the presence of a windy, rattle-trap rake such as ye'self. Now, 'ave I made meself perfectly clear?"

He gave a sympathetic grin and replied, "My poor little

flower. I see now how frightened you are. Otherwise you would not try so hard to get rid of me. Afraid that you might melt in my arms, are you? Afraid that you'll enjoy my attentions all too much?"

"'Course not!" she protested.

"Prove it, then."

Prudence put her hands on her hips and narrowed her eyes. "I don't 'ave ta prove anythin' to the likes o' you."

"Ah, you see? You *are* afraid to test yourself," he pronounced. "And I must say, I can't blame you. There isn't a woman alive who can resist my embrace, or my kiss. I wouldn't trust myself either, if I were you."

Oh, the absolute cheek!

Prudence stared silently at him for some moments.

How she would like to humiliate this man! But that was not why she had come out to Drury Lane this evening. She was wasting time. Even though she had lost the first girl, there were others she could help tonight, if she could just get rid of this pest of a man.

Still, if she could embarrass him—obviously a regular customer, perhaps she would be doing some good after all. Perhaps she could eliminate one more patron from buying the favors of the poor girls she was trying to help.

"Oh, I trust meself completely, sir," Prudence replied haughtily. "I'll prove it to ye, then."

"Shall you, now?" he said, cocking an eyebrow.

"Yes, I shall, sir. Ye'll see that yer embrace'll not affect me in the least."

"And my kiss?" he whispered, as he pulled her back around a tree and into strong, well-muscled arms.

"N-nor that, neither," she said, gulping as he brought her full against him.

Gads, was she really going to let this stranger kiss her?

As his wicked mouth descended toward hers, it seemed that she was.

The stranger's intoxicating kiss created the most alarming sensations all over her body—in parts that were nowhere near where she was being kissed! Tingles danced up her spine, heat flooded slowly through her limbs, and her knees seemed to forget their purpose in helping her to stand.

But strangest of all was that she didn't seem to care one whit about any of that.

All at once she felt the stranger being torn away from her, grunting in pain.

Opening her eyes, she saw a frightening figure looming in the shadows. Mungo—looking every inch the blood-thirsty pirate—had one hand around the man's throat and was lifting him practically off the ground.

"Ye wants I should squeeze 'is neck so 'is eyes pops out of 'is 'ead, miss?" Mungo said, grinning like a madman.

The dark stranger looked down at her and rasped something incomprehensible.

"That won't be necessary, Mungo," Prudence said, trying to regain her composure.

"Oh, but it's been so long!" Mungo pleaded. "'Ow 'bout I slits 'is throat, then? I brought me nice sharp dagger, so I did." The shiny blade flashed in the lamplight as he raised it to the man's throat.

"If you had a dull knife, I might consider it," Prudence replied, crossly. "You shouldn't have come over, Mungo. I didn't call for you, did I?"

"But 'e was kissin' ye, miss, and gropin' ye like there was no tomorrow. Ye didn't want 'im t' keep maulin' ye, now, did ye?"

She glared up at the stranger who had just made a fool of her and watched him squirm in Mungo's grasp. "Of course not. But this creates a problem. This man might very well call for the constable—considering that you're strangling him—and I haven't even begun my work for the night. We must get rid of him, quickly."

"Well, I made me suggestions," Mungo shrugged. "Ye didn't seem t' like any o' those."

Prudence regarded the struggling stranger and tapped her chin as a plan formed in her mind. Reluctantly, she said, "I'm afraid there is only one thing to do."

Gadzooks, but he was cold.

Alfred struggled to open his eyes. He blinked several times to try to focus his vision, but saw only the dimness of the lamp-lit night.

After a few moments, he realized the reason the world looked so strange was because his head was lying on the cold, wet grass, and everything that normally stood vertically now seemed to be horizontal. He must have been royally in his cups tonight to end up like this.

He tried to get up, but a sharp pain in his head made him groan and stay where he was.

Which was a good question. *Where the devil was he?*

As he lay immobile, he realized that he was shivering, and his teeth were chattering. All in all, he felt quite decidedly terrible.

He opened his eyes again and willed himself to get up. Ughh.

With all the strength he could muster, he pushed himself up and leaned on one arm. It was then that Alfred realized why he was so bloody cold.

He was naked.

Damnation, he was naked!

Then, it all came back to him—the flame-haired prostitute teasing him on the street, the heated kiss, the huge man who came out of nowhere, holding Alfred aloft and nearly strangling the very breath from his body.

And then, blackness.

Alfred reached back and felt the lump on the back of his head. The big oaf had knocked him out with those meaty fists of his. And then the pair had robbed him.

He slammed his fist against the ground in frustration. At least they had seen fit to deposit him behind some bushes, so that all of London wouldn't see him in nothing more than his skin.

He looked around to see if anyone was about. How on earth was he going to get himself home like this? He couldn't exactly walk down the avenue without a stitch of clothing on.

Then in the faint lamplight he spied his hat just a few feet away, sitting up-ended on the ground. He grabbed it and looked inside, and found his wallet—still holding all his money. His watch and quizzing glass were also there.

Standing, Alfred held the hat in front of the most private part of all and hid behind a shrub. With any luck, a coach would drive by and he could hail it without the whole street seeing him. At least he still had money to hire a coach.

He turned his head at the sound of voices approaching.

A man and a woman strolled down the street. They would soon pass by.

God in Heaven, let them keep walking.

They stopped directly in front of the bushes that hid Alfred from view. He held his breath and tried not to move, willing them to move on. But they paid his thoughts no heed.

"Oh, Lavinia...my dearest," the man whispered loudly.

"You are surely the most ravishing creature alive. Let me kiss you."

Alfred couldn't help but watch this uncomfortable display through the lamp-lit branches. He recognized the man as Viscount Seton, a member of Alfred's club.

Damnation! He didn't want to have to explain himself to this dimwit. If Seton got sight of him, the story would be all over London in a matter of hours.

Alfred held still and watched Seton drool slobbering kisses over the poor creature in his arms. Though she was obviously a member of the *ton*, the young woman didn't seem to mind Seton's attentions.

Probably counting his money in her head to keep herself occupied, Alfred thought.

As the sneeze came upon him, Alfred tried vainly to hold it in. But it only made his lips smack together loudly as a resounding "Ahh-CHOO!" echoed in the night.

At the noise, Lord Seton opened his eyes and stared directly at Alfred. It seemed to take a few moments for Seton to recognize that the thing he saw lurking in the bushes was a man's face.

And it was the face of someone he knew.

"Egads...*Weston?*" the man asked, incredulous. "Is that you in there? Whatever are you doing lurking about in the bushes, man?"

"Lurking?" Alfred said, non-chalantly. "Certainly not. Just looking for my wallet. I seem to have lost it."

Seton nodded. "Ah, bloody bad luck. Lady Fairfax and I will help you look for it, then."

"No!" Alfred exclaimed, then cleared his throat and said more calmly, "I mean—there is no need. I would not want to interrupt your evening, Seton. I'll find it soon enough, I'm sure."

"Don't be such a bloody hero, Weston," Lord Seton

said, moving about the bushes. "We would not dream of leaving you here to look for it alone, would we, my dear?"

Alfred ducked into the bushes, wincing as the branches scratched his skin.

The little red-haired strumpet would pay for this indignity.

"Weston?" Seton called. "Where on earth have you got to, man?"

"In here," Alfred replied from the sanctuary of the foliage. "I think I've found it. Yes, there it is. Bloody good luck. I thank you for your help, Seton. You need not detain yourselves further."

"At least join us for a late supper, Weston," Lord Seton pressed, peering into the dark branches that hid Alfred from view. "Come out of there and we'll make an evening of it, the three of us. Eh, Weston? Weston?"

In desperation, Alfred pushed himself through the bushes. He felt the sting of more cuts from the dense branches as he forced his way through to the other side.

"Weston? Where are you?" he heard Seton calling.

Now Alfred was stuck out on the street, which was, for the moment, blessedly empty. Still holding his hat in front of him, Alfred ran, feeling the cold cobblestones beneath his feet and the chilly night air touching him in places he usually kept clothed.

"Weston!" he heard Seton shouting from behind him. "Have you gone bloody daft? You're *naked*, man!"

At the commotion on the street, a few doors opened and heads popped out to see what was amiss. The gawking faces passed by in a blur as Alfred rounded the next corner and dashed behind a hedge. Panting, he stopped and caught his breath.

Now, all he had to do was pray that a coach would

come by in the very near future. He folded his arms in front of him and did a little dance to keep warm.

He wanted to leap for joy when a coach rolled toward him, but decided against drawing any more attention to himself than he already had.

Alfred waved his hat furiously from around the hedge. The driver saw the movement and stopped, craning his neck to see who hailed him. Alfred sprang out of the dark foliage and dashed into the safety of the cab. Sighing with relief, he leaned out the open window and called his address out to the driver.

The coach jerked ahead and started down the street. Alfred settled back in the seat, trying to ignore the strange feeling of being completely naked in the cab of a coach. He would be home soon, he told himself, home and in his robe, drinking a nice brandy by the fire.

And while he drank the brandy and warmed himself up and stared at the orange flames of the fire, he would plan how to find the red-headed strumpet who had robbed him and left him naked in the night.

And exactly how he would make her pay.

CHAPTER THREE

Alfred reached for his cup of coffee and downed a gulp. He looked across the table at his Great-Aunt Withypoll, who was still engrossed with the *Times*, then back at his plate of poached eggs, braised ham and biscuits with raspberry compote.

Cook had served up another magnificent breakfast this morning. And it was a good thing, too. Great-Aunt Withypoll had a very discerning palate.

"I say, what's this, now? What's this say?" the ancient lady said, squinting her eyes and bringing the paper right up to her nose.

"My dear Auntie, you must arrange to get spectacles," Alfred said, taking a bite of ham. "Dr. Trask has recommended it."

Lady Weston lowered the paper and glared at him. "You know I refuse to listen to that imbecile. Spectacles! Do you think my ancestor, the great Saxon Queen Withypoll—for whom I was named—wore spectacles? I think not. And I don't need spectacles to see that you've made the *Times*, m'boy." She whacked the paper with a gnarled hand and stared at him with disapproving eyes.

Alfred reached for the paper, but she grabbed it away. "I'll read it, young pup," she said, then cleared her throat and read aloud:

"WHO IS THE MYSTERY MAN OF DRURY LANE?

London theater-goers were treated to a unique sight last evening, as a mysterious man wearing nothing but a *beaver* was seen skulking about the bushes in wait there, to expose himself thus unclothed to innocent passersby.

Lord S_____ and his *companion*, Lady F_____ encountered the strange fellow after taking in a performance of 'Much Ado About Nothing,' at the Theater, though there is speculation as to the mystery man's identity as being that of Lord W_____, younger son of the Earl of H_____.

Apparently, after laying in wait and spying on Lord S_____ and Lady F_____ in his naked state, Lord W_____, having been caught indulging in any number of lewd solitary amusements, ran down the street wearing nothing so much as his hat (though not upon his head!).

It is a mystery as to what may have caused Lord W_____'s confounding actions last evening in Drury Lane. But tonight's theater-goers are advised to keep watch for the be-hatted Mystery Man, as they may forgo the price of a ticket and be just as entertained."

Alfred remained silent, waiting for the second wave of the onslaught.

The little woman stared at him with ice-blue eyes, which though clouded with age, still had the power to make a man quake in his boots.

As Alfred was trying not to do now.

"Nothing to say, eh?" she asked. "Nothing to say about all of London laughing at your schoolboy shenanigans?" Lady Weston shook her head in disappointment. "My word, a man your age running about naked as the day you were born. Is it true?"

Alfred sighed. "I'm afraid it is."

"Well, I never heard of such a thing," Lady Weston replied. "No doubt a bad habit you picked up in Italy when you were on your Tour—well, I don't hold with it! You may be my favorite great-nephew, Alfred, but you try my patience. And it would be unwise to take advantage of an old woman's affections, even if you no longer need me."

"I will always need you, Auntie," he replied, truthfully.

She looked unimpressed. "I admit, I favored you while you were growing up, and I fully supported you as my late husband's heir to the barony, but now I am not so sure. Your brother Richard would never indulge in such scandalous actions."

"My brother Richard is no fun," Alfred replied, rising from his chair. He took her hand and pressed his lips to the back of it. "I swear, Auntie, it was all a misunderstanding. You must believe me."

"Too much like my Bertram, you are, my boy," she said, reluctantly giving a smile. "Same devilish eyes. Hmph. If I didn't know better, I'd say you were playing me like a violin, as you do with all the women."

She laughed then and patted his arm. "Ah, Alfred...you always could make me laugh, even when I was angry with you. And that is why you are my favorite. But I am still quite cross with you. All of London will be tittering with amusement at your unfortunate adventure...and the Weston name should *never* be tittered at. You will have to find a way to make amends."

"Anything, Auntie," Alfred said, leaning back against the table. "My wish is your command, as always,"

Lady Weston gave a devilish smile of her own and said, "I have something in mind—though it would not be a difficult task for a man such as you. And it may help to quiet the gossip's wagging tongues, as well. But tell me more of what happened last night."

"It is quite embarrassing, Auntie, and I shall spare you the details," Alfred replied. "But last night, as I was returning from the Theater, I was set upon by thieves—a man and a woman. As the woman distracted me with conversation and pretty smiles, her man, a big burly oaf, came out of his hiding place and with one hand about my throat, tried to choke the very breath from me. For a moment, I thought they had murder on their minds, but at the woman's order, her man knocked me out with a blow to the back of my noggin, see?"

Alfred pointed to the lump on his head, and heard Great-Aunt Withypoll gasp as she felt the hard bump there.

"My dear, boy, are you alright?"

Alfred turned back to face her and waved away her concerns. "Oh, yes. Good thing I also inherited Great-Uncle Bertram's hard head. At any rate, the next thing I knew, I woke up on the ground, hidden below some bushes, without a stitch of clothing on. This woman and her accomplice had made off with my clothes—but curiously left me my hat, watch and wallet—still full of money."

Great-Aunt Withypoll nodded, looking suitably

impressed. "A strange tale, indeed. What sort of thief would steal only the clothes upon your person and leave your valuables behind?"

Alfred shook his head, saying, "I've asked myself the same question. And my clothes would never have fit that big ape who so enjoyed choking me. It is a mystery, Auntie."

"But however did you get home?" she asked.

"After being spotted in my state of dishabille by Lord Seton, who obviously felt obliged to share the story with the *Times*, I ran down the street and took refuge in a hedgerow until a coach came by. I flagged it down and returned here."

Great-Aunt Withypoll's sapphire eyes twinkled with mischief. "And what did you use to flag down the coach, Alfred? Do tell."

Alfred smirked, amazed at her cheek. "My hat, madam...nothing but my hat. You know, for a woman at the grand age of eighty-seven, you have a terribly naughty mind."

"From whom do you think you inherited yours?" she asked, deadpan.

"Well, I would have hoped it was from Great-Uncle Bertram."

"No, no. Though you are the spitting image of him." Lady Weston began to rise from her chair and Alfred assisted the tiny white-haired woman to her feet. "Let us go outside into the garden, Alfred, where I will tell you more about your task."

They walked slowly down the hall, each step short and carefully placed on the white marble floor. Alfred felt the frailty of the old woman's grasp on his arm, felt the brittle bones of the gnarled fingers clinging so dependently to him.

He looked down at her and felt his heart warm with affection. This indomitable woman had been the closest thing he'd had to a mother for most of his life. She and her late husband, Bertram, had practically raised Alfred and his brother, Richard. She and Alfred had always been very close.

His father, the Earl of Harrington, had insisted upon naming his sons after great English kings. But he'd never had much time for them, and even less when his wife, Lady Harrington, abandoned her family and ran off to Italy. Alfred was only eight at the time.

Soon after, Lord Harrington had placed his sons with his uncle, the eleventh Baron Weston, and his wife, to raise. Lord Harrington's business commitments kept him very busy and he didn't want his sons raised by servants.

It was strange, but sometimes Alfred still dreamed of the day his mother left...that cold winter day when his world had changed forever. He, a grown man of thirty, was still haunted by an eight-year-old's broken heart. How pathetic.

He led Great-Aunt Withypoll outside into the back gardens of the townhouse. They walked slowly across the lush grass at the same steady pace, just as they did every day that she was in residence.

Great-Aunt Withypoll insisted on taking in an hour of fresh air each day, weather permitting, to invigorate her health, and it was obviously quite effective. For though her bones were becoming frail, her constitution was surely as strong as that of an ox.

He helped her to her seat on the marble bench next to her favorite pink rose bush and sat down beside her. "Now, Auntie, tell me what I must do to win back my place in your heart."

"Foolish boy," she replied. "I believe you are probably there to stay, after all. But you will certainly strengthen your position by fulfilling my task. All you need do is act as an escort to a young lady that I have taken under my wing—"

"Oh, Auntie," he said, sighing. "I am still not recovered from my last assignment as escort to one of your protégée's. Do you not remember Miss Honoria Walters and her penchant for eating onions? I squired her most dutifully without complaint about her breath, or her high-pitched giggle, or her propensity for tears, or the attentions of her tiny dog. Though I must say, Miss Walters was an improvement on the others you've forced me to escort about of late."

"You are too critical, Alfred," Great-Aunt Withypoll admonished. "And I am not getting any younger. I want to see you settled with a wife, and babies for me to spoil. And what does it matter *who* you marry, as long as she is young and healthy and able to provide you with children?"

"Well, it matters to the man doing the marrying."

"Ah, but you cannot refuse me this request, Alfred," she said. "Not ten minutes ago you promised that you would do anything I asked. Appearing in public will show your utter disregard for that offensive article in the *Times*. And though it is unfortunately true, you must take pains to act as if it were not true. Escorting a proper young lady to an entertainment of the *ton* will show you to be the picture of propriety. It is the only course of action, I'm afraid."

Alfred resigned himself to defeat. If his Auntie asked for the moon, he could not deny her.

"Alright, I'll do it," he said, finally. "I only hope that I survive this one."

"Oh, stop whining, m'boy!" she replied. "This one's a gem. You'll see. Miss Prudence Atwater is a very unique young woman."

"*Unique*? Is that your way of saying she looks like Medusa and has a temper to match?"

Great-Aunt Withypoll whacked his arm and he yelled, feigning injury.

"Behave," she warned, "or I'll give you something to yell about, m'boy. Now, you will escort Miss Atwater to Lady Townsend's ball in a week's time. I, of course, will be in attendance. I do so like to see the young people enjoying themselves."

Alfred looked at her quizzically. "Just who is this Miss Atwater, Auntie? Not another vicar's daughter, I hope?"

"Her father was a scholar, I believe," Lady Weston answered, thoughtfully. "Well, he must have been, for I met her at the library last month when you were away to Devonshire. She was carrying a stack of books almost as tall as herself. And then she dropped them all. Terribly unfortunate. Made a very loud noise. I of course commanded Barkley, who had escorted me there, to assist her in picking them up. She was wonderfully grateful and I was taken with her charming manner. Very bright girl. Pretty, too. She runs her late father's school—the Atwater Finishing School for Young Ladies, and *I* am its newest patroness."

"Patroness?" he asked, suddenly worried. "Auntie, is this wise? You should have consulted with me first."

"Oh, for goodness sake!" Lady Weston retorted. "I may be old, but I am *not* feebleminded. I am quite able to make my own decisions on such matters, m'boy, and don't you forget it. I have a singular feeling about this girl, Alfred."

"Just like you had a singular feeling about Miss Honoria Walters, and Miss Gertrude Tibbets, and Lady Clementia Bagley?" he asked.

Lady Weston waved her hand and chuckled. "Oh, no. I was wrong about all of those silly girls. But you'll see, m'boy. Miss Atwater is quite different. In a week's time, you'll see. You might even like her."

"In a week's time, then, Auntie," he said. "As you wish."

He helped her to her feet and they walked slowly back to the house. Alfred resigned himself to his fate with a sigh. If escorting his Great-Aunt's young protégés made her happy, then he would do it.

This wonderful lady had given him so much. It was the least he could do for her. Yet, in his heart he knew he should be doing much more. Great-Aunt Withypoll was right. She wasn't getting any younger.

Didn't he owe her the joy of holding his children in her arms before it was too late? Didn't he owe her the knowledge that the Weston name would carry on?

He had been putting off the idea of marriage for years, now. But perhaps he didn't have as long as he thought. Just because the great old lady seemed healthy as a horse, didn't mean she would live forever.

The only problem was that Alfred found the very thought of marriage abhorrent. Truthfully, it was nothing but a charade...an arrangement in which a man gave a woman his name and a share of his earthly possessions in exchange for the rights to her body—most importantly, her womb.

It was all about breeding, about heirs, and preservation of the family fortune. It was almost never about love.

Most husbands and wives he knew merely tolerated each other. They lived apart and saw each other only when necessary.

Except for his friends, Beckett and Isobel, of course. Lord and Lady Ravenwood, late of Barbados, were a true love match. Sometimes, when he watched Beckett and his wife together, speaking to each other only with their eyes, Alfred would feel a stab of jealousy. He knew that what he was seeing was so precious and so rare, he doubted that he would ever truly understand it, let alone possess it for himself.

His parents' marriage had been a sham—as his father told it—and at any rate, his mother wasn't around to explain her side of the story. She'd been traipsing about the continent since she'd left them, or so they'd heard, living in sin with an Italian Count Something-or-Other.

Alfred had looked for her on his Tour in Italy…

He'd looked everywhere he went.

They reached the back step to the house and Great-Aunt Withypoll leaned more heavily on Alfred's arm as he helped her up onto it. She stumbled a little and he stooped to catch her, feeling the old woman's frailness as he held her steady in his arms.

"Oh, thank you, my dear," she said, shakily. "I'm afraid my knees aren't what they used to be. Ah, well. I shouldn't complain, as I am still breathing."

Alfred chuckled. "I have no doubt you will be doing that for a long time, Auntie."

But would she? She had already lived to a very impressive age of eighty-seven years. How many more did she have, really?

As they made their way back to the salon, Alfred found himself thinking about Miss Prudence Atwater. And he hoped, for the sake of his Great-Aunt Withypoll and her fondest wishes for him, that Miss Atwater truly was different.

A week later, Alfred squired Lady Weston to Tattingstone's Circulating Library in Bedford Square.

Alfred's arm was becoming stiff, but he held it straight

and sturdy, supporting Great-Aunt Withypoll as they walked about the shelf-lined rooms. Of course, they had yet to peruse any books, as Tattingstone's was a favorite place for the *ton* to indulge in daytime socializing.

"Of course, you are coming to Lady Townsend's ball tomorrow night, Dorothea?" Great-Aunt Withypoll asked as they passed by the elderly Lady Abercrombie, who nodded and smiled in reply.

Alfred chuckled to himself. It seemed that practically the whole place would be attending Lady Townsend's ball tomorrow.

Since they had arrived a quarter of an hour ago, Alfred had noticed a few curious looks, a few whispers and knowing glances, undoubtedly about the unflattering article in the *Times*.

He'd been ribbed about it at his club but had succeeded in brushing it off—dismissing it as pure bunk. This appearance at the library would also work in his favor. And the ball tomorrow night would be the final stage of his campaign.

Alfred had no idea what to expect, really. When he pressed Great-Aunt Withypoll about details to the girl's appearance or temperament, she would merely answer that Miss Atwater was pretty and bright.

Must be unbearably ugly, then, he thought.

And overbearing.

And loud.

Well, it would all be over tomorrow night. He would have fulfilled his duty and would be free to engage in his own pursuits about town. He could hardly wait.

As they made their way around the south side of the gallery, Great-Aunt Withypoll stopped for a moment and squinted at something in the distance. Alfred followed her glance, but could not see who she was staring at.

"I say...is that...can it be she?" Great-Aunt Withypoll said.

"Who, Auntie?" he asked.

She sighed, replying, "Perhaps you are correct in advising me to acquire spectacles, Alfred, for I cannot say for certain, but I do believe I see Miss Prudence Atwater there."

"Where?" Alfred said, regarding a group of people milling about at the other end of the room.

"Yes! I was right," Lady Weston said, happily. "It is Miss Atwater. Come along, Alfred. You will be able to make her acquaintance before the ball tomorrow. Oh, what luck!"

This time, Great-Aunt Withypoll dragged him across the room toward the dense crowd.

"Miss Atwater? Miss Atwater!" Great-Aunt Withypoll called to a girl whose back was toward them, her head buried deep in a book.

Even before the girl turned, Alfred felt a familiar jolt of recognition in his gut.

Perhaps it was the fiery red hair that, even though pulled back into a demure knot, unavoidably caught the eye. Perhaps it was her bearing—the way she held her head and shoulders as she turned.

As the girl faced them, Alfred saw the look of surprise and shock spread over the girl's face.

He felt his blood heat with anger...and something else just as dangerous. For the girl standing before him was none other than the Drury Lane strumpet.

CHAPTER FOUR

Prudence stared at the dark stranger who stood next to Lady Weston, and found herself quite unable to speak.

It was him.

The man from Drury Lane.

The one who had kissed her.

The man she had left laying naked and unconscious under a hedgerow.

For a fleeting moment she had thought he wouldn't recognize her—thought that perhaps he'd been in his cups that night and wouldn't remember much of what happened.

But the controlled fury that smoldered in his dark brown eyes made it quite clear that he *did* remember her...as well as everything that had happened between them.

Suddenly, she dropped the book she'd been reading. *The Complete Works of William Shakespeare* landed with a great thunk on the floor.

"Oh, my—Miss Atwater," Lady Weston exclaimed, "you are forever dropping your books. Alfred, my dear, would you be so kind as to retrieve Miss Atwater's book for her?"

The man stooped to pick up the heavy tome. He stood and handed it back to Prudence silently, but his eyes spoke their message quite clearly.

I know who you are.

"Miss Atwater," Lady Weston began, "I would like to introduce to you my great-nephew, Alfred, Baron Weston. He is the one I told you about. Lord Weston will be escorting you to Lady Townsend's ball tomorrow evening." She turned toward him. "Alfred, I am pleased to present to you Miss Prudence Atwater, proprietress of the Atwater Finishing School for Young Ladies."

Prudence felt her heart beating as if it were lodged in her throat.

Would this man expose her secret in front of Lady Weston?

With his dark stare never leaving her eyes, he slowly took her hand in his. It was warm and strong—just as she remembered. She struggled to keep her composure as Lord Weston performed a courtly bow over her hand.

"Miss Atwater," he said.

When he stood tall again, Prudence took a shaky breath and forced herself to meet his eyes. "Lord Weston."

"I should think you two will want to become better acquainted," Lady Weston said, eyes twinkling. "I shall go and sit with Lady Merton. And perhaps Alfred, you should ask Miss Atwater if she would like to take a turn about the room."

"Yes, Auntie," he replied. His voice had a slight edge to it. "I can think of nothing I would rather do at the moment. Miss Atwater?" He offered his arm.

It would cause a scandal if she refused, so Prudence reluctantly slipped her arm through Lord Weston's, and forced herself to smile. What was his game?

Lady Weston was already making her way to where a group of ladies sat in nearby chairs along the wall.

Prudence felt the muscles in Lord Weston's arm tense under her fingers. She dared to look up at him. "I daresay you are surprised to make my acquaintance again, my lord."

His eyes blazed with anger as he replied, "I daresay that I am. What do you think you are doing passing yourself off as a schoolteacher to my great-aunt?" He kept his voice low as they began to go about the room.

"I *am* a schoolteacher—"

"A schoolteacher who also leads another life as a light-skirt and a thief?" he demanded. "I'm sure you neglected to mention that before you asked Lady Weston to be your patroness—a situation that I intend to remedy, I assure you."

Prudence felt her stomach tie into a hard little knot.

Oh, this was not going well at all...

"I understand your shock, Lord Weston—"

"Do you?" he said. "You understand my astonishment that the young woman I am to escort to Lady Townsend's ball is the same woman who not only tried to seduce me on the street, but also robbed me of my clothes and left me to be the subject of a rather embarrassing article in the *Times*?"

Prudence bristled at the accusation. "I did *not* try to seduce you! And we did not set out to rob you—"

"Oh, didn't you?" he said sarcastically. "Well, whether or not you set out to rob me, you and your large friend did exactly that, after he nearly choked the very breath out of me. And as for seducing me, I recall quite clearly both your lips and your body pressing wantonly against mine. Surely, Miss Atwater, you remember doing *that*?"

Prudence felt her face heat with color.

33

He stopped and looked at her, and lowered his face close to hers. "Do you remember kissing me, Miss Atwater? Opening your mouth to me and letting me take my pleasure there? Do you?"

Prudence remained silent, held prisoner by the expression in his eyes and the truth of his words.

"Well, *do you?*" he demanded, hotly.

"Yes," she whispered.

He glared down at her, saying, "Well, I am glad to see that you are at least honest about that. As for the rest of it—"

"It is the truth, I assure you," Prudence insisted. "I am not a thief! I run the Atwater School. And when you came upon me that night, I was out searching for new students."

He laughed, but it wasn't a pleasant sound. "What do you take me for? A complete imbecile?"

Prudence felt her own temper flare. "Whether or not I take you for a complete imbecile, Lord Weston, I shall repeat that I am indeed the proprietress of the Atwater Finishing School for Young Ladies. And the type of young ladies I endeavor to teach are the ones that walk the streets of London at night, scandalous though it may be."

He placed her hand in the crook of his arm again and they continued about the room. She could feel the power of the muscles in his arm. It was very distracting.

"And how much of this does my great-aunt know, if any?" he said.

Lady Weston smiled at them from across the room and Prudence forced herself to smile back. "She knows that my students come from the streets. And she supports my ideas about education. She wants to help these girls, Lord Weston, even if you don't."

"And does she know about your own nocturnal adventures, Miss Atwater?"

Prudence replied, "No. She does not. And I do not believe she would approve of such a thing, which is why I did not tell her."

"And how do you think she would react if she knew that you had lied to her?" he asked. "That having accosted her great-nephew and stolen his clothes, you are indeed a thief. And what's more, that you are responsible for an article appearing in the *Times* that was embarrassing to her as well as to me?"

Prudence tried to steady her breathing. It felt as if her heart was being crushed by a huge fist. "I don't know."

"Well, I do know," Lord Weston replied. "She would not be pleased. In fact, she might be persuaded to withdraw her support from your school, Miss Atwater. Quite easily, indeed."

This could not be happening.

Prudence desperately needed Lady Weston's support, or the future of the school would be uncertain. In truth, it might not have a future at all.

She took a deep breath and met Lord Weston's eyes. "Please...I implore you. Do not tell Lady Weston the truth of our association."

"You want me to lie to her, then? As you have done?" he said with unmasked contempt.

"I beseech you, Lord Weston," Prudence continued, "on behalf of my girls. They are depending on me in order to realize their dreams of a better life. Please do not turn Lady Weston against me. For myself, I accept the consequences of having Mungo knock you out and steal your clothes—"

"Mungo?" he asked, cocking a brow.

"Mungo Church," she replied. "My bodyguard."

"Ah...the one with the meaty fists," he said. "I'd thought him a pirate."

"He is," Prudence answered. "He *was*, I mean. I found him one night when I was out looking for students. He'd been injured quite badly in a brawl. I took him home with me to the school and we nursed him back to health. Since then, he's taken it upon himself to act as my bodyguard when I go about at night."

Lord Weston gave a bitter chuckle, saying, "Well, I can assure you that the man is very good at his job. I still have a lump on my head from his efforts."

"I am dreadfully sorry you were hurt, Lord Weston," she replied. "But knocking you out seemed the only course of action. I was afraid that you would have had us arrested."

"Perhaps I still should, Miss Atwater," he threatened.

She gulped down her fear at the prospect. "That is your decision, my lord. But I hope you will remember what I said about the girls at my school. It is *they* who you will be hurting, much more than me."

Lord Weston studied her with bold intensity, finally saying, "I will make an agreement with you, Miss Atwater. I will keep your secret. I will not tell my great-aunt anything about the first time we met that night in Drury Lane. But my silence will have a price. And it will not come cheaply."

What would this man deem to be a fair price? Prudence wondered. And what choice did she have but to pay it, whatever it was? "W-what exactly did you have in mind, my lord?" she stammered.

He looked thoughtful, obviously enjoying her uneasiness. "I do not yet know. But I assure you, Miss Atwater, I will think of something. I can safely say that it will not be anything of material value, but rather something you yourself will have to do for me. Those are my terms. Do you agree to them?"

Her heart thrummed painfully in her chest.

How could she agree to such a thing?

How could she not?

If she refused, she would lose the school. The girls would have nowhere to go but back to the streets that they were trying so hard to escape. But could she agree to be no better than this man's slave? What exactly would he ask of her?

The strange, cold feeling in her stomach told her the answer. She had no choice. She would have to pay the price for Lord Weston's silence, and pray that he would be honorable.

"I agree to your terms, my lord," she said. "In exchange for your silence, I shall pay whatever price you deem fit."

His dark eyes sparkled, and he gave a wry smile. "Very good, Miss Atwater. When I have decided on the price you are to pay, I will inform you. And now, I must return to my great-aunt. I fear that if you and I take anymore turns about the room, we will cause the gossips to speculate on the depth of our relationship. Until tomorrow night. We shall come 'round about eight to fetch you."

He bowed over her hand again, leaning toward her and said softly, "You might consider wearing that lovely little confection in red satin I saw you in that night. I must say, the plunging neckline suited you. And I very much enjoyed the view. Until tomorrow, Miss Atwater."

Prudence watched him walk away and tried to quell the wretched feeling that churned in her heart.

Until she paid her debt to him, the infuriating Lord Weston now virtually held her prisoner!

Alfred handed Great-Aunt Withypoll into the carriage and followed her inside. In a few moments they were heading away from the library and home to the townhouse in Mayfair.

"And how did you enjoy meeting Miss Atwater, Alfred?" Lady Weston asked as she settled herself into her seat. "Pretty little chit, is she not?"

"She was indeed pretty, Auntie, I agree."

"Mmm. And bright, as well," she said. "Whatever were the two of you talking about for so long? Lady Abercrombie speculated that you may have developed a *tendre* for Miss Atwater already, you seemed so enchanted by her."

Alfred huffed. "Hardly. I've just met the girl, and you are measuring me for my wedding clothes! Miss Atwater is bright, and pretty, and that is all."

Only it wasn't all, Alfred thought.

There was much more to Miss Atwater than anyone would guess.

"Well, there is no need to take that tone, Alfred," Lady Weston said. "You had better be nice to her at the ball tomorrow."

"It will be an evening Miss Atwater will never forget...I promise," he said, keeping his wicked thoughts to himself.

"I am glad to hear it," the old woman said, yawning sleepily. "I have had quite a day. I think I shall have a nap the rest of the way, my dear. Wake me when we are home."

"I will, Auntie."

In few moments Great-Aunt Withypoll was dozing off, and Alfred was left alone with his thoughts. He stared out the window as the carriage ambled through the streets of London.

But as he stared out the window, he saw only the girl's face. The full mouth...the vivid blue eyes...the autumn-red hair.

He had lied to Great-Aunt Withypoll.

Miss Prudence Atwater wasn't the least bit pretty.

The chit was most extraordinarily beautiful.

She was also a petty thief who liked to go out at night dressed as a trollop.

He chuckled as he thought of their first meeting, where she'd been trying so hard to convince him that she was a streetwalker. He'd known something wasn't right. At first he'd thought she might have been a bored countess, out getting her kicks for the night. Then, when she'd seemed almost panicky, he'd attributed it to virginal trepidation.

He'd been wrong on both counts.

The girl was a bloody school-marm! One who needed to be taught a lesson herself, it seemed. And he would be only too glad to oblige.

Now he had her right where he wanted her—indebted to him. She had agreed to pay the price of his choosing. It was a situation that he planned to take full advantage of.

Perhaps it was rakish, what he was doing. Certainly, a gentleman wouldn't put a young woman in such a position.

But he had never claimed to be a gentleman.

Never had been—never would be.

And what would he exact as a price? He couldn't help but grin as his mind raced with possibilities. She had looked so very enticing in that red satin, with her breasts spilling out of the tight bodice like pearls out of a jewel-case....

How much could he demand from her?

How far could he go?

An uncomfortable heat suffused his loins as he remembered the sensation of her mouth beneath his and her tempting little body pressing against him.

He would make her wait for awhile.

Make her fear the worst.

Then he would make her pay as he had vowed to do that very night.

Didn't he still have scratches all over his body from when he'd jumped through the bushes? Hadn't he had to put up with all the jokes at his club, all the curious looks and nudges? And hadn't he had to deal with Great-Aunt Withypoll's disappointment in him for sullying the family name?

Oh yes...Miss Prudence Atwater would pay for all of that, starting tomorrow night at Lady Townsend's ball.

CHAPTER FIVE

"Cup o' tea, Miss?" Dolly said as Prudence walked slowly into the kitchen. She sat down at the table, staring numbly at the brightly flowered tablecloth.

"I said, would ye like a cup o' tea?" Dolly said, again. "The kettle's just boiled. Miss Atwater? Is somethin' wrong?"

Prudence jolted slightly as she felt a hand on her shoulder. She looked up into Dolly's concerned eyes. "I'm sorry...what did you say?"

The housekeeper stood back and folded her arms across her ample bosom. "I asked ye if there was somethin' wrong, and I see plainly that there is. Now what's happened?"

"I—I met the man," Prudence stammered.

"The man?" Dolly said, frowning. "Could you be just a wee bit more specific?"

"The one that Mungo and I left under the hedge."

"Oh, no!" Dolly exclaimed. "Ye mean the one ol' Mungo clobbed on the 'ead? The one ye left naked as a wee babe after ye stripped 'im of all 'is fine clothes? The one that

41

kissed and fondled ye as if 'e had a God-given right to?"

"Yes, Dolly," Prudence said, finally. "*That* one."

"Lud! Well, ye better tell me everythin'," Dolly said.

As she poured two steaming cups of tea, Prudence related the tale, begging Dolly not to tell Mungo about the price Lord Weston meant to claim from her. Mungo would only go after the man and no doubt succeed in strangling him the second time around. This was one problem Prudence would have to solve by herself.

"Oh, my...," Dolly said, putting her hand to her face after Prudence finished her story. "An' now 'e's yer escort to the ball tomorrow. Dreadful! But ye can't do this, Miss! What does the rascal want of ye? 'Ave ye thought of that? 'E is a red-blooded man, after all."

"I know, Dolly, but I have no choice," Prudence replied. "I'll have to do whatever he says. Otherwise, the Atwater School will most certainly be forced to close its doors. I can't send you all back out onto the street again. I wouldn't be able to live with myself."

Dolly clasped her hand. "Per'aps me or one o' the girls could...y'know. Change 'is mind."

Prudence looked at Dolly, alarmed. "No, Dolly. That part of your life is over. You'll never again be forced to sell your body to a man. I promised you that."

"But ye will in our place?" Dolly asked. "'Ow is that fair?"

"We don't even know what Lord Weston wants," Prudence replied, weakly.

"Oh yes, we do. 'E wants ye, flat on yer back! Mark my words, so 'e does. Ye must tell 'im ye've changed yer mind. There must be another way."

"There is no other way," Prudence said sighing. "The money Father left me is all but gone. I've been using my own money since the school's account ran dry last

Christmas. I'm afraid the only way we can survive is through the generosity of a wealthy patron. And we have secured one in Lady Weston. If we lose her, I don't know how long it would take to find another. Or if we *could* find another one."

"But ye've sacrificed so much, Miss," Dolly said, "If not for us, you could have been married by now."

"I don't want to be married, Dolly. You know that," Prudence said, clearing away the teacups. "I am doing what I love. And I am not going to let Lord Weston—or anyone else—stop me."

Dolly sighed, joining Prudence at the sink. "Well, yer a clever girl, Miss. I'm sure ye can outsmart this nasty rogue, if ye try. And ye'll look so beautiful tomorrow night, 'e'll lose 'is very senses when 'e sees ye. I'll make sure o' that. Now 'ow shall I do yer hair...?"

Prudence smiled and left Dolly dreaming at the sink.

She walked down the hall to the little classroom and went inside to prepare for tomorrow's lessons.

She had to keep her mind off of Lord Weston and their dreadful arrangement.

As she stood behind her desk, Prudence looked about the room at all the treasures her father had left her. There was the huge atlas he'd used to teach her geography. There were the shelves of books on everything from Alexander the Great to botany to the works of John Donne. And she had read them all.

They were like old friends, for in reality, they were the only friends she had ever truly had. As a girl, she had never fit in with children her own age. Father had taught her to read and from then on, she'd always had her head buried in books. They'd been much more interesting than the neighborhood children. More fun, too.

As Prudence grew up, she always seemed to be too

smart for the boys who tried to court her. Intimidated by her talk of ancient history and philosophy, they soon disappeared.

But Prudence didn't mind. She'd found most of the boys a little boring, anyway.

And now, at twenty-one, she was the proprietress of the Atwater Finishing School for Young Ladies. This had been Father's dream, and together they had worked hard to make it a reality. Then, only a week after they had opened their doors, he'd collapsed. The doctor had said it was his heart.

So Prudence had kept her father's dream alive, and carried on with the school. Now it was her dream to help the girls who had given up on dreams.

And Mungo, who—though he didn't like to proclaim himself a graduate of a Finishing School for Young Ladies—had nonetheless learned to read there.

The current class showed just as much promise as the previous ones. Prudence couldn't take those dreams away from them, not after they had worked so hard to achieve them.

Lord Weston wasn't going to scare her off by demanding a price for his silence. And yet, that little knot was forming in her stomach again as she thought about what he might want from her.

Would he ask for her favors? She tried to prepare herself for that possibility, tried to imagine herself kissing him again. Certainly, she had to admit that kissing him hadn't been entirely unpleasant.

But what if he wanted more than just kissing?

What would she do then?

Oh, it was no use trying to predict the future. She would make herself sick if she kept worrying like this.

She had done the right thing. Why, just a few days ago,

she had used some of the money that Lady Weston had donated to purchase five new readers for the primary class, and five new books of poetry for the secondary class, as well as embroidery thread and needles.

The rest of the money would be needed for Dolly and Mungo's wages, for food, clothing, coal, and other necessities. And that would only last a few months. Though Lady Weston had assured Prudence of her ongoing patronage, the lady's future support was now uncertain.

At least the Atwater School owned the building they were in. Her father had secured it as a donation before he died. Though the building was not large by any standards, it was in Putnam Lane, a lovely residential area of town.

It had a schoolroom, a kitchen, a salon, and three large bedrooms for the students and staff to share. And it had a very nice sign above the door that she and her father had painted, which announced to the world in swirling black letters that this was *The Atwater Finishing School for Young Ladies.*

And the Atwater Finishing School for Young Ladies was worth fighting for.

Prudence picked up her chalk and began listing the kings and queens of England on the blackboard for tomorrow morning's history lesson.

Perhaps it wouldn't be as bad as she thought. Perhaps Lord Weston's price would be quite innocent, after all.

And perhaps she was Queen Eleanor of Aquitaine.

Alfred paused before lifting the brass knocker. The lion looked quite angry with him for swinging the ring in its mouth, but he did it anyway with gusto. The heavy ring clanged against the brass plate on the beautifully painted olive-green door.

Well, at least from the outside the school looked respectable.

The door opened, and Alfred gazed up into the scarred face of Mungo Church—Miss Atwater's faithful bodyguard. The man recognized him immediately, and instead of taking pains to hide it, smiled a big, gap-toothed grin at Alfred as if they were old friends.

He bowed his hulking form and asked, "May I help ye, sir?"

Although Alfred could still remember the disturbing sensation of the brute's hands around his neck, he curiously felt his anger dissipating.

Still, he would have words with him later.

Now wasn't the time. Not with Great-Aunt Withypoll waiting out in the carriage for him to fetch Miss Atwater.

"Good Evening," he said to Mungo. "Would you be so good as to tell Miss Atwater that Lord Weston is here. I believe she is expecting me."

"Very good, sir. Will you await Miss Atwater in the salon?" Mungo directed him to a modestly decorated but quaint little blue salon. He stood near the fireplace while the man went to fetch his mistress.

Absently, Alfred picked up a miniature that stood on the mantle, and studied it. Surely it was Miss Atwater as a girl, he thought as he regarded the vibrant red hair, bright blue eyes and rosy cheeks of youth. Even as a girl she had possessed a startling beauty.

"Miss Prudence Atwater," Mungo announced.

When Alfred turned to greet her, he was unprepared for the vision before him.

God help him....

She was absolutely stunning.

Miss Atwater wore a satin gown of soft pale green. A thin braid of gold trimmed the bodice and drew the eye to the creamy curves of her breasts, which, though more demurely covered than they'd been the night at Drury Lane, were just as impressive.

Her wavy auburn hair was piled on top of her head in the latest Grecian style, and had been woven with the matching gold braid that trimmed her dress. Tear-drop ear bobs dangled on each side of her exquisite neck, and matched the fine jade necklace that adorned her.

Her face was all soft lines and curves, her skin smooth and pale as alabaster, her eyes vibrant as turquoise, her full lips red as garnet.

And she smelled as sweet and bewitching as a fresh rose.

Damnation, she was attractive.

"Lord Weston," she greeted him, formally.

"Miss Atwater," he said, making a bow. He bent to kiss her hand, feeling the softness of the skin against his lips.

He couldn't help but smile at her as he stood, for tonight, this beautiful creature was his. Oh, he would have to try very hard not to demand his payment tonight. He wanted to draw this out as long as he possibly could.

Besides, he hadn't yet decided on his price.

However, one thing was certain—he now had Miss Prudence Atwater right where he wanted her.

"Shall we, Miss Atwater?" he said, offering his arm.

She curled her arm through his, and he immediately felt the warmth of her hand through his coat-sleeve. Her hand was small, and her touch light, but it was maddeningly feminine. The sensation was very distracting.

For a fleeting moment, he had the image of her hand reaching to touch him in other places....

They proceeded to the door in silence, and Mungo closed it behind them.

Soon they were in the carriage with Great-Aunt Withypoll, rolling along to Lord and Lady Townsend's grand house back in Mayfair. In fact, they lived only a few streets away from Alfred. They were old friends of the Weston family.

Great-Aunt Withypoll and Miss Atwater immediately engaged in a conversation about poetry, so Alfred sat back and watched the red-headed beauty as she talked. Her eyes sparkled with enthusiasm over the latest offerings of Lord Byron, though for himself, he didn't hold much with Byron. The man himself was a bore.

As the ladies talked, Alfred thought about the price he would demand.

He could have anything he wanted from Miss Atwater.

Anything at all.

What would it be? A few kisses would not suffice. She had caused him injury, not to mention humiliating him in the Times.

No, the price would have to be quite steep to make up for all of that.

She glanced at him suddenly, and when he gave her a wicked smile, she quickly looked away. That made him smile all the more.

Whatever price he demanded of her, he would enjoy receiving payment very much indeed.

CHAPTER SIX

Prudence accepted the crystal glass from Lord Weston and raised it to her lips. The raspberry punch was cool and sweet and very refreshing after their turn about the room. They had yet to dance, and in truth, Prudence had been hoping Lord Weston would refrain from asking her. But of course, he *had* asked her. And it would be impossibly rude to refuse him.

How she loathed the man!

His gaze seemed always to be on her, and that devilish twinkle in his eye told her exactly what he was thinking about....

The power he held over her.

The fact that she was practically his slave.

The fact that she would have to obey his commands, whatever they might be.

Oh, it was simply too much!

"They are beginning the next dance, Miss Atwater," Lord Weston said, offering his arm. "And I believe I have asked you to do me the honor of being my partner. But instead of dancing, perhaps we might go out onto the balcony. It is a lovely night."

Prudence forced herself to smile back at him, though she knew his despicable game. He wanted to get her alone so that he could torment her further. Or worse.

She set her glass on the table and took his arm, replying, "Of course, my lord."

As the lines of dancers formed in the middle of the room, they walked to the expansive French windows that opened onto the balcony. As they walked, Prudence tried to look as if it were her dearest wish to be forced into the private company of London's most exasperating lord.

It would do no good for Prudence to show him just how much he irritated her. This was no doubt part of her earthly trial. And every time she felt her courage wane, she would think of her girls. She would picture their faces bright with enthusiasm and hope as they learned in her classroom. And it would give her strength.

The music began behind them, and they went out into the night. The balcony was deserted. The warm glow of candlelight spilled through the French windows and gently lit the night.

Lord Weston led Prudence down to the end of the balcony, which had a bench and several tall, potted shrubs. In fact, it was like a little garden.

Very quiet.

Very isolated.

Prudence felt a thread of fear weaving its way through her stomach. But no, surely he couldn't, he wouldn't—not here!

Would he?

She soon had her answer, for in a moment she was in his powerful arms, only inches away from his broad, masculine chest. Forced to look up into eyes as dark as midnight, and a face as hard and handsome as the statue of Apollo, she struggled to keep her composure.

"Once again, you are in my arms, Miss Atwater," he said, his voice softly dangerous. "Once again, you are standing quite close to me. Close enough so that I may feel the heat from your body. Close enough so that I could kiss you, if I chose. Shall I kiss you, Miss Atwater?"

"Is that your price, my lord? A kiss?" she asked, pushing back against his chest.

"No," he answered. "That is not my price."

"Then you shall not kiss me," Prudence countered.

"Yet you were not averse to kissing me the night we met."

"That was a different circumstance," she pointed out, weakly.

"Yes, quite." He regarded her for a moment, though he made no move to release her. "Your choice of attire was completely different that night, as was your cockney accent."

"I was playing a part," she replied.

"And are you playing a part now?" Lord Weston demanded.

"Yes...and no."

"Ah, a decisive reply."

She ignored his sarcasm and continued. "Yes, I am playing the part of your happy companion, and no, I am not the girl from Drury Lane. Tonight I am myself. Prudence Atwater."

"And Prudence Atwater usually allows a virtual stranger to take her in his arms, like this?" he asked, pulling her close once again.

Prudence glared at him. "Only if the virtual stranger holds something over her head, my lord. Which you do."

He slowly released her, saying, "So you think me unfair? I am merely demanding that you pay a price for all the woes you've caused me—injury to both my person and my family name. Surely that is not unfair, Miss Atwater."

She stepped away from him, needing to put distance between herself and his alarmingly masculine body. "I think it unfair of you to take advantage of the situation, which you have just done by forcing me into an intimate embrace. Will you not decide on a price tonight, so that I may begin to satisfy my debt to you, my lord? Or do you plan to drag this out for as long as you can?"

To her surprise, he laughed.

"You make me sound so dreadful," he admonished. "And the embrace was not so intimate. At least, not in my experience."

Prudence watched his eyes glitter as Lord Weston stepped toward her again. She wanted to back away, to run away. But she would not lose any more ground to this man. She would not let him see how afraid she really was.

As he studied her, she saw that he understood. He knew how difficult this was for her. And yet...he would still hold her to this scandalous agreement.

Black-hearted scoundrel that he was.

"Come," he said, motioning toward the marble bench. "Let us sit for awhile. I promise to be a perfect gentleman...for the time being."

"Alas, that is something I fear you will never be, my lord," she retorted.

"How you wound me, Miss Atwater!"

"If only that were true," she grumbled, sitting as far away from him as possible.

"Pardon me?" he asked.

"I said, 'what a lovely shade of blue!'" She pointed to his jacket.

He laughed, and his amused expression showed that he had heard her the first time. Would the man never tire of playing games with her?

What sort of other games would he want her to play?

Another couple wandered out onto the balcony, and Prudence breathed a sigh of relief.

"Come now, Miss Atwater," Lord Weston said with annoyance, "stop being so theatrical. I shan't ravish you right here on the balcony, I promise."

"And why should I trust you, my lord?" she asked, incredulous. "You hold the entire future of the Atwater School in your hands. You have threatened me with the loss of your great-aunt's patronage if I do not willingly become your slave. You have used my unfortunate situation to your advantage, which you have undoubtedly done many times before with other women, most likely the very girls I have sworn to help."

Prudence stood, as haughtily as she dared. "You, sir, are the most dangerous man I have ever met."

Lord Weston quickly rose to his feet, staring down at her with eyes blazing. "Me—dangerous? You mean, more dangerous than the men who ask for your favors when you walk the streets of London dressed as a trollop?"

"Yes," Prudence replied, anger swirling in her veins, "more dangerous than that. Because those men are not trying to close down my school as you are. Those men are not trying to ruin the chances of my students making a better life. They are not trying to put an end to my father's dream of helping those less fortunate than ourselves. Those men could never hurt me the way you could."

"You are not only naive, but reckless, Miss Atwater," Lord Weston said, darkly. "And far too independent for your own good."

"Naive? *Reckless*?" Lord, but she wanted to slap him.

"Yes, and—"

"Far too independent for my own good?" she demanded, hotly.

"At least we have established that your hearing is as sharp as a pin," he muttered.

Prudence glared at him with all the fury she could muster. "How dare you, sir! How dare you even think to assume that you know what is best for me? That I do not know what is best for myself?"

Lord Weston folded his arms across his broad chest, saying, "Traipsing about London at night dressed as a trollop is reckless, Miss Atwater! With or without your bodyguard, you are putting yourself in grave danger. Mungo Church is a formidable opponent, I assure you, but make no mistake—he could be subdued. He is but one man. Against three or four, he might very well lose. Have you considered that possibility?"

"I carry a dagger with me when I go out," Prudence countered. "Mungo showed me how to use it."

"Well, then—I stand corrected," he said sarcastically. "It is no guarantee of your safety."

"And what do you care about my safety?" she demanded. "You, who wanted to buy my favors that night in Drury Lane. You, who now hold me prisoner to your whims in this devil's pact. You do not care about anyone but yourself, my lord."

"How little you know me, Miss Atwater."

"Pardon me if I consider it a blessing," she replied.

"Don't consider it one for too long." He took a step toward her and pulled her against his chest in a steely grip. "You will get to know me much better when you pay the debt that is owed me. You will learn much, I think...about me, as well as yourself."

Prudence met his stare and gave a bitter smile. "As you wish, my lord. After all, I have no choice but to obey you, do I?"

"No," he answered. "And you would do well to

remember that. Perhaps it is time for the teacher to learn a much-needed lesson of her own."

Prudence shook him off.

Unable to bear his presence a moment longer, she turned on her heel and stalked off down the long balcony. She didn't care if it was scandalous for her to return to the ballroom without her escort. She didn't care about anything except getting as far away as possible from the fiend.

Prudence heard the sound of his boots hitting the stone floor behind her, and she quickened her step. Then she heard a man say Lord Weston's name. It was the couple who had ventured outside earlier.

She stepped through the doorway, and looked back through the panes of the French windows. Lord Weston's dark gaze pierced her right through the glass. But his acquaintances were talking animatedly, and it seemed he had no choice but to let her go.

Prudence pushed through the crush, and made her way across the ballroom. She had no idea where she was going. She just knew she had get away from Lord Weston.

As Prudence neared the far side of the ballroom, she felt someone tugging at her sleeve. She turned to see Lady Weston sitting in her chair by the wall, looking up at her with concerned eyes.

"Is something amiss, my dear?" she asked. "Where is Alfred?"

Prudence forced a smile and replied, "He is talking to some old acquaintances outside on the balcony, Lady Weston. I was cold, so I came inside."

"And he did not escort you in, my child?" Lady Weston said, frowning. "I must say, I am displeased with his lack of manners. I shall speak to him about it."

"Oh, no, my lady," Prudence protested, "you see, it was

my idea. I did not want to keep him from his friends. In fact, I insisted on returning alone. It is not so scandalous, is it?"

"No, I suppose not," Lady Weston said, not looking quite convinced. "Perhaps it is my age, my dear. I am from a different era. And you are such a young, modern girl. Will you sit with me and tell me all the news of your lovely school?"

Prudence smiled. She could not refuse this great old lady anything. And she would be safe with Lady Weston. If Lord Weston came by, he would surely behave himself in his great-aunt's company.

So Prudence sat, and related all the new lessons she was planning, as well as each student's individual progress. Lady Weston seemed enthralled with even the smallest detail. She was truly the most wonderful patroness the Atwater School could have hoped for.

Prudence knew that she must do whatever it took to keep Lady Weston's patronage—even if it meant willingly submitting herself to blackmail.

Lady Weston patted Prudence's hand and smiled, saying, "I must say, I especially enjoyed your girl's singing at Lady Braxton's assembly a week past. Miss Linton has a lovely soprano. I should like to hear her in a duet with Alfred. He is an accomplished baritone, you know."

"I confess, I did not," Prudence answered, reluctantly intrigued.

"Oh yes, my child," Lady Weston replied. "Why the richness of his voice is enough to make your knees go weak."

"Make your knees go *where*, Auntie?" Lord Weston asked, suddenly towering above them.

"Never you mind, m'boy," she said, winking at Prudence. "How are you young people enjoying yourselves? Is my great-nephew providing a satisfactory escort, Miss Atwater? Hasn't made you dizzy with dancing, has he?"

Prudence felt herself flush under Lord Weston's stare.

"No, my lady," she said brightly. "Your great-nephew has been an attentive escort. He has taken great pains to ensure my comfort, and not to overtax my health by dancing. Along with that, I have found Lord Weston to be a most stimulating partner in conversation."

He bowed gallantly and pressed her hand to his lips, then said, "I am honored that you find me a stimulating partner, Miss Atwater. It would be my greatest desire to explore more diverse areas of stimulation with you."

Prudence almost choked on her tongue.

Lord Weston, the rogue, didn't even bat an eyelash.

"What?" Lady Weston said, putting her hand to her ear. "Tribulation? Of what sort, m'boy? Oh, I fear my hearing is not what it once was," she commented to Prudence.

"Your hearing is quite correct, my lady," Prudence replied. "Lord Weston was indeed referring to what I would consider a tribulation indeed."

He put his hands on his hips, stared directly at Prudence, and chuckled—as if she were nothing more than an amusement to him.

She fought vainly to control her fury. Oh, how she wanted nothing more than to take the sugar spoon from the nearby table and plunge it straight through his wicked black heart!

"Whatever are you laughing about, Alfred?" Lady Weston asked. "I see nothing in our present circumstance that would inspire such a degree of mirth."

"My apologies, Auntie," he said. "You are quite correct. There is nothing in our present circumstance, but there certainly will be in the future. Now, I've promised to meet Lord Kendall in the card room. I shall return after I have fleeced him of a good portion of his wealth."

He kissed his great-aunt's hand, and bowed to Prudence, saying pointedly, "Miss Atwater."

She watched him stride confidently across the room and saw most of the ladies' heads turn as he passed by. As he walked away, Prudence made a silent and furtive prayer that someone would trip him.

CHAPTER SEVEN

Prudence was happy to keep Lady Weston company for the remainder of the evening, sitting attentively beside her while the patroness told stories about her great-nephew's escapades.

She learned that Lord Weston had also distinguished himself fighting in the Peninsula. He and his friend, Beckett, Lord Ravenwood, were two of Wellington's finest Exploring Officers. They executed daring missions behind enemy lines, gathering intelligence on enemy troop movements, fortifications, and battle plans.

"There is one story about the wife of a French General becoming absolutely besotted with Alfred," Lady Weston explained. "He and Lord Ravenwood had infiltrated a fortress being held by the French, with orders to steal important documents from the General's quarters. The way the boys tell it, Alfred was to keep the general's wife distracted while Beckett searched for the papers. But in the end, the woman developed such a *tendre* for my great-nephew that she told them where to look!"

"That is quite amazing," Prudence said.

"Well, can you blame her?" Lady Weston said,

chuckling. "After all, Alfred is a handsome man. Apparently the French General wasn't much to look at. The poor woman would probably have thanked Wellington himself if she'd had the chance."

Prudence squirmed uncomfortably in her seat. She didn't want to think about Lord Weston—or how handsome he was—at the moment.

"He is utterly devoted to me," Lady Weston continued. "I consider myself quite blessed to have both his affection, and his protection. A woman my age could be a victim of any number of unscrupulous villains, trying to separate me from my fortune. But Alfred sees that I am kept away from such riff-raff."

Prudence forced a smile. "Good of him."

"Why, just last year," she said, "I met a young man from Kent who told me the most awful story about his father having lost all his money, and asked if I would invest in his schooling, so that he might become a physician as he'd always dreamed. Well, I was quite willing to help the young man. He was indeed most charming and very adept at pulling at one's heartstrings. But after Alfred investigated him, it was discovered that he had already collected hundreds of pounds from wealthy widows in a similar manner!"

"It was very lucky that Lord Weston could spot him out," Prudence replied.

"And I must say, Alfred had his doubts about you, Miss Atwater," Lady Weston said. "But I assured him that you were most honest and forthright—a young woman of the most honorable character. And that there was no one more deserving of my patronage than you and the Atwater School."

Prudence felt her heart sink with guilt.

It was obvious that Lady Weston would not be amused

if she discovered Prudence had not been truthful with her about her night-time adventures. If Lady Weston withdrew her support, any further patronage from the *ton* would be in jeopardy.

There was simply too much at risk.

She had to settle the situation once and for all.

Prudence would go to Lord Weston directly, and demand that he fix a price for her debt this very night.

Taking a deep breath for courage, Prudence stood. "I must excuse myself, Lady Weston. Will you be alright until I return?"

"Of course, Miss Atwater," the lady replied, genially. "I have been keeping you all to myself for far too long, and you must be tiring of my endless propensity for conversation."

"Oh, no, Lady Weston, not at all," Prudence began.

"It is quite alright, child. I will keep myself occupied with Lady Abercrombie, who is eyeing your chair even as we speak. Dorothea!" Lady Weston called, waving. "Dorothea and I are old friends. She will no doubt want to inform me of all the goings-on with her twenty-two grand-children, and her forty-six great-grand-children, which should keep her talking for at least an hour or more. Now, why don't you go and find where my great-nephew has gotten to."

"That is exactly what I shall do, Lady Weston," Prudence said.

Though not for the reason you would expect...

Lord Weston had gone to the card room, she thought. Heading for the hallway, Prudence fairly walked right into him, stopping just short of slamming into the same broad chest that she had been pulled so closely against only hours before.

Lord Weston looked down at her with dark, penetrating eyes. "Miss Atwater. Are you enjoying yourself?"

"No," she said, trying to pull him out of the doorway. "I need to speak with you, my lord. At once."

He paused, then said languidly, "About...?"

"You know very well what about!" she hissed in a whisper. "About settling my debt to you."

"Oh," he replied, calmly. "That."

"Yes, that!" Prudence said, looking around to see if anyone had noticed them. "I beg you—"

"I must say, I like where this conversation is going," he said, grinning devilishly.

Prudence's hands balled into tight fists at her side. It was all she could do to keep them still, and not flying at his face.

"As I was saying before I was so rudely interrupted, I would ask that we go somewhere private—"

"A *very* good idea," he intoned.

"To discuss your price!"

He shook his head, saying, "You could never afford me."

She glared at him and stretched up on tiptoe, so that they were almost nose to nose. "I pity the woman who could."

Lord Weston chuckled softly, amusement sparkling in his coal-black eyes. Indicating the hallway, he said, "Shall we, then?"

He led her into a library. Prudence found the familiar smell of books comforting. She turned to face the man who had infuriated and confounded her since the first night they'd met.

Standing as tall as she could, Prudence looked him in the eye, and said, "My lord, I demand to know the price you would have me pay. I will not spend one more day with this vile thing hanging over my head. Whatever it is, I would pay it and be done with it. Now tell me what it is you want from me."

"In truth," he said, "I had not yet been able to turn my mind to it."

"A convenient answer, my lord," she replied, "but I'm afraid it won't do. Though I admit my actions on the night we met injured both your person and your family name, I cannot abide this waiting. So for those reasons, as well as your promise to keep the truth from Lady Weston in exchange, I wish to make amends as quickly as possible." She took a deep breath. "If you would just fix a price."

"I see that you will not be dissuaded," he said, finally. "And I must say, I am happy to see you so eager to do my bidding. So, in that regard, I shall endeavour to please you with an answer."

Lord Weston smiled down at her like a cat making friendly with a mouse. He reached out and took one of the curls that dangled next to her face, rubbing it gently between his fingers.

Strange how he wasn't really touching her, and yet Prudence felt her skin heat at such blatant intimacy. She should have been bristling at his touch—ripping his hand away from such a bold move.

And yet, she did neither.

"All I can tell you, is that you shall know by tomorrow. The rest," he said languidly, raising her hand and pressing his lips to her skin, "is a surprise."

Alfred sat back in the plush wing chair and sipped his brandy. The fire blazed warmly in the hearth. He took his feet out of his slippers and wriggled his toes in front of the glowing logs.

He and Great-Aunt Withypoll had arrived home hours

ago, but he was still awake in his chamber. That was why he'd decided on the brandy.

Still, he would need more than brandy to get Miss Prudence Atwater out of his head.

Damn, but the chit irked him!

Defied him, patronized him, and frustrated him beyond belief.

And aroused him....

She'd looked like a Greek goddess tonight. Aphrodite couldn't have done better.

Damned if she wasn't the most prattling, pig-headed little baggage that he had ever had the misfortune to meet. She was most certainly reckless, and too independent for her own good. Heaven help the man who would fall in love with such a creature.

However, she was about to learn a lesson she wouldn't soon forget.

He ran his hand through his hair and took another swig of the brandy, this time draining the glass. He rested it on the table and folded his hands.

Great-Aunt Withypoll had certainly enjoyed herself at the ball. She was truly taken with Prudence Atwater. The two had talked together for most of the night. He knew that his great-aunt was hoping for a match between he and the schoolmarm. Well, he would have to break the news to her that her latest protégé would not be in the running. Miss Prudence Atwater would be a terrible choice for a wife, not only for him, but for any man.

For one, she had too many thoughts. Secondly, there were too many subjects that she was knowledgeable about. More knowledgeable than most men. And she was impossible to control, like a new filly that foolishly wanted to be her own mistress.

Still, the uncomfortable fact remained that he couldn't

seem to dispel her from his mind. The creamy skin, the flame-colored hair, the sapphire eyes, and the curvaceous body that would make even Aphrodite weep with envy.

He'd held her in his arms—was so close to kissing her, to tasting those ripe lips again. How he'd wanted to feed on them...to feed on her.

Damnation, but he desired her.

He wanted, no *needed* to have her in his arms again. And for more than just a kiss. Prudence Atwater tempted him and plagued his thoughts like no other woman ever had. She was all at once infuriatingly impudent, maddeningly innocent, and bewitchingly beautiful.

She aroused his passion, much more than he wanted to admit.

Perhaps that was why he found himself unable to release her from this 'devil's bargain', as she'd called it, even if he wanted to. Perhaps it was cruel, what he was doing.

But was it not cruel to allow her man to bash him in the head and render him unconscious? Was it not cruel to have stolen his clothes and left him under a hedge that night in the busy Theater District where anyone might come upon him—and did? Was it not injurious to both he and Great-Aunt Withypoll to have had the Weston name slandered in the Times? Not to mention the fact that Miss Atwater had secured the patronage of his great-aunt, without Lady Weston knowing all of those details?

By rights, he was only settling a score that needed to be settled.

Teaching a lesson that needed to be taught. If not, might not Miss Atwater do this again to some other unsuspecting man out for a night's entertainment? Was it all part of a grander scheme to fleece the pockets of wealthy widows like his great-aunt, not to mention rich rakes like himself?

One thing was certain.

There was much more beneath Miss Prudence Atwater's schoolmarm exterior than she wanted anyone to know.

Tomorrow night, he would play the role of the teacher.

And Miss Atwater—the inexperienced student.

CHAPTER EIGHT

Prudence walked to the corner again, trying to ignore the chill of the night air. She looked past the trees where Mungo waited, hidden from view, and sighed.

It had been a long day in the classroom, and before that, another long, sleepless night. The previous evening's events with Lord Weston had done nothing to alleviate the pressure that weighed upon her mind concerning this whole sordid situation. Though he had promised that she would know his price today, she had not heard a word from him. He obviously intended to break his promise, and keep her a prisoner of his whims even longer.

And to top it off, tonight was not going well, either.

She'd been walking the street for over an hour, and had met with little success. Soon after her arrival, she had talked to two young girls, newly to London from Yorkshire. The girls were sisters, and obviously beginners at the light-skirt trade. Their frightened eyes and thin faces had nearly broken Prudence's heart.

But try as she might, she'd been unable to convince them to return with her to the school. One of the girls,

Lizzie, had been tentative, but genuinely interested in Prudence's offer. Her sister, however, was suspicious.

Prudence had encountered the same problem before. If the girls saw her a few more times, perhaps they would grow to trust her.

But something else was bothering her.

As Prudence had talked to the girls, she had seen the shadowy figure across the street again, watching them. When she'd first noticed him weeks ago, she had taken him to be just another patron, waiting for his favorite light-skirt to stroll by.

But the tall, wiry man never talked to any of the girls at length. And he certainly never hired any of them. He just stayed in the shadows, watching. Though she had never seen his face—it was always obscured by the brim of his cap—she knew that he was watching her.

It made her shiver.

Perhaps he was harmless. Perhaps he was a clergyman, out for the same reason she was. But the feeling in her gut told her otherwise.

Thank heavens he was gone, now. The uneasiness in her stomach was just now starting to dissipate.

Prudence looked back at the sisters, huddled at the opposite corner, still glancing her way every now and then. They were so young. And they deserved so much more in life. Prudence hoped they would give her—and themselves—a chance at the Atwater School.

She would stay for another hour or so. The Theater Royal had already let out, and after the initial crowds had dispersed, the street had remained empty.

But there came a carriage down the cobblestone street. Perhaps letting off a girl who had finished an evening's employment.

Prudence fluffed her hair and pushed her cloak back

over her shoulder, displaying her wares as a streetwalker would. She tossed her head a little, pushed out her bosom—and tried to look friendly, yet rough.

The coach stopped in front of her, rolling slightly as the big black horse took a step back. For a moment, nothing happened. The only sound was the horse breathing in the dark, quiet night.

Then, the door opened.

A glossy black boot emerged from the shadows, followed by a man in hat and greatcoat. The brim of his hat shielded his face as he emerged, but Prudence knew who it was.

He stepped onto the street, his boots crunching the ground beneath.

Prudence swallowed.

It was him.

Lord Weston.

His dark, powerful gaze told her exactly what he had come for.

Her...

His mouth curved into a wicked smile. He was half-devil, half-angel—and all dangerous.

"You know why I've come?" he said.

"Yes," Prudence said, taking a deep breath. "I believe I do."

"You had given upon me, I suppose."

"Yes." Her heart was beginning to beat in an odd, heavy rhythm.

"I have finally decided on a price, little flower," he said, stepping closer. "The pleasure of your company for an evening. Only the pleasure of your company. It is what I asked for the first night we met—before you had me knocked unconscious. I think it a fair and fitting price. I promised to release you from our agreement today. You will see that I keep my promises, Prudence."

"As do I, my lord." She met his dark, powerful gaze, and he held her there for a moment, with only the heat in his eyes. She felt like a puppet on a string—weightless—and in someone else's control.

Lord Weston's arms circled her waist, pulling her against him. He touched her face, tilting it up toward his.

"Everythin' alright, Miss?" Mungo said from behind her, a dangerous edge to his voice.

Just inches from covering her mouth with his own, Lord Weston stopped and eyed Mungo, then gently released her.

Prudence took a moment to regain her bearings. She turned to face her trusted bodyguard.

"Yes, Mungo," she stammered. "Everything is fine."

"Ye *sure*, Miss?" He asked, looking unconvinced.

"Yes, Mungo, I am quite sure," she replied. "You know Lord Weston. He has graciously asked to drive me home, tonight. And I have consented."

Mungo gave a look of warning.

As if in reply, Lord Weston said, "Have no fear, Mr. Church. Your mistress will come to no harm while in my presence. You have my word upon it."

Mungo seemed appeased by this assurance, and even smiled good-naturedly. "I 'ave no fear o' that, milord. For I know ye still remember me 'ands about yer neck, squeezin' it like a grape." He nodded to Prudence. "I shall see ye tomorrow, Miss." With that, the huge man disappeared into the shadows.

And then she was alone with Lord Weston. Save for the hired coachman who sat placidly on top of the carriage, seemingly detached from the whole scene.

Lord Weston opened the door. He took her hand. And in a moment, she was sitting beside him in the plush cab as they rolled down the dark street. Where they were going, she didn't know or care.

"You have nothing to fear, Prudence," Lord Weston said. "I would never hurt you."

"I know that," she said.

"Nothing will happen tonight unless you wish it. As I said, I want only the pleasure of your company. Nothing more."

"Nothing more," she repeated.

She saw the angled planes of his face in the shadowy darkness, lit by the coach lamps that swung outside. She was drawn to his eyes—dark and glittery like a moonlit pool she was being dared to dive into.

"I thought we'd drive for awhile," he said, his voice velvety soft. "See the sights of London at night."

Prudence nodded.

"But while we're driving," he said, "I might do this..."

He raised her hand to his lips, pressing his mouth to her skin. Over and over he kissed the back of her hand...the palm of her hand...the length of each finger. Prudence felt hot shivers dance up and down her spine at his wicked attentions.

He pushed the cloak further up her arm, exposing more of her bare skin to the ministrations of his mouth. His lips were soft, yet completely masculine. They blazed a possessive trail over her wrist, up her forearm, in the crook of her elbow, and at that, she caught her breath.

He looked up, then bent his head again. In fascination Prudence watched as he continued slowly kissing her trembling skin. The subtle smell of him, soft and spicy, invaded her senses.

All in all, she thought she might swoon.

No other man had ever done this to her before. She found herself entranced by the sound of his breathing, the sound of his big, solid body moving around as he inched closer and closer to her.

Certainly, she'd endured a few chaste kisses from the suitors of her youth, but nothing like this.

It was unbearable, and yet she didn't want it to stop.

Prudence closed her eyes as Lord Weston's lips reached her bare shoulder. Gently, he turned her face toward his, and Prudence heard herself give a little moan as his mouth finally touched hers.

What his lips had been doing all the way up her arm, they now did to the mouth that trembled beneath his. Warm and wet, his mouth caressed hers with perfect skill.

At least, Prudence thought it must be perfect—it *felt* perfect—even though she hadn't much to compare it to. With his tongue, he parted her lips further, and she obeyed his command without protest.

He pressed her back into the plush seat, encircling her with his arms and pulling her powerfully against him.

Her limbs were going to jelly. She was dizzy...yet how she could be dizzy while sitting down, she didn't know.

He cradled her face in his hands and regarded her, his eyes heavy-lidded and filled with undeniable passion.

"Oh, my beauty," he murmured, burying his face in her neck and kissing her there, too. Prudence felt delicious little shivers ripple over every inch of her skin and steal her breath away. And as he continued kissing her there, Prudence pulled him closer, for she could do nothing else.

"Patience, my sweet," he whispered.

"Prudence," she corrected breathlessly.

"I know," he said, chuckling. "*Patience*, Prudence."

"Oh, I see. Of course." And she laughed at herself, too.

All this kissing must be addling her brain, she thought.

Perhaps that was why some people campaigned against it. But it was no matter. The only thing that mattered to her right now was the wicked, wicked pleasure that this devilish lord was tempting her with.

"You've never done this before, have you?" he asked, bending his head to kiss the hollow of her neck.

"No," she breathed, closing her eyes.

"Then one could say, you are learning something new."

"I most certainly am."

Oh why was he talking and not kissing?

He looked into her eyes again, his mouth curved into a sensuous smile. "Then, you are enjoying the lesson?"

She looked away, feeling her face flush.

But he tipped it back to look at him. "It is a simple question, Prudence. And an honest one. Doesn't every teacher want to know if the pupil is enjoying the lesson?"

He kissed her shoulder again, and her collarbone, and nibbled her ear. "I just want to know," he murmured, "if you are enjoying it?"

She swallowed and looked into eyes that seemed to gaze right through to her very soul. "Yes, my lord...I am."

"Don't you think it's about time you called me by my Christian name?" he asked. "I confess, I have a desire to hear it on your lips." To further his point, he kissed them.

"Alfred," she said, finally.

"Hmm," he purred, kissing her nose. "You are an apt pupil. And you have made your teacher very proud. I think you deserve a reward—*more kissing*."

Prudence gripped his shoulders as he kissed her more deeply. She pulled him closer, revelling in the sensation of his strong, solid body against the softness of hers.

His kiss grew more fervent, more demanding, yet she felt light as air. A flood of warmth seemed to take over her whole body. She was growing uncomfortable, restless. She wanted something—but what?

For all her book-knowledge, Prudence knew terribly

little about the affairs between men and women. Though she knew the basic facts of physiognomy, she knew nothing of what would really happen during any intimacies with a man.

This kissing, for instance. She had known what it was. Had even done it herself a few times. But never like this.

No one had ever told her the physical reactions it would ignite within her trembling body. No one had ever told her that her limbs, and her willpower, would turn to mush. No one had ever told her how she would feel feverish, weak and dizzy. And certainly, no one had ever told her how wonderful it would feel to be held in a man's arms and kissed absolutely senseless.

Alfred lowered his mouth and began kissing a trail between her breasts. Prudence felt her heart race alarmingly, but not with fear.

With something far more frightening.

Just then, the carriage jolted to a halt.

Alfred paused, then raised his head and looked around. His hair was slightly tousled, and his eyes blazed with heat as he sat back, running his hands through his hair.

Prudence was confused. Why had they stopped? And more importantly, why had *he* stopped?

Alfred adjusted his jacket and cuffs, saying, "We have arrived, Miss Atwater."

"What?" Her mind was muddled. "Where?"

"At the Atwater School. I promised to see you home, and you are now home," he said, and his voice seemed to be tinged with frustration.

He seemed so cool sitting there across from her. Where was the heated angel who had made her melt in his arms only moments ago?

"I encourage you to arrange yourself," he said. "The

coachman has hopped down, and will soon open the door."

Something made her obey him, though it wasn't conscious thought. She was still too muddled from all the kissing for that. Quickly, she pulled the cloak around her bare shoulders, and covered her head with the hood.

The door swung open.

Alfred hopped out onto the street, and then reached in to help her down.

When her feet hit the ground, she wobbled slightly, and she clutched at Alfred for balance. He walked her to the door, one strong arm about her waist, and his other hand holding hers. In moments they were at the front door, and he turned her to face him.

Prudence looked up into Alfred's eyes, which moments ago had been heated with fire, and now were shuttered and unreadable. He made a courtly bow, and chastely kissed her hand.

"Thank you for allowing me to see you home, Miss Atwater," he said.

She saw a flicker of something in his eyes, but what it was, she couldn't say.

"Consider your debt paid in full," he said, abruptly heading toward the coach.

With that, he opened the door and disappeared inside.

Then the carriage rolled away, leaving Prudence standing at the steps of the Atwater School, as she tried in vain to make sense of what just happened.

CHAPTER NINE

M r. Cage tasted the girl's lips again. She was putting on a good show, trembling in his lap, clad only in her chemise. He had to give her credit. After all, little Effie was a virgin.

He had paid top price for her. And her drunken oaf of a father hadn't seemed to mind. When his pretty young daughter cried out for mercy at being sold to a stranger, the repulsive man had pushed her away. His only concern had been counting Mr. Cage's gold guineas.

And now little Effie Sinclair, late of Shropshire, was the 'Silver Rose's' newest acquisition. Cage was certain that the sixteen-year-old beauty would earn back what he'd paid for her within a week.

A knock sounded on the chamber door.

"Come in, Mr. Grimes," he said, knowing exactly who it was, and why he had come.

The oak door opened, and the tall, thin form of Jeremiah Grimes passed through into Cage's private rooms.

Cage always had rooms on the first floor of each of his brothels, usually off the main salon. This one, at the favorite of his clubs, was the height of luxury, boasting zebra-hide rugs, silk draperies from his travels to the Orient, furniture in plush burgundy velvet, and a huge four-poster bed that was, of course, the centerpiece. After all, it was where he did his best work.

Grimes stepped through the doorway and Cage felt Effie tense in his arms. She looked fearfully from one man to the other.

Cage patted her arm. "Not to worry, my dear. Mr. Grimes has not come for you. He has come to see me on important business." He pushed her off his lap like an indulgent parent now tired of his child's company. "Run along, now, Effie. Pierrette will continue your lessons. She is waiting for you upstairs. Go on now, child."

He scooted her back through the study and toward the door. She looked over her shoulder at him with those wide, uncertain eyes. He closed the door, then slowly turned to his visitor.

"Now, Mr. Grimes. You have news?"

"Yes, sir," the man replied. "I saw 'er again, tonight. In Drury Lane. Seems to be 'er favorite spot."

"Are you certain she's the one?" Cage asked.

Grimes nodded, folding his cap in his hands before him, demonstrating that he knew his place.

"Yes, sir," he answered. "I talked to a couple o' girls who said she'd been tryin' to get them to come home with 'er. To some school or other."

"Intriguing. What else?"

"Said 'er name was Miss Prudence Atwater."

Cage leaned back on his desk, running his fingers through his thick silver hair. "And she is the one who has been talking my girls into leaving the streets? She is the one who has been stealing money from me?"

"Could be, sir," Grimes said. "Though she did go off

with a man last night in a fancy carriage. Looked like 'e was a customer."

"Was there a coat of arms on the coach?" he asked.

"It was hired, sir. No way to tell who it was had 'is pleasure with 'er."

"Pity," Cage said, annoyed. He was not used to Grimes being unable to answer every question with perfect certainty. That was why he had Grimes on the payroll. The man was very, very good at finding things out.

And if you wanted someone to disappear for awhile, or to disappear forever...he was good at that, too.

"Find out more, Grimes," he poured himself a glass of claret. "Look into this school. See if it's the same girl who runs it. I want to be absolutely sure before we act further. Keep me informed."

"Sir," Grimes said, giving a nod, and then left Cage alone in the study.

He sat down in the leather wing chair, sipping the claret, taking the time to taste the exquisite flavor. He never rushed such things. He had learned a long time ago to be patient when taking his pleasure.

Soon, Grimes would have the information he wanted. And then he would carry on with the next stage in his plan. First, they would need irrefutable proof that Miss Atwater was the one responsible for his recent financial losses. And if she was, then she would be taken care of. But first, the chit would be forced to pay back what she owed him.

And as Cage thought of the endless possibilities in that regard, he couldn't help but smile.

Prudence walked down the busy street and clutched

her cloak closer around her. Unlike her purple silk, this heavy grey wool was very good at keeping out the cold. It would do just fine as she walked to the library.

It had been a week since she had seen Lord Weston.

A whole week.

In all of her life, she had never known days could pass so slowly as they had since the carriage ride with Alfred.

Before she could stop it, his face materialised in her mind's eye. She had learned that it was senseless to try to stop Lord Weston from invading her thoughts. He had been doing so quite successfully now every day this week.

And every night, too.

Somehow when she closed her eyes in the dark, she was there again with him in the carriage—his strong arms around her, his skilful lips pleasuring hers.

Prudence side-stepped the lamppost she'd been about to walk into, and continued down the congested street. Yesterday, she had bumped into a doorframe, dropped a heavy stack of books on her foot, and spilled a pot of ink on her skirt, along with all sorts of other clumsy things.

Everyone at the school was concerned for her health. They were perplexed. This was not the thoroughly unflappable Miss Atwater they knew. Only one person knew the truth of the matter. Dolly had guessed it almost immediately. And there was no use lying to her about it. Dolly could read her mind.

So Prudence had told her about Lord Weston...Alfred.

About his kisses.

About him deeming her debt paid in full.

Dolly had listened with utmost understanding. The kindly housekeeper had merely patted Prudence's hand, and said she could talk to her more about it any time she liked.

Now, as she ambled down Ridgely Street, she found

herself wondering what Alfred was doing, this very moment. Was he at one of his clubs, lunching with friends? Was he at Mr. Jackson's boxing salon, taking a bit of exercise? Was he perhaps, thinking of her, too?

She wondered if she would ever see him again. She would certainly have future dealings with Lady Weston, to discuss the funding of the school. But would Alfred come to call as well? If he did, what would she say to him?

Prudence knew this was all terribly foolish. She had been swept off her feet by a man who was skilled at seduction. That was all. For heaven's sake, she didn't even *like* the man.

She and Lord Weston were completely incompatible. They had opposing views on just about everything.

She found him infuriating.

He found her exactly the same.

And yet, in the carriage...they had been very compatible indeed.

But the fact remained that he was simply not the man for her. And even if he was the man for her, she wouldn't want him as a suitor.

Or a husband.

Marriage had no place in her future. The Atwater School was her life. And that was just the way she wanted it.

A husband wouldn't let her keep operating the school, let alone go searching for streetwalkers dressed as one of them! He would want her to stay at home, play the pianoforte, invite ladies over for tea, and have babies. He would not want her to teach classes in ancient history, read Plato's 'Republic' in Greek, or be more intelligent than he, in any way, shape, or form.

Once, at one of Lady Abercrombie's assemblies, Prudence had unintentionally embarrassed a wealthy colonel by knowing more about Alexander the Great's military strategies than he did.

Needless to say, he did not ask her to dance—nor did he become her patron. After that, she'd learned to bite her tongue. And she could not, in good conscience, go through life forever biting her tongue. Which is what she would have to do if she married.

But what about babies, Dolly would ask? *Didn't she want to have babies of her own?*

It was a sacrifice she would have to make, she'd replied to Dolly. And it was worth it, to be able to realize her and Father's dreams of running their school, and making a difference in the world.

But there was another reason Prudence had reconciled herself against ever having children. A reason even Dolly didn't know....

From a purely scholarly interest, Alfred's sensual skill intrigued her. She was curious about what other responses he could illicit from her. He'd heated her blood to scorching with the expert touch of his hands and mouth, and yet, she knew there was more. The power of her own desire had surprised her, to say the least.

She would consult some books on physiognomy, in an effort to understand the biological reasons for such distracting feelings.

To clear her head, Prudence concentrated on her destination. The library stood only a few blocks away. But as she neared the familiar building, she saw a tall figure waiting by the steps, looking directly at her.

It was him—the man who watched her in Drury Lane only last week.

So, she had not been imagining things....

Her heart pounded in her chest as she frantically searched for somewhere to duck out of sight. Quickly, she stepped into the alley. She picked up her skirt and ran as fast as she could, which, considering she also carried an armload of books, didn't seem fast enough at all. Looking over her shoulder, Prudence saw the man turn the corner, then stop when he saw her.

He followed in pursuit.

Fear shot through her anew, and a bolt of energy quickened her step. The skirt of her frock flapped around her knees as she hiked it higher, lengthening her strides as much as she could. The heavy books fell from her arm, and she used both hands to hold her skirt.

But what did all that matter, when he was getting closer!

She came to a turn in the alleyway and dashed left, immediately regretting her decision.

It was a dead end.

Prudence whirled around, her back against the cold stone wall. There was nowhere to hide. She was trapped. Scanning the ground for a weapon, she swooped down to grab a loose stone, and held it in front of her. If only she had her dagger.

The man ran past the alleyway, but she soon heard his steps come to a jolting halt. He re-appeared at the corner and came toward her.

Prudence heard her jagged breathing, half from running, half from fear. She raised the stone so he could see it.

"Don't come any closer!" she said, struggling to keep her voice even. "I warn you."

To her surprise, he didn't laugh at her little threat. He just kept the same serious expression as he continued toward her.

She raised the stone higher. "I mean it, sir! I may not kill you with this, but make no mistake, I will injure you. Of that you may be certain."

He regarded her with flinty grey eyes, stepping closer. "Ye better put that down, Miss. 'Afore ye gets hurt."

"I'll smash your skull with this," Prudence said. "I swear I will!"

"Be nice, now, Miss Atwater. Ye don't want to make 'ol Grimesy mad."

Her blood went cold. "How do you know my name?"

The man gave a slimy grin, saying, "Miss Prudence Atwater, proprietress of the Atwater Finishing School for Young Ladies. Oh...I knows all about ye. About 'ow ye takes in the girls who walk the streets at night, and tries to turn 'em into ladies. A very noble endeavour."

"What do you want?" Prudence demanded.

"I'm 'ere to deliver a message from someone...someone who doesn't like what you're doing at all. You're interferin' with 'is business, ye see?" He jabbed his finger at her. "Stop takin' those girls off the streets. For if ye don't, it could be very bad for yer 'ealth. *Very* bad indeed."

He stepped back, adjusting his cap, and turned back down the alleyway. As he reached the corner, he turned back to her. "Remember what I said, or next time, I won't be so nice."

With that, the odious man disappeared around the corner.

Prudence stood frozen, still helplessly holding the stone in case he should change his mind and return. She remained there for some moments, as if rooted to the spot. The only sound in the deserted alley was her labored breathing.

She put down the stone, and on shaking legs, made her way down the alley. She took a deep breath and glanced around the corner. He was nowhere in sight. Then, forgetting the books she'd dropped along the way, Prudence ran for home.

CHAPTER TEN

Miss Atwater cleared her throat and regarded the class. "That concludes our study of 'Measure for Measure'. Next we shall travel to Imperial Rome as we study another of Mr. Shakespeare's plays, the tragedy of 'Julius Caesar'."

The girls looked at each other excitedly.

"Fanny, Jane, and Matilda, as you are new readers," she explained, "you shall be studying from our new books of poetry, which were, as you know, purchased with funds generously donated by our patroness, Lady Weston. But as with 'Measure for Measure', you will be invited to listen and participate in our discussion of 'Julius Caesar.' Class is now dismissed."

Great-Aunt Withypoll looked at Alfred with a beaming face. "*Wonderful!*" She clapped her hands enthusiastically. "Oh, my dear boy, was it not exciting? Were you not impressed with Miss Atwater's knowledge and skill? And the girls—the precious, precious girls! To think that I am helping them in their quest for knowledge...it warms my heart so."

Alfred smiled down at Great-Aunt Withypoll and put

his hand over hers, squeezing gently. "I am glad to see you enjoying yourself, Auntie."

Her eyes twinkled. "And what of you? Did you not enjoy watching Miss Atwater teach with such aplomb? You might as well admit it, m'boy—because I know that you did."

"How do you know?" he asked, quirking a brow.

"Well...though the play was a comedy, you smiled a bit too much throughout parts which were not at all amusing," she explained. "And earlier, during the botany lesson, you barely moved, you were so transfixed. Indeed, your eyes were quite glassy from staring so long at Miss Atwater. My word, for a moment, I feared you had died sitting up."

"Hmpf," he replied. "You are imagining things, Auntie. I was merely attempting to be an attentive student. Nothing more, I assure you."

"After all your shenanigans at Eton, I must say I find that sentiment surprising. But you would do well to learn from Miss Atwater, Alfred. She could teach you a thing or two."

"About what?"

"Well," Lady Weston whispered, "perhaps you should investigate. I'm sure that Miss Atwater has many more talents that you would find most impressive."

He stifled a chuckle. Curiously, he was sure of that too.

After her passionate response to him that night in the carriage, he had speculated that Prudence possessed many hidden talents, of which even she was unaware. Oh, how he would like to teach her the finer points of using them....

He and Great-Aunt Withypoll had come to visit the Atwater School at the elderly lady's insistence. The fact that the classes had been taught by a beautiful flame-haired enchantress, the very same vixen who had so bewitched him almost a fortnight ago, had nothing at all to do with his interest in attending. While undeniably lovely to look at, the fact of the matter was that Miss Prudence Atwater was a gifted teacher.

He felt a grudging admiration for her. And though he didn't want to admit it, he was, all in all, quite impressed.

Oh, he still found her irritating—like a bee buzzing about one's ear. But she was an intelligent little bee. And obviously committed to her cause.

Meeting her students in the flesh, he'd found it difficult to dismiss them and their school as easily as he had been doing. He'd been uncomfortable at first, but upon introduction, the girls seemed as well-mannered and proper as any others he had met in London society. And indeed, thanks to Prudence Atwater, they were.

What were their stories? How long had they walked the streets before Miss Atwater had come upon them? Had he once passed by these very same faces in the dark streets of the Theater District, on his way to enjoy a night of gambling?

The thought left him with an odd feeling that he did not at all like.

Prudence walked across the classroom toward him and his great-aunt, and he rose to greet her.

As she neared them, a bright smile lit her face with a beauty that was almost painful to regard. The sombre dress of smoky-grey only served to sharpen the blue of her eyes and accentuate the rosiness of her full lips. All of a sudden, Alfred remembered exactly what those lips had tasted like, yielding bewitchingly beneath his....

"Did you and Lord Weston enjoy yourselves, my lady?" Prudence asked. "I hope you did not find the lesson too long."

"No, no, my dear," Lady Weston said, as Alfred helped her get to her feet. "If anything, it was not long enough! Oh, I was entranced, was I not, Alfred? And I daresay Alfred was as well. I remarked on it not a moment ago. I mentioned that I had noticed him *staring*—"

"At your detailed notes on the board," Alfred interjected, pointing. "Fascinating stuff."

Prudence turned to look at the scant few jottings she had put on the board during the lesson.

"Really?" she asked, confused.

"Oh, I can assure you, Miss Atwater," he continued, "the lessons seemed to stimulate my brain quite intensely...as well as several other organs. And my physician advises such stimulation of the organs as imperative for a man's good health. Keeps the blood flowing."

At that, Prudence raised an eyebrow.

"Whatever are you going on about, Alfred?" Lady Weston said, craning her neck to look up at him. "I do not see what your *organs* have to do with Miss Atwater's lesson."

"Figure of speech, Auntie," he replied.

Prudence gave him a warning look, then turned to Lady Weston. "Would you like to take a turn in the garden while we wait for tea, Lady Weston? The girls are anxious to show you the different plants that they've studied."

"Oh, I should like that very much. I do so enjoy the out-of-doors." Before Alfred could offer his arm, his Auntie was half-way to the door.

"But Auntie, don't you want me to escort you?" he asked, concerned.

"No, m'boy," she said. "Though I do appreciate the lending of your sturdy arm on most occasions, you would be wise to note that we are not attached, nor should we be.

I shall walk on alone. I have my cane." She waved it in the air and smiled mischievously before leaving them alone in the classroom.

He turned slowly toward Prudence. "Alone again, Miss Atwater."

"Indeed," she replied, looking at him with those disarming blue eyes.

He saw an errant curl, like russet ribbon, and fought the desire to touch it, to smooth it back. For if he reached to touch its silky perfection, he would have to pull her into his arms, just as he was doing now....

"My lord...?" she whispered, but he silenced her mouth with his own.

He hardened instantly as her body curved into his, her soft supple lips surrendering beautifully. With his tongue, he parted them, so that he might kiss her more fully—might taste her more deeply.

Damnation.

He had promised himself he'd keep away from her.

Suddenly she broke the kiss, pushing him away, and looking quite insulted. "I thought my debt to you was paid, my lord."

"So it was."

"Then why did you make so bold as to kiss me just now?" she demanded.

"I suppose I thought you might be yearning for my kiss as much I was yearning for yours," he answered. "Judging by your response to me just now, I'd say that you were."

Her eyes glowed blue fire. "You...You...!"

Alfred couldn't help but chuckle. "Pray, continue, Miss Atwater. After all, what man doesn't like to hear about himself?"

"Ooohh!" Prudence clenched her fists at her sides.

"I hope no one can hear you," he pointed out, "for it sounds as if you truly are enjoying yourself. Or, shall I say, enjoying whatever it is I am *doing* to you."

She gasped loudly.

He pointed at her. "That is exactly what I am talking about."

"You rake!" she said, hotly. "You scoundrel. You unseemly rogue!"

Alfred covered his heart. "Unseemly? Gads! You wound me, Miss Atwater. Sensitive creature that I am."

"The wound is not nearly enough, my lord," she retorted, "as I see you are still breathing."

"Now, now, is that any way to speak to your patroness' favorite great-nephew?" he asked, innocently. "The one she adores and relies upon for protection and advice? It seems the teacher still has a few lessons to learn, herself. Lessons that I will be only too happy to teach."

Alfred listened attentively as Miss Annabelle Banks described the different plants in the garden to him. She proudly gave their Latin as well as common names, as well as their origins.

"Very impressive, Miss Banks," he said. "You do Miss Atwater proud."

"Thank you, my lord," she replied, beaming. "I feel very fortunate to be able to pursue an education here—a *real* education—not just needlepoint and cookery. We all owe so much to her and the Atwater School."

"She is an inspiration to us all," he said.

Annabelle smiled, saying, "I know that you and Lady Weston also hold Miss Atwater in as high regard as we do. She is so very brave—putting her own safety at risk time after time. And especially now, with that awful business on her way to the library...."

"What awful business?" he asked.

Annabelle looked surprised. "Miss Atwater did not tell you?"

"Tell me what?" Alfred felt his blood begin to heat with anger...and something else that tasted very similar to fear.

"If she did not tell you," Annabelle said uncomfortably, "then perhaps I am not supposed to say."

"You had better tell me what you know, Miss Banks," he ordered sternly. "This is no time to be concerned about proper etiquette. If Miss Atwater is in danger, then I must know."

Annabelle gulped. "Well...it seems that yesterday, as Miss Atwater was walking to the library, she was accosted by an awful man who told her to stop taking girls off the streets."

"What else?" he ground out.

"He said that the message was from his employer, who was very unhappy with Miss Atwater for ruining his business. Something like that," she explained. "Lord Weston—where are you going?"

"To see your teacher," he said as he stalked across the grass. "She has some explaining to do."

CHAPTER ELEVEN

Prudence put the last of the books back on the shelf, and adjusted the spines so that they were all completely even. If there was one thing she insisted on, it was a neat and orderly classroom.

The sound of boots stomping down the hallway made her turn just in time to see Alfred, his expression dark as a thundercloud. He stopped in the doorway, filling it with his towering form.

"You little fool," he said, his voice low and dangerous.

"I don't—"

But before Prudence could finish, he had crossed the room in only a few strides. With firm hands he took hold of her arms and pulled her up in front of him, so that she had no choice but to meet his accusing gaze.

Prudence tried to shake him off, but it was useless. "Let me go! I shall call for Mungo."

"Go ahead." His face hovered only inches from hers. "I should like to have a word with him as well."

Prudence opened her mouth to call for her trusted bodyguard, but nothing came out. All she could do was stare up into Alfred's dark eyes—eyes that burned with fire. He held her close—so close that she felt the tips of her breasts touching his chest.

Then, in exasperation, he released her. He let out a breath and ran his hands through his hair, stalking across the room. "Don't you realize that you could have been hurt—you could have been killed!" He shook his head. "I forbid you to go out on the streets at night—"

"You what?" Prudence said, incredulous. "You *forbid* me? Oh, no. You do not forbid me anything, my lord!"

"I most certainly will forbid you. For you, madam, do not have the sense God gave a chicken!"

"Oh!"

"That's right," he continued. "For all your books, and all your Shakespeare, and all your reading Plato in Greek, you, Miss Atwater, are the most mutton-headed, cork-brained, foolishly misguided female I have ever had the misfortune to meet."

"*Misguided*?" she said. "I take offense to that, sir! Is it misguided to help those unfortunate girls who have no choice but to sell their bodies on the streets at night? Well, I for one cannot, in good conscience, sit in my pleasantly warm salon, enjoying my pleasantly warm tea when I know that right now, as we speak, there are girls out there—girls who have no one looking out for them, no one who cares whether they live or die, except for me. I care enough to risk the same dangers they do, and if you think I am going to let a few threats stop me from doing my duty, you, sir, are mistaken."

He stared at her, saying nothing, but fairly humming with anger.

"And don't try to threaten me with the loss of Lady Weston's support," she added. "You may say whatever you like to her. If I lose her support because of you, then so be it. We will find some way to manage. But I will not stop helping those girls."

Alfred folded his arms, regarding her coolly. "And you will not be dissuaded?"

"No."

"I see," he replied. "Call Mr. Church, if you please."

Confused, she asked, "Why do you want to speak to Mungo?"

"For once," he said, with an edge to his voice, "will you simply do as you are told, Miss Atwater?"

His words made her fume, but she obeyed, and rang for the burly bodyguard. In a few moments, Mungo appeared, his massive form filling the doorway.

"Yes, Miss?"

"Lord Weston wishes to speak with you, Mungo," Prudence said reluctantly.

"I wish to speak to Mr. Church alone, if you please, Miss Atwater," Alfred said, folding his arms.

Prudence huffed. "Fine. I shall be outside in the garden, while you two discuss me as if I were nothing but chattel."

With that, she removed herself from the infuriating company of Lord Weston.

"Ye wanted to speak to me milord?" Mungo asked warily.

"Yes, I did." Alfred hated the way he had to look up at the enormous man before him, for it made him feel at a disadvantage. "Would you mind explaining to me what in the devil is going on?"

"Of course, sir," Mungo replied. "What is it you're confused about?"

"I'm not confused, man!" Alfred barked. "I'm infuriated with that girl out there—and with you, for letting her go about as she pleases, getting herself into trouble that she can't get herself out of."

"She got out of it yesterday, alright," Mungo answered, folding thick arms across his barrel-sized chest. "But I agree, the little lady does 'ave a penchant for danger. What d'ye want me to do about it? Ye know as well as I that there's no talkin' her 'round. Miss Atwater is as stubborn as a mule and a goat put together...ye better understand that right now. Keepin' her still is like tryin' to catch a greased pig. The only thing that comes of it, is the pig gets away, and ye find yerself covered in muck."

Alfred disagreed, saying, "We can't just let her go about, putting herself in dangerous situations."

"We?" Mungo raised a bushy brow. "I assume this 'we' means me an' you. That right?"

"Yes, that's right," Alfred stated, resting his hands on his hips. "What I'm proposing is that you and I join forces in looking out for Miss Atwater's welfare. You'll be working for me. I'll double your wage—"

Mungo made a face. "Don't insult me, milord. After twenty years on a pirate ship, ye come to understand that money don't buy loyalty. I work for Miss Atwater. I do what I do for her out o' loyalty—not for what she pays me. I would do anythin' for her. But sometimes, a woman that headstrong needs protectin' from herself. As for the wages, give it to her school. And then, I'll let ye team up with me. That's the deal. Take it or leave it."

Alfred paused for a moment. Certainly, he was unused to such frank talk from a subordinate. But Mungo was an important ally. Alone, neither would be able to fully protect Prudence. But together, they would be a formidable team.

Alfred nodded. "I accept your terms, Mr. Church. Now, let us decide on a plan—"

"Just a minute, there," Mungo interrupted. "Why are you so concerned with Miss Atwater's welfare? What's it to you what she does? And don't go tellin' me it's because o' your great-aunt's patronage."

Alfred pondered, for he didn't know the answer himself. "It is my duty, as a gentleman."

Mungo looked unconvinced, saying, "Yeah. And I'm the Prince Regent. You've got eyes for Miss Atwater. I'd 'ave to be blind not to see it. Just make sure ye treat 'er as a gentleman should, milord, or 'ol Mungo will 'ave to rearrange that pretty face o' yours. Understand?"

Instead of being insulted by the man's words, Alfred felt a grudging admiration. Mungo Church obviously cared a great deal about Miss Prudence Atwater.

Alfred nodded his agreement. "Not to worry, Mr. Church. I have the utmost respect and admiration for Miss Atwater. Now, let's get to work on our strategy."

As they planned their next move, Alfred discovered that he hadn't been totally honest with Mungo about his motives.

It wasn't just that he cared about Miss Atwater's welfare. It was, he realized reluctantly, that he cared about her.

"Lizzie, isn't it?" Prudence asked the thin, pale girl who stood nearby on the dark street corner.

The girl eyed her warily. "Yeah. So what?"

"You remember me, don't you?" Prudence gingerly approached her, sensing that if she moved too quickly, the girl would spook like a frightened horse. "I spoke to you a few nights ago."

"Yeah. I remember now. The lady from the school, or something." Lizzie wiped her nose with the back of her hand.

"But where is your sister? Wasn't she with you last time?"

"Meg," the girl replied, "oh she got promoted to a fancy 'ouse on Bricknell Street."

"Really?" Prudence asked, unhappy to hear such news. "Well, why didn't you go there too?"

Lizzie shifted her feet and looked at the ground. "They didn't want me. Said I was too old for that place."

"Too old? But you can't be more than seventeen."

She looked up at Prudence, and then laughed. "Truth is, I don't know 'ow old I am. I thinks I'm about that age. But me sister, Meg, she's younger by a few years. Looks about fifteen, the man at the fancy house said. She's gonna 'elp me out with 'er extra earnings. I'm allowed to visit 'er once a week, the man said. Every Sunday. That's only a few more days!" The girl's face beamed.

"But surely, this is not good news for you, Lizzie," Prudence said. "Won't it be difficult coming out here every night by yourself?"

Lizzie's chin rose with defiance. "Yeah. But I'll manage."

"Will you, Lizzie?" Prudence asked. "Have you had any customers tonight?"

The girl remained silent, scowling slightly.

"And when did you eat last?" she inquired. "Yesterday? The day before?"

Prudence saw tears well up in the girl's eyes—angry tears which trickled down her dirty face. Lizzie wiped them away and stared at Prudence with a grim frown.

"It don't matter—'cuz I ain't hungry!"

Prudence felt her heart near to breaking at Lizzie's misfortune.

"My poor dear," she whispered, reaching out her hand. "Let me help you. Please, Lizzie. I can help you, if you'll let me."

"Why should you?" Lizzie demanded. "Why should you 'elp the likes o' me?"

Prudence put her arm around the girl's shoulders. "Because, my dear, it's what I do."

At that, Lizzie choked back a sob and buried her face against Prudence's shoulder.

"It's alright, Lizzie," Prudence said gently. "I'm going to take you home now. To the Atwater School. There, you'll meet many other girls who were just like you. You'll be fed and cared for. You'll acquire an education. And one day, you'll take your place in society. I think you'll be very happy there. We'll try to get your sister to attend the school, too. You'll be together again, as you should be."

"Thank you, Miss—?" Lizzie said, snuffling.

"Miss Atwater."

Lizzie managed a smile. "Thank you, Miss Atwater."

"Let's get you home, now," Prudence said. "I just have to call Mungo to bring the coach—oh, here he is now."

Prudence saw a black coach hurtling toward them. That was strange—it looked like a different driver on top. The door swung open, and Prudence stepped toward the coach.

"Mungo, I'd like you to meet—"

But it wasn't Mungo stepping out of the cab.

It was the thin-faced man who had chased Prudence down the alley.

Before the thought had fully registered in her brain, the man grabbed her arm.

"Come on now," the thin man growled. "Settle down—

Ow! Little she-cat!" He wiped his hand across where Prudence had scratched his rat-like face.

"Unhand me, ruffian!" Prudence yelled. "Mungo! Help!"

The man pinned Prudence's arms to her sides and lifted her off the ground. She flailed and kicked her feet as hard as she could, hearing him groan in pain as the heel of her boot struck his shin.

If only she could reach her dagger.

"You'll pay for that later!" he spat.

"The only person who'll be paying tonight is *you*," a deep voice said from behind them.

Prudence turned, recognizing the voice, but still astonished to see Alfred lunging for the man who held her, as Mungo went after the giant who held Lizzie.

Prudence stumbled as she was abruptly released, then regained her balance and turned to see Alfred duck a punch. Swift as a cat, he bounced back up and landed a fist in his opponent's gut.

The thin man doubled over, but managed to recover, and swung again at Alfred. But Alfred's training at Mr. Jackson's boxing salon gave him the advantage. He seemed to effortlessly avoid the man's fists, while landing a few well-placed punches of his own.

Mungo seemed to have a more equal opponent in the giant, and the two of them bellowed and lunged at each other like mad bulls.

Lizzie stood off to the side, immobilized with fright. Prudence quickly pulled her away from the brawling men and retreated to a safe distance.

Just then, Mungo's opponent landed a crushing blow to his jaw that sent her trusted bodyguard reeling.

"Mungo!" Prudence cried.

He tried to get up, but was flattened by another blow.

Prudence screamed, and at that, Alfred looked toward her. The thin man pressed his advantage and landed a hard jab in Alfred's gut, which knocked him backward.

"Let's get out of 'ere!" The thin man jumped in the door of the coach. "Come on, Piggott!"

The giant looked up and dropped Mungo back on the ground.

Prudence bent down and grabbed a nearby stone, hurling it at the giant as he climbed aboard the carriage. The rock hit the back of his head, and he fell onto his partner, pushing them both into the cab.

Alfred gave chase, but it was no use. The coach turned the corner and disappeared into the dark night.

Prudence ran toward Mungo who lay on the cold cobblestone street. "Mungo, are you alright?" She lifted his head and wiped the blood from his face. "Mungo!"

Then Alfred was beside her, examining the unconscious bodyguard. "He's suffered a blow to the head. We must get him home at once and send for a doctor. You stay here, and I'll get the coach."

His footsteps echoed down the lonely street as he disappeared around the corner.

Prudence tried to keep the tears from filling her eyes, but it was no use. Mungo, her bodyguard and friend, was hurt because of her.

"Is 'e going to die, Miss?" Lizzie asked, her eyes like saucers. "Who is 'e?"

"He is my bodyguard," she replied. "His name is Mungo Church, and he is also a dear friend. Oh, poor Mungo!"

Prudence cradled his head in her lap, offering a silent prayer for his recovery.

Then, a muffled voice said, "I can't breathe."

Prudence sat back. "Mungo?"

"Ugh...," he croaked, opening his eyes. "That brute packed a mean punch. But why are ye upside down, Miss?"

She laughed, replying, "I'm not upside down, you great oaf!" She helped him sit up. "Oh, Mungo-—are you alright? Truly?"

He slowly got to his feet, rubbing his jaw. "Yeah. I'll be fine. I'm afraid 'ol Mungo ain't as young as 'e used to be. That young fella was a real scrapper. 'Ow long was I out, anyways?"

"Oh, not long. Just a few minutes, I think," she replied.

"Good," he said. "Any idea who those two were, Miss?"

"Yes. The thin one, the one who fought with Lord Weston, he was the one who chased me the other day. The one who warned me to stop helping the girls off the streets."

"Seems they were miffed that ye didn't obey their wishes, doesn't it?"

Prudence nodded.

"Now who's this, then?" Mungo pointed to Lizzie, who was hiding behind Prudence.

Prudence brought Lizzie round beside her, keeping her arm about the frightened girl's shoulders. "Mungo Church, may I present to you Miss Lizzie... What is your last name, dear?"

"Jones, miss," the girl whispered.

Mungo made a bow. "Pleased to meet ye, Miss Jones."

"This can be your first lesson, then, Lizzie," Prudence said. "It is customary for a young lady to curtsey when being introduced. And to reply in kind to the gentleman or lady you have been introduced to. Now, you try."

Lizzie looked from one to the other, and then made an awkward curtsey to Mungo. "Er, pleased to meet ye, sir."

Prudence smiled at her newest student. "You shall do

very well at the Atwater School, Lizzie. Very well indeed."

The coach came rumbling down the street, and pulled to a stop beside them.

Alfred hopped out, and the sight of him made Prudence's knees go to mush. He looked like a knight just returned from battle. His shirt and neck cloth were in disarray, and his jacket was dusty. His hair was ruffled, and his eyes glowed with dangerous heat.

He was the most handsome man she'd ever seen.

In an instant, he was beside her, encircling her in his strong arms. "Are you alright, Prudence? Did that villain hurt you?" He touched her face, her hair, as if she were a delicate china doll.

"I am quite alright, my lord," she said.

He closed his eyes in relief. "Thank God we heard your call for help."

"Which reminds me," Prudence began, "whatever were you doing out here with Mungo?"

Alfred looked at the older man and said, "Good to see you're back on your feet, Mungo. In answer to your question, Prudence, when I was unable to dissuade you from coming out here at night, Mr. Church and I decided to join forces in looking after your welfare. As you can see from tonight's events, it was a good thing that we did."

Prudence made to reply, but Alfred cut her off.

"But now is not the time to be chattering," he pronounced. "We would do well to get you home, Miss Atwater, and off the street from which you and this young girl were almost abducted."

Mungo helped Lizzie into the coach, and Prudence waited for Alfred to hand her in.

But before he did, Alfred pulled her tight against him, holding her prisoner with the power of his gaze. He covered her mouth in a heated kiss, plundering her, branding her there with his lips and tongue. It was wicked and passionate and possessive all at once.

He broke the kiss and held her in front of him, his eyes blazing.

"What was that for?" Prudence asked, breathless.

"I just wanted to remind myself why I came out here tonight, Miss Atwater." He touched her chin, tipping her face up to look at him. "And to remind you, as well."

As they rode home together in the carriage, Prudence knew she wouldn't soon forget.

CHAPTER TWELVE

A knock sounded on the bedroom door, waking Alfred from his slumber. No matter, he thought as he rolled onto his back, rubbing his face. It hadn't been a very satisfying slumber anyway, as he had spent most of it in fitful dreams about the infuriatingly beautiful Miss Prudence Atwater.

It seemed that he was destined to be tormented every waking moment—and every sleeping moment too—by the memories of Prudence's soft lips and sensuously curved body. The fact that she was stubborn, headstrong, and outspoken did nothing to quell his desire for her. If anything, it only added fuel to the fire. And if the flame got much hotter, it might very well consume him.

"Milord?" the valet asked, knocking louder.

"Yes, Downing, I am awake," he said. "Come in, man."

Downing entered the room quietly—just as he did everything else—and addressed his employer. "Milord, you have a guest waiting to see you downstairs. I have shown her to the library."

Alfred instantly sat up. "Is it Miss Atwater? Is she alright?"

He threw back the covers and reached for his trousers, now fully awake.

"It is Lady Harrington."

Alfred froze.

"Your mother, milord."

His blood turned to ice-water in his veins, snaking through his body like cold lightning, and finally pooling in his heart.

"My *mother*, did you say, Downing?"

The valet nodded. "I did, sir."

Alfred shook his head, saying, "This is unusual. Tell Lady Harrington that I will attend her shortly. Has Lady Weston risen?"

"She has, milord," Downing answered. "I was told that she will be down soon, and that in the meantime, she would like you to receive Lady Harrington on her behalf."

"I'm sure she did," Alfred growled. "Well, don't just stand there gathering dust, man. Help me get ready."

He and his valet rushed through his usual preparations, then he descended the staircase, to greet his guest. As he neared the library, Alfred felt an uncomfortable sensation stab his chest, and he recognized it as something he hadn't felt in a long time.

Fear.

Inside, he was an eight-year-old boy again, chasing after his mother's carriage in the snow as she left them forever. How he had hated her for that—for choosing a carefree life on the Continent over a life with her own children. But he and his brother had managed without her.

He would show her just how well they had managed without her in their lives.

The silver-haired butler, Crawford, opened the door to the library and announced him.

Alfred stepped into the room. A flurry of butterflies danced in his stomach as he saw her turn.

She was beautiful, still—her appearance not much changed from that of the miniature he had gazed at and secretly cherished while growing up.

He saw something flash in her eyes, the same dark walnut-brown as his. But then it was gone.

He steeled his features and approached her, unwilling to give anything away to this woman who had broken his heart so long ago. Stopping in front of her, he made the customary bow, and raised her gloved hand to his lips.

"Mother." He straightened and met her gaze. "You look well. The Italian climate obviously agrees with you. And what, pray tell, brings you to London? Why, it must be twenty years or so. Am I right?"

Lady Harrington regarded him for a moment, then answered. "Yes, Alfred, you are right. I have not been in England for many years. Since you were—"

"Eight years old," he replied. "I'm surprised you remember how old I was when you left us. In fact, madam, I'm surprised you even remember my name.

He saw pain in her eyes, and it unnerved him.

"I remember everything, Alfred. *Everything*."

"Do you?" He fought to keep the anger out of his voice, but it would not be held back. "Do you remember when I called out to you? When I begged you not to go—"

Crawford opened the door just then and stepped inside. "Lady Weston."

Alfred and his mother turned to see Great-Aunt Withypoll enter the library, leaning heavily on her cane. Alfred quickly went to her side. Her hand felt so frail upon his arm as he guided her toward the sofa.

"Thank you, Alfred," she said, settling herself. Then she

reached out to Lady Harrington. "Alicia, my child—come and give your old auntie a kiss."

In a moment, Lady Harrington was beside the great old lady.

Alfred saw tears in his mother's eyes.

"Oh, Auntie!" Lady Harrington clutched Great-Aunt Withypoll's hand and pressed it to her lips. "I came as soon as I could."

"I know, dear." Great-Aunt Withypoll smiled. "I thank you for responding to my summons so quickly."

"Summons?" Alfred said, sharply. "What summons? You sent for her, Auntie?"

His mother turned to look at him. "Yes, she sent for me. I am surprised that you didn't do it sooner, knowing that she is ill."

"Ill? But she isn't ill," Alfred said, surprised. His gaze went to the aged lady beside her. "Are you?"

She nodded calmly. "I am afraid so, my dear."

"But why didn't you tell me?" he demanded. "We shall consult a specialist, then. Whatever it is, you will be cured. I'll see to it."

"No, Alfred," Lady Weston replied. "I'm afraid there is no cure for what I have. For it is a chronic case of old age."

"But—" Alfred protested.

"But, what? I'm old, m'boy! It's perfectly natural—for a woman my age. So, now that you know I am not going to live forever, let us have some tea. Alfred, would you ring, please?"

Not knowing what else to do at the moment, Alfred obeyed.

Great-Aunt Withypoll—*dying*?

She was right, of course. He had refused to think about such a thing, hoping that somehow he could keep her with him forever through sheer force of will. He ought to have learned long ago, that such things were impossible.

What a way to start the day.

First, his mother arriving out of the blue, and now the threat of losing his beloved great-aunt—the only mother he had ever known. He hoped the afternoon would be more promising.

Soon Crawford appeared, wheeling in the silver tea service. Along with the tea was a tray of *petit-fours* and raspberry scones. Great-Aunt Withypoll helped herself to the *petit-fours*, as they were her favorite.

Though Alfred's appetite was negligible, he dutifully took a scone. He noticed his mother nibbling hers as unenthusiastically as he was.

He sat in the wing chair near the end of the sofa and sipped at his tea, barely noticing that he had forgotten to put milk in it. His heart was a swirling mixture of emotions. He had been so sure that he'd blocked his mother's memory out of his mind forever. And now, here she was, turning his life upside down, bringing back feelings he had sworn to keep buried in the recesses of his heart forever.

He had a sudden a memory of her laughing and holding him close on a warm summer day, twirling around and around in their garden.

Then he remembered doors slamming down the hallway at night. His father's voice yelling. And his mother crying.

But the most vivid memory of all was the day her carriage drove away in the swirling snow. The tears had frozen on his face in the bitter cold.

And now, here she was, sitting only a few feet away from him after all these years.

Why had she come back?

And why had she ever left in the first place?

She looked up at him then, and he saw questions in her eyes as well. He hardened his gaze and she looked away.

One thing was certain.

Before his mother left London he vowed to find the answers to his questions.

Mr. Cage puffed on the cigar, drawing the fragrant smoke slowly into his lungs. It tasted good.

Dark.

Hot.

Just the way he liked most everything.

Behind him a young girl stood, clad in a sheer chemise of finest lawn, massaging his shoulders. Another one sat at his feet, doing the same.

"So," he said, puffing the cigar. "She got away."

"Yes, sir." Grimes stood before him, cap-in-hand. "Won't happen again, sir."

"I know, Grimes. I know." Cage smiled, pointing his cigar at him. "You're a smart man. I know you won't disappoint me again."

"'Twas just bad luck this time, sir. We'll get 'er next time."

"Yes, about that. I've been thinking we should become a bit more aggressive in our plan." Cage stood up, brushing away the girls' hands, and stepping over the one at his feet as if she were no more important than a foot stool.

He walked to his liquor cabinet and poured himself another brandy. He didn't offer any to Grimes.

"It is obvious to me that Miss Atwater is a tenacious young woman," he said. "And while I admire that in her, I will not tolerate her interfering with my business. She must learn to understand that. So, we must look at the problem a different way. Since Miss Atwater will not be dissuaded from her cause, we must remove part of the equation."

"'Ow do we do that, sir?" Grimes asked.

Cage watched the end of his cigar glow orangey-red. "You know what they say. It's best to fight fire with fire."

Alfred looked out the carriage window and watched the darkened city roll by. Restlessness churned in him like the waters of a stormy sea.

Thoughts swirled in his head—of his mother, of Great-Aunt Withypoll, and of Miss Prudence Atwater.

He had been unable to see her today due to his mother's unannounced arrival. And after the previous night's episode with the thwarted abduction, he'd meant to check in on Prudence today.

Now, as his carriage headed toward the Theater District, he felt an uncomfortable surge in his heart. And though he was reluctant to admit it, he realized the true nature of his mission.

He needed to see her.

For some reason, when the pain of seeing his mother had bitten at his heart, he'd wanted to go to Prudence—as if perhaps she would have the answers he sought.

The carriage turned onto Drury Lane, and Alfred immediately noticed the shadowy forms of the girls as they walked along the lamp-lit street. He sat up and peered out, looking for Prudence's unmistakable red hair.

He didn't see her.

Instead, he met the eyes of the girls she hadn't yet reached. They regarded him with wariness. He could feel their desperation like a physical thing.

He knocked on the roof with his walking stick, and the carriage rolled to a stop. Without waiting for the driver, he opened the door and hopped down onto the cobblestone street.

"Just be a moment, Tomkins," he called up to the driver.

Two young girls stood huddled under the leafy branches of an oak tree. When they saw him approaching, they ventured forward, letting their tattered shawls fall away from their bare shoulders to better display their wares.

"Good evenin', sir," one of them said. "D'ye fancy some company?"

"Actually, no." Alfred brought out his pocket-book and took out a few pound notes.

"Then what's the money for?" the other one asked, eyeing Alfred skeptically.

"It's for you—for both of you," he said, holding out the notes to each of them. "I don't want anything in return, just your assurance that you'll use it to get yourselves some supper."

"Supper? But it's so much, milord!" the first one exclaimed.

"Yes, well, you should be able to eat on that for awhile then, won't you?" he answered.

"What's your game, then?" the other one said. "What d'ye want from us? No man gives away money if 'e don't expect somethin' back."

"Well," he began, "perhaps as a way of offering your thanks, you can provide me with some information. I'm looking for a girl with curly red hair, quite beautiful and well-put together. Wears a purple silk cloak."

"Oh yeah, her," the first one said. "A real fancy one. We seen 'er. Down the end o' the street, there."

Alfred made his bows and headed back to the waiting carriage. "I thank you, ladies. To you both, I bid a good evening." He hopped back inside and watched the girls stare at him with open mouths, still holding the pound notes in their grimy hands.

Soon, the carriage pulled to a stop again at the end of the street. Alfred scanned the darkened shadows for any sign of Prudence.

He looked to the other side of the street, and his heart clenched uncomfortably as he took in the scene across the street.

Prudence stood near a lamppost, her wild red hair spilling over creamy bare shoulders. Her red skirts were hiked up, showing off a generous length of thigh, which had certainly caught his attention the first night they'd met. And he was convinced that the neckline of her scarlet gown was even lower than she usually wore it.

But her appearance was not what made his throat constrict.

It was the sight of her talking to a man—one who obviously wanted to give her a night's employment, among other things.

Hadn't he himself tried to enlist her services the very same way this blackguard was now doing?

Of course, he had.

He was a rake and a rogue, and an unapologetic one at that.

But it was one thing for *him* to proposition Prudence. It was quite another for *someone else* to do it.

Especially now that he—

He refused to finish that thought, and instead leapt from the cab and stormed toward Prudence and the unidentified man.

She smiled and batted her eyes coquettishly at the cad

in front of her. Then her expression changed as she caught sight of Alfred stalking towards them.

Alfred stopped short and gripped the man's shoulder. "Pardon me, my good man, but the lady is engaged." He jerked the man away from Prudence.

Lord Rigglesford squinted his beady eyes up at Alfred and squeaked, "Weston? What the devil are you about?"

Alfred glared at him, saying, "What I am about is resuming my conversation with this beautiful lady, whom I made an appointment with earlier this evening."

"What previous engagement?" Rigglesford said, turning to Prudence. "She didn't say anything about a previous engagement."

Prudence gave a wide-eyed look of innocence. "Well, I didn't mention it before, milord, as 'e was a bit late, ye see? Didn't know if 'is lordship was comin' at all. But now he's 'ere."

"Yes, now he's here," Alfred repeated, pulling Prudence toward the waiting carriage. "Good evening, Rigglesford. Next time I see you at Jackson's, I'll try not to knock the stuffing out of you, alright?"

Alfred helped Prudence into the cab and tried to contain himself. "Where is Mungo? And why wasn't he doing his job?"

"Mungo is where he usually is," Prudence answered, crossly, "out of sight of the street. And he *was* doing his job."

"Well, I didn't see him come to your defense when that little rat of a man was harassing you," Alfred countered. "Why, Rigglesford was practically undressing you where you stood. Which wouldn't be difficult, considering how little you are wearing."

"And who are you to act in such a manner?" she

demanded, hotly. "Who are you to say anything at all about what I do or how I do it?"

"Who am I? Who am I, you say? Well, I'll tell you. I seem to be the only person in this carriage who has a brain, that's who!"

"Of all the nerve!" Prudence said, eyes blazing.

"Me—*I* have a nerve?" Alfred retorted. "Don't you know that it tears me apart to even think of another man putting his hands on you, let alone being forced to watch it?"

Before she could reply he leaned forward and pulled her into his arms.

"You're wondering why I came to you tonight," he said. "Why I sought you out. The reason is simple. I needed to see you, Prudence. I needed *you*. Like this, in my arms—beautiful and wild and infuriating, just as you are. And most of all, I needed to kiss you...like this."

He buried his hands in her hair and brought her mouth up to be captured by his. She gasped as he parted her lips with his tongue.

The challenge of such a kiss—of such a woman—thrilled him. Holding her was like holding a thunderstorm in his arms. He could feel her passion, her wild unpredictability warming every inch of his skin.

The taste of her, like sweet honey, made his body hum with desire.

She moaned, and he felt her soften in his arms.

He trailed kisses down her face, the soft skin at the hollow of her neck. Her fingers twined in his hair, and her breathing quickened as his mouth moved lower.

He couldn't stop his hands from reaching out to touch the exquisite curve of her breast. Softly, his lips brushed the soft skin exposed by the plunging neckline of her dress. He wanted so much to see all of her, to touch all of her, it was driving him mad.

His mouth dipped lower, to the hollow between her breasts.

He tasted her there, and felt his pulse quicken to a thrilling pace. He reached up to slide her dress down off her shoulder. Yes, this was exactly what he needed....

"Alfred?"

"Yes, my sweet?"

He supposed he should have seen the slap coming. But he didn't.

Before he knew what he was about, his head was snapping sharply to the side, and his cheek was on fire.

He wanted to be angry, but couldn't seem to muster anything at all to that effect. Because he knew he deserved it. Reluctantly, he met Prudence's fiery gaze.

"Don't even begin to think that I'm through with you yet, Lord Weston," Prudence said, haughtily. "I've only just begun!"

CHAPTER THIRTEEN

Prudence stared at Alfred, indignation shining bright and hot in her eyes.

"Just what did you think you were doing? And just *who* did you think you were doing it with?" she demanded.

"I—" he sputtered.

"You, ox-brained, meaty-handed oaf!" Prudence proclaimed. "You think that just because I wear these clothes, and pretend at being a light-skirt, that I *am* a light-skirt. That you may have your way with me whenever and wherever you choose. Or perhaps you think that I am so weak-minded and spindly-spined, that you can ply me with kisses until I leap into your arms, wearing nothing but the ribbon in my hair, and beg you to take me then and there."

"That is not how I think of you, Prudence," he said.

"Is it not?" she replied. "Well, you most certainly do not think of me as a lady who demands the respect of a peer of the realm. Perhaps it is simply my lower station in life that makes you try to seduce me with kisses, then."

"That is *not* why," Alfred said, angrily. "I think you are a passionate woman, Prudence. Far more passionate than you know."

"And because of that, you may take liberties with me which are far more serious than kissing?" she retorted. "I suppose you know more about my own nature than I do."

"Perhaps I do," Alfred answered. "I know that you enjoyed my lips on yours. The least you can do is admit that."

Prudence's eyes flashed with fire as she sat forward and jabbed a finger in his face. "Perhaps I did, but I did not ask you to undress me, my lord. You went too far."

He couldn't argue with that. "You're right, Prudence. Tonight I was an unthinking oaf with the sense of a randy bull. I came to you seeking comfort. And like a man, I sought it in your arms—the arms of a woman who has been driving me mad with desire since the first time we met. Though you may not believe me, I meant no disrespect. I wanted, no *needed* to see the beauty of your face, to touch the perfection of your skin. To somehow be washed clean by your innocent passion."

He continued, "There's a bit of a beast in every man, Prudence. I'm no different. But do you know how fearful I am for you, when I know firsthand what's in the hearts of the men who proposition you out here? Perhaps I was brutish just now—blinded by my own desire—but it was just that. Above everything else, I want you to know that you are safe with me, and that I would never, ever hurt you."

Finally, she said, "I know that you would not hurt me, Alfred. Not in the way you fear another man might. But I have Mungo to protect me—"

Alfred waved a hand in dismissal. "The attack on you

the other night has established that one man's protection is not enough. You are in danger, Prudence. Every night that you go out walking the streets, searching for girls to help, you put yourself in grave danger. A danger so insidious, so dark that you cannot possibly imagine it. Have you not thought what might happen if you are abducted by whoever it is that is harassing you? Well, I have thought of it. I cannot sleep for thinking of it."

Her chin rose in stubborn refusal. "I will not give up my work with the girls."

"I know," he answered, taking her hands in his. "Your bravery is both admirable and infuriating. And it might well land you in a great deal of trouble... Trouble that Mungo and I might not be there to help you out of. If I were your husband—"

"My *husband!*"

He smiled. "Yes, thank God that I am not, but if I were your husband I've a mind it would be quite easy to keep you home at night, and not roaming the streets."

She lifted a brow. "Oh? And pray, however would you do that?"

He let his smile widen slowly, all the while watching her mind work.

"*Oh...*"

He imagined her saying that over and over again, riding waves of pleasure as she straddled him—hair wild, eyes glazed.

"You shouldn't have said that, Prudence. It's giving me ideas."

"Well, then I should be glad that you are not my husband," she answered. "But you see, there will be no chance of that, Lord Weston, as I intend never to marry." She sat back on the seat with a satisfied smile.

"What? Never marry?" he asked, shocked. "You mean,

you intend to become a spinster—never have children or a family of your own? Well, I must say, that's dreadfully unsociable of you."

"It is not unsociable," she said, "it is my *choice,* you infuriating blockhead!"

"Well, I find it unsociable," he replied. "Keeping everything you have to offer a man—your intelligence, your beauty, your extremely kissable lips—hidden away forever? Not to mention what you will be losing; an opportunity to study the intricacies of a daily relationship with another human being, in this case, a man. Why, if I didn't know better, I'd wager to guess that the real reason you have decided not to marry is that you are, quite simply, afraid."

She sat ram-rod straight. "*Afraid?* You are quite mistaken, my lord. It is not with fear that I regard the institution of marriage, but with disdain. Why, I would sooner throw myself from London Bridge than marry any man."

"A drastic, if effective measure," Alfred answered, amused. "But why, my dear?"

"Because the institution of marriage is much like another institution I am sure you have heard of," she explained. "Prison."

"So, you view marriage as a prison, do you?" He was intrigued.

"For me it would be."

Alfred chuckled. "Funny, it is usually the man who sees it as a life sentence, and the woman who sees it as a necessity."

"For many women it is a necessity," Prudence agreed. "They need a man to support them, provide a home, and give them children. But in exchange, the woman gives away her freedom, such as it is. But I do not want or need any of that. All I want is the freedom to help others, as I do now with the Atwater School."

"Perhaps you are right to give up the idea of marriage," he said. "In that regard, you have more freedom than I do. I have a duty to carry on the Weston name and ensure that the family fortune is passed on. Just as a woman becomes a breeding mare in matrimony, so too a man is put to stud."

He shifted in his seat. "Time is running out for me, Prudence. Great-Aunt Withypoll is ill, and she won't live forever. She wants to see me settled with a wife, to start filling up our nursery. And yet, I fight against the very thought of it. I have seen the most unhappy marriages... aside from Beckett and Isobel, of course, but they are an exception. It was never like that for my parents. Their marriage was—and still is—a complete disaster."

Just the thought of it made his head hurt—his parents' failed marriage, his mother's unexpected return, the old wounds it opened and left raw and exposed.

"What will you do?" Prudence asked quietly, as if she could read his very thoughts.

"About what?"

"Marriage."

He shrugged. "I will do my duty, I suppose. I will marry a quiet, biddable girl of good breeding who will be content to attend assemblies and balls, do needlepoint and bear my children. The sooner the better."

"Sounds completely awful."

"I know." He looked across at Prudence and noticed her gaze transfixed at something out the window.

Before Alfred had time to stop her, Prudence was out the door and running toward the Atwater School.

Alfred felt his own gut harden in fear as he raced after her.

The Atwater School was on fire.

The sky glowed orange, as clouds of smoke were lit by the flames that rose into the night sky. The building itself seemed to be choking on the smoke that poured out of the third-floor windows and poisoned the air.

Prudence ripped off the hindering cloak and ran toward the school. She could hear Alfred shouting something behind her, but paid no attention.

Were they all still inside?

Dear God, protect them!

At the front steps Prudence reached out desperately for the door, recoiling from the smoke. She fished for her key in her reticule and hastily put it in the keyhole. But something was stopping the key from going in all the way. She tried frantically to push it in, but to no avail.

"The key, I can't get it in. Something's jamming the keyhole*!*"

"Get back, Prudence!" Alfred yelled, grabbing her shoulders and wrenching her away.

"No! Let me go. I have to save them!"

Mungo appeared beside her—he'd undoubtedly been close behind them the whole way home from Drury Lane. Tomkins, the driver of Alfred's carriage ran to join them.

"She says the lock is jammed," Alfred said. "We'll have to break down the door."

"I've got something in the coach," Mungo said, then headed back toward his carriage with Alfred's driver.

A window crashed from above. Dolly's head poked out as she yelled, "Help us! For the love of God, we'll burn alive!"

"Dolly!" Prudence cried, reaching her hands up futilely.

She swallowed and tried to ignore the rising panic in her chest. She had to be strong, now, for Dolly and the girls. She shouted up to her frightened friend, "They're coming to break down the door. Are the girls alright?"

Dolly looked frantic. "They're all with me, except for Emma. We couldn't find her. She must be on the first floor. And we're trapped in 'ere. There's fire at the top o' the stairs!"

Mungo and Tomkins ran by with a sledgehammer and an iron wedge, joining Alfred at the door.

"Come on, boys!" Alfred waved them up and helped them place the wedge in the lip of the doorframe. "Tomkins, help me with it here, like that. Now, hit it, Mungo—hit it for all you're worth!"

The huge man grimaced and swung the sledgehammer back. It hit the wedge and the door creaked, but didn't give way.

"The door is made of oak," Alfred said. "She won't give way easily. Try it again!"

Mungo swung his arms back and growled, hitting the wedge dead-on. Splinters of wood went flying, and Alfred and Tomkins jerked their heads away to keep from being blinded by shards of wood.

"Almost there, Mungo," Alfred yelled. "One more, man. One more and we're in!"

Prudence looked up at Dolly, saw the terror in her face.

"Oh, hurry, Mungo, please!" Prudence cried.

Mungo lifted the hammer, bellowed and swung it back again. With a loud groan, the door finally gave way, sending more splinters into the air. The three men pushed against the heavy door and it seemed like a mouth from hell opening, belching smoke as it welcomed them into the fiery haze.

Alfred turned to Prudence, commanding, "Stay outside, Prudence. Promise me—"

"No, I must help them!" Prudence protested.

"For once, do as I ask of you!" He jabbed a finger at her as he turned to enter the fiery abyss. "Obey me in this, Prudence. *Stay here!*"

Prudence watched him disappear into the smoke, a war of raging emotions burning in her heart.

Fear...anger...helplessness, they all swirled together in her gut as she reluctantly stepped back from the door.

She looked up at Dolly's window, and felt white-hot fear take over.

"Dolly!" she shouted. "Dolly, they're coming. Hang on, just a little longer!"

But there was no reply.

The window was empty.

For a moment, Alfred found himself disoriented. The smoke stung his eyes and burned his lungs. He coughed, lifting his sleeve to his mouth and breathing through it. He could see shapes up ahead, illuminated by flame and clouds of orange-colored smoke.

"Mungo! Tomkins!" he shouted, and saw the men turn. He hurried toward them.

"Fire's at the top o' the stairs, sir." Mungo pointed up at the crackling flames. "If we don't get up there soon, the stairs will give way."

Alfred nodded. "We have to split up. Tomkins, you search the first floor. Mungo and I will go upstairs. Go!"

Tomkins gave a nod and turned down the opposite end of the hallway, shouting that help had arrived.

Alfred and Mungo exchanged a look, and each took a

deep breath in preparation for what they were about to do. Then, knowing there was nothing else for it, they bounded up the stairs.

Flames licked down at them from above, like the tongue of a hungry beast. The fire seemed to growl and moan like a demon from hell. All around them the glow of the flame mocked and beckoned them, drawing them deeper and deeper into the fire's lair.

The two men headed for the room where Dolly had poked her head out the window. They came to the door and heard screams beyond it.

Both men hurled themselves against the door, and when it gave way, they almost fell into a gaping hole that shot flames from floor to ceiling. The fire had burned through the floor from the room below. Now, the flames climbed greedily up the bedroom wall, feeding on the wood and wallpaper like a hungry babe at its mother's breast.

"Dolly!" Mungo shouted. Dolly lay unconscious on the floor, while the other girls stood huddled around her with frightful faces, coughing from the thick smoke.

"Wait," Alfred held the big man back. "That floor's ready to cave in. You weigh a lot more than I do—I'll go in and bring her out, then pass her to you."

Without waiting for Mungo's approval, Alfred gingerly stepped through the door, and kept to the side as the flames reached closer.

He reached Dolly, squatted down, and lifted her into his arms. He headed back to the door, hugging the side of the wall. He felt the floor shift slightly under the extra weight, and practically danced his way across it.

Upon reaching the door, he quickly transferred Dolly into Mungo's waiting arms.

Turning back, Alfred dashed into the room again,

gathering the girls together. He ripped off his jacket and vest, handing them to the frightened girls.

"Breathe through the cloth," he ordered, "We're going to go out into the hallway, then down the stairs as quick as you can. Stay close to me. Are you ready? Follow me!"

Alfred stepped quickly across the deteriorating floorboards, and reached the door, passing the girls out into the hall one by one. As the last one neared the door, she stopped and stood frozen to the spot and stared transfixed as the flame seemed to creep across the floor toward her like a serpent.

"Come on!" he shouted, recognizing the girl he had talked to in the garden. "Annabelle, come on!"

But Annabelle just stood there, eyes wide with horror as she watched the flame lick across the floor with its bright orange tongue.

With a hideous shriek, the floor gave way, and Annabelle fell through, screaming.

"Annabelle!" Alfred bolted, but slowed himself when he felt the floor heaving under his feet.

He looked down into the gaping hole that seemed to lead to the fires of hell itself, and saw Annabelle dangling there, just out of the flame's reach. Her housecoat had caught on a jagged beam, and she now hung helpless above the burning room below. Her screams sliced through the air, sharp with terror.

"Hold on, Annabelle! I'm going to get you out of there."

Alfred lay down on the floor to make himself more stable and reached his hands over the side of the hole. Her hands frantically tried to grasp his. She slipped out of his grasp and he swore an oath, grabbing her in an iron grip. He grit his teeth, pulling her up with all his might. He gave one last pull, sitting back and bringing her up over the side.

The flames shot higher and Alfred felt the floor giving way. He scrambled to his feet and grabbed Annabelle, practically throwing her out the door ahead of him. They had just made it to safety when the floor of the bedroom crumbled into the mouth of the fiery beast.

We've got to get out of here, now!" Alfred shouted, heading for the stairs. The girls were close behind him as he led the way out.

Alfred could see the doorway at the end of the hall. He stopped at the foot of the stairs and looked back to see that all the girls were close behind him. They huddled close, fearful eyes peeking out from over his jacket and vest as they shared them to breathe through the smoke.

"Alright, out you go, now. I'll stay back here and follow you out."

He herded them toward the door and watched them scurry out like little mice. When the last one was safely through, he dashed out as well, coughing and sputtering more than he would have liked.

He saw Mungo attending to Dolly, and Prudence checking her girls like a mother hen counting her eggs. Tomkins stood by with blankets from the coach.

Prudence saw Alfred, and came rushing over to him. "But where is Emma?"

"She isn't with you?" he asked.

Prudence looked stricken "No..."

"Tomkins!" Alfred beckoned his driver, who dutifully trotted over. "You didn't find anyone on the first floor?"

"No, sir. I searched everywhere. Not a soul to be found."

Prudence covered her hand with her mouth. "She must be on the third floor." She moved toward the door but Alfred stopped her.

"You're not going in there, Prudence. I'll go." He looked

up at the third floor and saw orange flames reaching out the window as if to welcome him back in.

One of the girls passed his vest to Prudence, and she handed it to him. He looked into her eyes, her beautiful face, and knowing it might be the last time he did so, swept her up into a fervent kiss.

Without looking back, he covered his mouth and ran back into the burning house.

CHAPTER FOURTEEN

Alfred raced up the stairs, dashing from side to side as bits of flaming wood dropped from the ceiling. The house was in its last throes, now. Soon it would be completely consumed.

The smoke had grown thicker, and he coughed almost constantly as he pushed upward.

Perhaps it was a fool's mission. But he would rather die trying to beat the cunning flames than to let them win without a knock-down, drag-out fight.

He came to the second floor landing saw that the bedroom that he'd rescued the other girls from was now almost completely engulfed in flames. As he neared the top floor, he could hear the flames raging above him.

The smoke forced him to stop for a moment. Even breathing through his jacket seemed futile here. His lungs fought for air, and his eyes burned from the smoke.

He was almost to the third floor landing.

It would be no picnic when he got there, either.

Flames ate at the walls and curled up and over the ceiling. The heat was at its most intense here, and Alfred felt it weaken him. Another of the fire's dirty tricks, he thought.

He called out and though he was trying to shout, his voice rasped like an old man's. "Emma!" he called again.

There was no response.

He made his way to the first doorway, and saw a room full of flame. He shielded his face from the heat and pressed on, moving to the other side of the hallway and found a room filled more with smoke than fire. Alfred called out again, but there was only the sound of the cackling flames.

He was about to turn and go when he saw her.

There in the far corner, Emma lay unmoving on the floor. He rushed to her and pulled her into his arms. Dizzy from the smoke, he struggled to lift her.

If only he could get a breath!

He grit his teeth and headed for the stairs. He'd be damned if he let this fire get him now.

The stairway was still clear, just barely. Alfred dashed down steps, hugging the wall as the flames reached out long hot fingers.

A thick beam cracked as it broke free above them, and Alfred leaped out of the way as it crashed down onto the staircase.

They were almost there.

He dashed down the hallway, hearing the staircase crumble behind him, the fire devouring the structure as if it had teeth.

With a sheer act of determination, Alfred pushed forward and ran out the front door.

Unable to do anything else, he sank to his knees with Emma still in his arms, while Prudence and Mungo rushed to his side.

Alfred coughed uncontrollably as Prudence crouched

down beside him. Mungo ministered to Emma, and soon the girl regained consciousness, looking weakly about at everyone. Her fellow students surrounded her and wiped away tears of joy.

And though she tried to hide it, Alfred saw Prudence wipe away a tear or two as well.

"Please, don't cry on my account," he croaked. "I'm quite certain that I shall live."

Prudence regarded him, with a mixture of rage and relief in her expression. "Don't you dare make jokes at a time like this!"

"Nothing like kicking a man when he's down, eh?" He coughed again, quite pitifully, he thought.

Prudence opened her mouth to say something, but shut it. Instead, her eyes filled up with glistening tears. Alfred watched in wonder as a fat, twinkling teardrop ran down her cheek, glittering like a diamond.

"My word, I must be in terrible shape if I'm making you cry. Tell me, my dear," he said with all the melodrama of a true thespian, "will I ever walk again?"

"I said no jokes!" she said.

"Alright, no jokes." He sat up, duly chastised, and reached out to wipe another tear that slid down her cheek.

"What shall we do, Alfred?" she asked. "The school—"

"Hush, now." He pulled her into his arms and cradled her close, thankful that she didn't care who might be watching. "It will be taken care of. You shall stay with me in my house in Mayfair."

She pulled back for a moment, her expression confused.

He explained, "You *all* shall come to stay with me, Prudence. I have more than enough room. I would be pleased to provide a temporary home for the Atwater School. Great-Aunt Withypoll will insist upon it. *I* insist upon it. No arguments, now."

Lifting her chin, Alfred gently placed a soft kiss upon her lips—effectively ceasing any arguments Prudence might have made.

The ride to Mayfair was quiet. They had piled everyone into the two carriages and drove in a somber procession along the dark London streets.

Alfred kept his arm around Prudence for the length of the journey.

She'd felt so lost, so afraid. He had simply offered the comfort of his strength—quietly and without ceremony. He would never know how grateful she was for that.

Upon their arrival, the butler effortlessly mobilized the house staff and organized the preparation of food and rooms for the guests. A physician was summoned, the authorities were notified, and before long, Prudence saw the girls to their beds.

The house was quiet, now.

Though she knew she should be exhausted, sleep eluded her. All she saw when she closed her eyes were the flames.

Oh, what was she to do now? The Atwater School—her father's dream—was now no more than a pile of cinders.

She'd heard Alfred and Mungo talking in the hallway. They were trying to shield her, but she knew their suspicions. They thought the fire had been deliberately set—to keep her from taking the girls off the streets.

Could it be true?

Could someone have planned to murder them all?

It was a chilling thought.

All she'd been trying to do was help these girls. To give them a chance at a better life. And tonight, it had almost cost all of them their lives.

She was in danger. They were all in danger, because of her.

A hideous knot formed in her gut, heavy and sour. Fear crept up her throat with cold fingers that threatened to strangle her.

She threw back the covers. Dolly stirred in the other bed but did not waken. At least one of them could get some rest. Prudence hastily donned the robe that matched her white lawn nightdress and tied the satin ribbon.

Somehow, Alfred's butler, Crawford had arranged for them all to have nightclothes. There would be dresses for the morning, as well.

Prudence turned the door-handle and stepped out into the hallway. Crawford had mentioned that his master's rooms were down the adjoining hallway, if Lord Weston was needed during the night.

She crept silently around the corner, hoping she wouldn't become lost in such an enormous house. Finally she came to the door, and praying it was Alfred's, knocked softly.

The door before her opened silently.

Alfred stood in the doorway, his tall frame a dark silhouette against the warm glow of the room. His white shirt was open to the waist, revealing a broad, muscular chest, the sight of which had Prudence almost swallowing her tongue. His black hair was wild and unruly about his face, and his eyes, though dark as midnight, shone down at her with intensity.

"Prudence," he said, finally. "What is wrong? Is someone ill?"

She shook her head, muttering, "I can't sleep."

He rested his hand against the doorframe and shifted his weight. "I haven't even bothered trying."

"May I come in?" she asked.

Alfred stepped back, sweeping his arm into the room in invitation. "I was just having a brandy. Perhaps a glass might help you sleep."

Prudence walked past him and felt a tingle when her arm brushed against his. She smelled the spicy soap he'd used to wash away the ash from the fire. It lingered on his skin, teasing her with its bewitching fragrance.

"I'm afraid the tea didn't settle me as much as I'd hoped." She looked about the room, so as not to stare at him. "Perhaps you are right. A brandy might calm my nerves."

Wordlessly, he poured a glass and handed it to her, then poured himself another.

She looked up at him, and felt her heart tighten with emotion. This was the man whose bravery had saved so many lives tonight.

The man who had offered her his strength, and demanded nothing in return.

The man who had generously taken her and her students—not to mention Mungo and Dolly—into his home.

And now he stood before her like a dark god, dangerous and mysterious as midnight, offering her shelter once again.

"Aren't you going to taste the brandy, Prudence?" he asked, his voice like velvet.

She lifted the glass to her lips, and took the brandy into her mouth. It burned her throat a little, but she liked the sensation.

Alfred took a swig of his as well, all the while studying her with those dark eyes. He made no move to close his shirt together as a proper gentleman might.

She had an urge to slip her fingers inside and feel his skin there, knowing his chest would undoubtedly be as warm and hard as it looked.

Instead, she met his riveting gaze.

"The fire wasn't an accident, was it?" she asked.

He shook his head. "No. I don't believe it was."

"But why?" she said, shaking her head in confusion. "Why would someone do this? If we hadn't come along when we did—"

"Dolly and the girls would be dead, yes," he interjected. "But our villain was hoping *you* would have been in there, too. Someone tried to kill you tonight, Prudence. And the fact that they failed only means they'll most likely try again."

Prudence turned away. She didn't want to hear such things.

"You are in grave danger," Alfred continued. "I don't know how else to say it. You must be protected from this villain. To do that may mean protecting you from yourself."

"From myself?" She felt anger rising and fought against it.

Was he going to blame her for this?

"From now on," he said, "I want you to do as this criminal wants. You must stop going out on the streets and stealing his girls away from him."

"What? But they need my help!" she protested.

"I agree," Alfred answered. "They do need your help. And if you want to continue helping them, you will have to leave them alone for awhile. Until we can make a plan to trap the bastard."

"But—"

"No 'buts', Prudence," he argued. "You and your girls narrowly escaped a fiery death tonight. Your school was burnt to the ground. Don't think that this person is going to leave you alone with just a good scare. Oh, no. He'll want to finish the job, I assure you. Unless, of course, you back off."

"How can you ask me to do that?" she demanded.

"I'm not asking, Prudence—I'm telling you," Alfred countered, pulling her toward him and against the hard wall of his chest. "Don't you know how afraid I am for you? Don't you know that if anything happened to you, I'd never forgive myself? This madman tried to kill you tonight. He tried to abduct you only days ago. I won't lose you, Prudence. Not now."

He dipped his head and covered her mouth possessively. His hands molded her body to his own, and she heard him groan in need.

Sensation rocked through her, dancing across her limbs and making her feel light as air. His mouth was doing wonderfully wicked things to her, and she wanted it...needed it. More than she'd ever needed anything before.

This man could bring her to the edge of desire. He was her protector, her dark knight—battling fiery demons for her. In his arms, she'd be safe.

His lips trailed hot kisses down her neck, across her breasts. This time, she wasn't afraid.

Delicious shivers danced up her spine as his mouth tempted and teased her.

Suddenly he stopped and stared down at her, his gaze dark with heat.

To her surprise, Alfred gently pushed her away. "You'd better go, now, Prudence."

She looked up at him, confused.

"If you don't go now, I won't be able to stop myself," he said. "*I want you too much.*"

His words sent a thrill through her belly.

"But I don't want you to stop," she said, finally. "I want to be with you. Please let me be with you."

"Alright," he said, smiling wickedly, "if you're going to be pushy about it...."

He tugged at the ribbon of her robe and slid it slowly down her shoulders, where it fell to the floor at her feet. She was now clad only in the delicate lawn nightdress.

His eyes raked over her body, and she could see his desire, heavy and dark, burning there.

"I'm going to make it good for you. So good." He took her hand gently in his. "Touch me, Prudence. I can see that you want to. And I want you to. I want to feel the softness of your hands on my skin, like this."

He closed his eyes and tilted his head back as her fingers slipped inside his shirt.

Prudence stared in wonder as her hands explored him. His skin was so soft, yet the hard muscles were like granite beneath. His breath caught as she brushed a taut nipple. She smoothed her hand down to slide over his flat stomach.

"Take this off," she said, pulling at his shirt. "I want to see all of you."

He chuckled under his breath, and obeyed.

The warm glow of candlelight made his skin glow golden, made shadows play in places that Prudence ached to touch. He looked like a bronze statue of an ancient god, standing ready for battle.

Unable to help herself, she ran both hands up over his chest, down his powerfully solid arms, up over broad, well-muscled shoulders. Then daringly, she skimmed back down his chest and toward his narrow hips.

She looked into his eyes and saw the raw desire there, saw him fighting to retain control as her hands took their pleasure with his body. She touched his waist, brought her hands around, down the sides of his muscular buttocks, and finally to rock-hard upper-thighs.

"Are you through with me, Prudence?" he asked, his voice low and heavy with passion. "Or would you like to see more of me? Would you like to feel more of me under those delicate hands? Undress me, then. If that's what you'd like."

Unable to resist his command, Prudence let her hands roam downward to the laces that fastened his trousers at each side. They were tied with innocent-looking bows that seemed to beckon her hands of their own accord. She pulled gently and each bow unraveled itself in her fingers. She spread the laces apart, dipping her fingers in to feel his warm skin.

He hissed in a breath as she reached back to touch the roundness of his buttocks. Slowly, she pushed his trousers down to rest on the top of his hips.

He winced as if in pain, closing his eyes and turning his head away. Then he looked back at her, his eyes glittery in the soft light. "Touch me, Prudence. I beg of you...."

She reached down over his trousers, and with a mixture of desire and unabashed curiosity, pressed her hand against his hardened sex.

He moaned.

She felt the masculine power of him in her hands, felt the thrill sing through her veins, and let her fingers explore the mystery of him. He gripped her shoulders as if he needed support, and letting her have free reign over him.

"You witch...," he said, his voice rough. "As hot and dangerous as fire. You'd think a man would learn his lesson."

He pushed her hands away then and pulled her into his arms, holding her captive against the wall of his chest. Backing her against the bedpost, his mouth covered hers as a low growl rumbled in his chest.

Sensation flooded through her, hot, wild, and dizzying. She felt his hands, large and rough, roam up her sides and cup her breasts over her nightdress. Now it was her turn to moan as he rubbed his hands over her breasts, skimming his thumbs over the sensitive tips.

"I want to see you...." He kissed her neck, her shoulders. "I want to touch you. *All of you*, Prudence. I've dreamt of touching you like this. Of making you tremble with desire."

He picked her up and lifted her onto the bed, and when the weight of him pressed on top of her, Prudence almost cried out with delight. He was so solid, so powerful, it quite took her breath away. Her hands twined themselves in his hair as she pulled his mouth down for a feverish kiss.

She felt his hands undressing her, but her mind was too muddled to understand just how deftly they accomplished their task. Then she felt his naked skin next to hers—all of him—warm and heavy as his body pinned her easily to the soft bed.

Alfred leaned back on one arm, and she watched him looking at her, taking his pleasure with his eyes now. It sent a fresh thrill through her body. Softly, he ran his fingertip from the tip of her chin, down her neck and between her breasts, across her stomach....

Prudence closed her eyes in helpless pleasure as his strong hand caressed between her legs. She dug her fingers into the flesh of his arms and she moaned as his hand moved against her in sweet torture.

His mouth covered hers and she clawed at him as he stoked the flames of her desire ever higher. The intensity of feeling frightened her, and yet she knew that she had no choice but to go through the fire, and that Alfred would be there on the other side to catch her.

It was madness, sweet, hot madness, and she cried out, thrashed against him—against her own desire because she knew it was near, it was almost there now—consuming her, melting her heart and shattering everything that she ever was.

She felt something wet on her face, and realized in a haze that they were tears, her tears, and Alfred was brushing them away.

"Oh, my darling," he said, kissing her neck, her hair. "My glorious beauty. To let me see your passion, to let me hold you in my arms as you yourself discovered it. It's more than a man could dream of."

Prudence held his face in her hands and kissed him. "Can I make you feel like that, too?"

"Oh, yes, Prudence."

He rolled on top of her and she reveled in the weight of him. When he pressed his mouth to hers, she opened her lips to him, letting him take his pleasure there. She ran her hands down his shoulders, over his muscular back, thrilling as she felt the muscles bunch beneath her hands. Then, lower, to his hips and hard buttocks as she pressed him close against her.

"I don't want to hurt you," he said, his voice rough with desire, "but I want to be inside you."

"You could never hurt me, Alfred, never." She kissed him hard, spurring him on as the heat of her own desire grew stronger. "Please, Alfred...."

He answered her with a kiss, deep and hot. And while he kissed her, she felt him ease her legs apart, and then he pressed himself against her.

Prudence gasped at the quick shock of pain. But then the pain was gone, and in its place was the wonder of this man, the pleasure of his body.

He leaned up on one arm and shifted his weight so that he could thrust deeper inside her. Prudence closed her eyes at the glory of it.

She felt the heat of passion singing in her veins again, only this time it was hotter, more wicked than before. She opened her eyes and saw Alfred throw his head back, gritting his teeth as he groaned.

Was she doing that to him?

He leaned down and buried his face in her neck, and she knew his pleasure was getting nearer, like her own.

She felt it then as it grabbed hold of her, and she clawed at him as it consumed her, as *he* consumed her—surrendering to his own pleasure with a tortured groan.

He wrapped his arms around her and held her close, feathering her face with kisses. "I'll always keep you safe, Prudence. I promise."

She snuggled against him and promptly fell asleep.

CHAPTER FIFTEEN

Prudence slowly opened her eyes to the golden pre-dawn light that crept through a crack in the heavy draperies. Absently, she burrowed closer to the warm male body next to her, rubbing her hand over the muscular arm that held her close.

She jolted slightly as she realized where she was.

Lord Weston's bed.

And she wasn't just *in* Lord Weston's bed. She was lying *naked* in his bed after a night of forbidden passion.

Heavens, she had to get out of here before the household awoke!

She only hoped that Dolly had slept through the night, and hadn't noticed her absence from their shared room.

Prudence gazed at the man who slumbered beside her, and felt her heart tingle with emotion. In sleep he looked boyish, and she couldn't resist the simple joy of watching him for a moment. She fought the urge to touch the dark lashes that brushed his cheek, or push away an unruly curl from his forehead.

Sleep seemed to make Alfred's masculine perfection even more powerful to behold. His lips, sensuous and full, were parted slightly, and she yearned to press her own against them in a soft kiss. The thought of what his mouth had done to her trembling body in the night sent a hot thrill through her veins.

If she woke him now, and asked him with a kiss to love her again, she knew he would do so slowly, softly, as tenderly as the morning light touched the window. But such joy would not come cheaply, Prudence knew. For if she allowed Alfred to take her again, he would end up with much more than he bargained for.

He would have her heart.

And if she gave him that, Prudence would have to give up everything that she held dear. Her dreams for the Atwater School, her promise to her father, and to herself.

It was far too high a price to pay for such pleasure.

Even with a man as strong and wickedly passionate as Lord Alfred Weston.

Her decision made, Prudence gently lifted his arm from around her waist. As she tried not to wake him, he obliged her in sleep by rolling onto his back and freeing her completely.

Prudence quietly slipped out from under the covers and tiptoed across the floor to find her nightdress and robe. The robe lay at the foot of the bed where Alfred had slid it off her, but the nightdress had somehow made it across the room and was flung upside-down over the wing chair.

Hastily donning the lawn nightdress and robe, Prudence headed toward the door, quiet as a mouse. She put her hand on the door-knob and began to turn it, when a rough voice stopped her.

"Just where do you think you're going?"

Prudence froze, afraid to look behind her. Knowing it was no use, she turned to see Alfred standing beside the bed, tall and naked, and staring at her with dark, dangerous eyes.

"I—was just—" she began to explain.

"*Leaving,*" he finished, walking slowly toward her. "And I was so looking forward to waking with you in my arms, pulling you close for a kiss, and more."

Prudence opened her mouth to speak, but no words came out. She simply stared at the man who stood before her, looking for all the world like Adonis himself.

"What's the matter?" he asked, cocking an eyebrow at her. "Haven't you ever seen a naked man before?"

He was playing her like a violin, and he knew it.

However, two could play at that game.

"I confess, I had not truly *seen* a naked man until now," she replied. "I have been quite close before, but I was so busy at the time, I did not have a moment to examine the gentleman's physiognomy." She looked him up and down, fighting to keep a straight face. "Yes, well, that was quite interesting. I am much obliged. Good day to you, Lord Weston."

She turned to go, but Alfred caught her arm gently. When she looked up into his eyes, she saw the obvious amusement there.

"Well," he said, "of all the things I thought might have happened between us this morning, that wasn't it."

"No?" she asked innocently.

"No." His brow furrowed with disappointment as he studied her. "What are you about, Prudence? There's no need to rush off. The house is not yet awake. And I want you again." He pulled her into his arms and placed a soft kiss upon her lips.

Prudence felt her resolve crumbling like stale bread. Perhaps she was truly weak-willed, because she was perilously close to jumping into Alfred's arms and begging him to make love to her for the rest of the entire day.

"I must go," she said, pulling away. "Dolly is sure to awaken soon, if she hasn't already. And I'll have the girls to see to. Really, I must."

He lowered his head for a kiss. As his mouth warmed hers, she felt her blood heat slowly with dangerous desire.

Goodness, she had to get out of here, now!

Prudence wriggled out of Alfred's embrace and squeezed the door open.

"Prudence, wait—"

She glanced back at Alfred, trying to keep her gaze from roaming hungrily over his muscular, nude body.

"There is something we must discuss," he said. "Later today."

"Yes, of course," she whispered and crept through the door. "Now, I must go. I hear someone about."

Then, closing the door quietly behind her, Prudence turned and tip-toed down the hall. She should have peeked around the corner first, but as it was, she narrowly missed slamming directly into Crawford and his stack of neatly folded towels.

"Oh!" Prudence stepped back and caught her breath.

The grey-haired butler peered down at her, completely unperturbed. "Have you lost something, Miss Atwater?"

"Yes, I have," she replied. "The way to my room."

"Is that all..." he muttered under his breath.

She cleared her throat, saying, "Would you be so good as to point me in the right direction, Crawford?"

"Of course, Miss Atwater," he said. "It is around the corner, at the end of the west hall. Shall I escort you?"

"No, no, that is quite alright," Prudence replied. "I am sure I can manage to find it myself. Have any of the girls risen, yet?"

"No, Miss. It seems that aside from the staff, you are

the only one about this morning. Lord Weston is not an early riser. Usually," he added.

Prudence forced herself to smile sweetly, saying, "I thank you for your assistance, Crawford. You have been most helpful."

She thought she saw a hint of a smile on the butler's lips as he nodded before turning down the hallway toward Alfred's rooms.

Once around the corner, Prudence bolted, running as fast as she could, and at one point almost slid into a bust of Julius Caesar that stood frowning in an archway.

Finally she reached the door to her room, terribly pleased with herself for avoiding any other servants en route. Now, if she could just sneak past Dolly.

The door opened abruptly, and Prudence found herself staring into a pair of angry green eyes. One hand reached out and yanked Prudence in. Dolly turned and shut the door behind her, folding her arms across her ample bosom and looking as cross as a mother bear.

Well, Prudence thought, it was obvious why she had hired Dolly to act as chaperone to the girls. She was clearly a force to be reckoned with.

"Where have you been?" Dolly demanded. "I've been worried about ye fer hours. I woke up and ye wasn't there. Thought ye'd been abducted, I did! I 'ad to go and fetch Mungo—"

"Oh, no—you didn't tell Mungo! Please say you didn't," Prudence said, closing her eyes and plopping down onto the bed.

"What else was I supposed to do?" she asked. "I thought the villain took ye—the one who came after ye in the coach.

Dolly came to sit beside her on the bed. She pulled her into a tight embrace. "I thought ye was gone, Miss. But

Mungo told me ye were alright, ye were with Lord Weston, and ye'd be back to the room in the mornin'. He said ye'd explain it all to me yerself."

Prudence looked at Dolly, dumbstruck. "How did Mungo know where I'd gone?"

"He's like yer own shadow, Miss," Dolly said. "He follows ye everywhere. Wants to make sure ye stay out of trouble, and I'm glad of it."

Mungo knew that Prudence had gone to see Alfred—knew that she had spent the night with him—and he hadn't interfered. For some reason, it touched her quite deeply.

Prudence sighed. "Well, at least this will save me from putting an advertisement in the *Times*, as everyone already knows where I was last night, as well as what I was doing there."

"What *were* ye doing?" Dolly whispered. "Come on, tell!" Seeing the guilty look on Prudence's face, she gasped with delight, "Oh, my! Did ye really? With Lord Weston?"

Prudence looked about the room uncomfortably.

"Ye did!" Dolly exclaimed. "Don't shilly-shally, tell me everythin'. What did 'e do? What did *you* do? And 'ow many times did ye do it together?"

"Dolly!" Prudence said, giggling with embarrassment.

"With a handsome man like that," Dolly said with a dreamy expression, "why, I'd pay *him*!"

Prudence laughed. "I can't keep a secret from you, Dolly. You've guessed the truth of the matter."

"Oh, my girl!" Dolly beamed. "Congratulations! I'm so proud of ye."

Prudence laughed and said, "I beg your pardon?"

"Oh, it's a wonderful thing when a girl becomes a woman," Dolly continued. "Of course, if ye happen to be with a man who doesn't know 'ow to use what the good

Lord gave 'im, it can be a very tedious business. But I'm willing to bet Lord Weston knows exactly 'ow to use 'is God-given talents! Or my name ain't Dolly Simms."

Prudence fell over on the bed, giggling.

"And let me tell ye, my girl," Dolly continued, "once ye've tried it, it's a terribly hard habit to break. Like having yer first taste of sugar. Just makes ye want more."

"Oh, don't say that, Dolly!" Prudence pounded the bed in frustration.

"Why not? Ye must be daft if ye don't want that lovely man again."

"I do. I do want him. That's the problem." Prudence sat up and looked pleadingly at her friend. "I don't dare ever let it happen again, Dolly. It was so wonderful, more wonderful than I could ever have imagined. And if I let myself feel that way again with him, I'll be lost. I know it. Last night I gave Lord Weston my body. But next time, I'll be giving him my heart."

"Oh, dear," Dolly said, looking dismayed. "It's like that, is it?"

"Yes," Prudence said, finally. "I wish it weren't so, but I felt it this morning when I awoke in his arms. I felt so secure, so cared for. I wanted to stay there with him forever."

Prudence felt her heart tighten painfully in her chest, as she continued, "I must be very careful, Dolly. Lord Weston made me feel things I could never have imagined. It is dangerous, for I know how easy it would be to trade everything I hold dear for such pleasure. Perhaps I'm not as strong as I thought."

"Oh, Miss," Dolly said, pulling her close in a motherly embrace. "Don't fret, now. Many a girl has felt the same way after their first time in a man's arms. It can be a wondrous thing, that's for certain."

A knock sounded on the door and a jolly-faced maid poked her head inside.

"Mornin', Misses," she said, bustling in and carrying fresh towels and a large pitcher. "I've brought fresh water fer ye both. Cook is making a hearty breakfast—Lord Weston's orders. I expect he'll be down after yer finished eatin'. A late riser, is the master."

Prudence and Dolly exchanged a look, trying not to giggle.

"Well, good to see yer in fine spirits this mornin'." The maid poured the water and set out their towels. "What with the fire and all."

The maid's words sent a sobering chill through Prudence's heart. After spending the night in Alfred's bed, she had almost forgotten about the fire for a few sweet hours.

"Thank you for your concern... Glynnis, is it?" Prudence asked, rising and smoothing her robe.

"It is, Miss." The woman nodded, smiling and looking quite honored that Prudence had remembered her name. "Glynnis Brodie."

"Thank ye for the water and towels, Glynnis, my dear," Dolly said, patting the woman on the arm as if they were old friends. "We'll be down quicker than ye can spit."

Glynnis's eyes widened for a moment at such plain talk, then she gave a nod and took her leave.

"It's a new day, Miss," Dolly said, pointing at the mantle clock. "We've only an hour or so before school should start. A full day of classes will keep yer mind off yer troubles, I'll wager. But first we've the girls to see to and breakfast to eat. Don't just stand there like a sheep, get movin'!"

Prudence couldn't help but smile as her friend bustled her toward the washstand and placed the screen around it.

"I'll give ye some privacy to wash up," Dolly said. "Just save me a little of that water before it gets cold."

Prudence chuckled. "Don't I always, Dolly?"

Her friend responded with an unconvinced grunt.

But as Prudence pulled the satin ribbon of her robe, she thought of Alfred's hands as they had done the same to her last night. The distracting images and sensations swirled in her mind, and she tried vainly to block them out.

Perhaps Dolly was right, a full day of classes would be just what she needed to keep her mind off her troubles.

To keep her mind off Alfred.

As her blood warmed with memories of the night's passion, Prudence wished the water she bathed with was ice cold.

Alfred looked at the clock again and felt his mood darken as it struck seven-thirty.

It seemed he'd been staring at the bloody clock all day, and not once had it helped him to see Prudence.

First he'd been told that she was conducting classes and shouldn't be disturbed. Then he had his own business to attend to, squiring Lady Weston to luncheon at Almack's. His mother did not accompany them, as she had gone to visit friends and would be away for a few days.

As Great-Aunt Withypoll shared her concerns about the fire, the future of the Atwater School, and the poor, poor girls, Alfred's thoughts were consumed with Prudence.

Flame-haired, passionate little Prudence.

The woman who had quaked and trembled in his arms, and taken him to new heights of desire without even trying.

Alfred had bedded his share of women, but until now, not one of them had haunted his thoughts like an apparition.

What matter if he couldn't stop thinking about the way she'd touched him with such boldness, such innocence? What matter if he could still imagine her little hands feathering his body, then growing more passionate, more wicked as she gave herself free reign over him, touching him as a queen would stroke a slave.

Then she had become the slave, helpless and panting in his arms, yet all the while casting her spell over him like a knowing witch.

He shook his head, as if that would help cleanse his mind, but it was useless.

She was still there, tormenting him.

Like a drunk yearning for his next drink, he was counting the moments until he could see her again, and take her into his arms where she belonged.

It was now thirty-five minutes past seven.

Supper was to be served precisely at eight o'clock, as it always was. He'd be sure to see her then. And it would be a new kind of torture for him to have to sit across from her, being forced to watch as she raised her fork, put her mouth around a delicious morsel of food, and closed her lips around it.

All the while he would want nothing more than to feel those lips on his body, wreaking havoc and reducing him to a panting beast.

He hoped Crawford had put out his favorite burgundy. To get through this dinner, Alfred would need all the help he could get.

Alfred escorted Great-Aunt Withypoll into the parlor, as he did most evenings. The students of the Atwater Academy—looking as polished as they could in borrowed clothes—stood or sat in small groups, waiting for their hosts to join them.

Prudence walked in on Mungo's arm, and Alfred felt an unwelcome stab of jealousy.

Damn, but she looked beautiful. And yet, that word alone could not do the distracting Miss Prudence Atwater justice.

Her hair was piled up into a Grecian style, and her gown of sapphire blue seemed to make her sparkle like the jewel itself.

Even though she was with Mungo—a man who Alfred himself would trust with his own life—he couldn't help but feel envious of him at that moment.

Lord help him. He should have joined the clergy.

Soon they were seated—Alfred at the head of the table and Great-Aunt Withypoll to his immediate left. The aged lady gave a hint of a smile, as if she knew exactly what her great-nephew was thinking, and about whom.

Prudence herself was seated opposite him.

Who had arranged that, he wondered? Most likely, it was Lady Weston. Though this time, he couldn't object to her matchmaking endeavors.

He *wanted* to be near Prudence Atwater.

Preferably when they were both naked.

Damnation, he was no fresh young buck, acting balmy after his first kiss! Yet, the headstrong beauty made him feel so. Prudence had turned his world upside down, and damned if Alfred could turn it right again.

She glanced at him then, and he felt his heart skip a beat. He had a vision of her in bed as their bodies entwined, her eyes glazed with passion, her mouth wet and open as she moaned in pleasure.

A footman began pouring the wine, and Alfred was glad of it. He needed a drink right about now.

"It has been unseasonably hot of late," Great-Aunt Withypoll said at last. "Has it not?"

"Yes it has, Lady Weston," Prudence replied. "I have noticed the heat myself."

"As have I," Alfred said, unable to stop himself from stirring the pot. "Last night in particular was quite warm. There was quite a lot of heat—at least in my chambers."

Prudence almost spit out her wine, but recovered quickly.

She stared at him quietly, an expression of bemused surprise in those sparkling eyes.

"Did you feel the heat as well, Miss Atwater?" he asked.

"Now that you mention it, my lord," she replied, "I did feel something of the sort. I thought perhaps I was coming down with a fever, but happily, the feeling has passed. I feel much more myself today."

"I have been acquainted with similar symptoms, Miss Atwater," Alfred said. "Make no mistake, these fevers of which you speak can strike out of the blue, with almost no warning. And when they do, there is nothing for it but to lie back and accept that you have no control over its power."

"The human body is a miraculous thing, to be certain," Prudence said, unfazed. "In fact, some of my students are about to start a detailed section on human physiognomy, including a study of the body's organs...*all* the organs."

Alfred quirked a brow. "How impressive. Do you know a lot about the organs of the human body?"

"I do now," Prudence replied, sweetly.

It was Alfred's turn to choke on his wine. He waved the butler over, saying, "Water, Crawford. And more wine, while you're at it. Dear God, bring it quickly."

"I admire your ambition, Miss Atwater," Lady Weston said. "The study of the human body is not a subject for men alone—nor is the study or application of medicine. I applaud your commitment to your students, my dear. You dare to give these girls a well-rounded education, no matter if it flies in the face of convention. It is my prediction that one day—perhaps not in my lifetime or even yours—our society will have both male and female doctors, and more. Education is the cornerstone of progress. And you, Miss Atwater, are essential to both."

She gave an appreciative smile to her benefactress, and Alfred couldn't help but agree. The only problem was that Prudence was becoming more and more essential to his happiness as well...and it would be a challenge to convince her of that.

CHAPTER SIXTEEN

Alfred had risen early the next morning, choosing to pass on breakfast with his great-aunt and their guests and instead went to his favorite coffee house on Hardwicke Square.

As he sipped Mr. Teagle's famous brew, he tried to turn his head to the problem at hand—that of finding the person behind the threats to Prudence and the Atwater School. Yet, his mind focused on the lady in question in a most distracting way.

He thought of Prudence possibly carrying his child right now, and felt a swell of male pride. Of course, it would be better for them both if she were not with child. Prudence had made her thoughts on the matter clear to him. She didn't want to marry him, or have children by him.

Not now, not ever.

Of course, she didn't seem to care what Alfred wanted. Only time would tell if she was with child. And if so, he would see them married, even if he had to hog-tie her and carry her down to the church in such a fashion.

He finished his cup of coffee and rose from the table,

placing his beaver hat precisely at the perfect angle upon his head, and gave a nod to the owner.

"See you tomorrow, my lord?" the portly man asked.

"Of course, Mr. Teagle," Alfred replied. "I cannot face the day without a taste of your exceptional brew."

"I'll have a cup waiting for you, sir."

Alfred headed out into the busy street. He sent his waiting coach to the Theater District to wait for him there, for he'd chosen to walk.

The sights and smells of London were a myriad of fascinations. Nearby, a father and his little daughter stopped to buy candied apples. Alfred watched with a pang of something, envy perhaps, as the flaxen-haired little girl held tight to her father's hand and gazed up at him with blatant adoration.

Would he ever have a daughter to buy candied apples for? And if he did, would she look like Prudence, all curling russet hair and sparkling eyes, with a mischievous little grin?

As he passed by, the smell of sweet candied apples filled the air, and he knew he'd forever think of the father and his little girl when he smelled such a thing.

There, an older couple walked arm in arm, but despite their age were obviously still besotted with each other. Would he and Prudence walk arm-in-arm together at that age, and gift each other with the same knowing smiles as these two silver-haired lovers?

A twinge deep in his heart told him that he hoped so, more than he wanted to admit.

He turned the corner onto a tree-lined street, a handy shortcut to the Theater District where he was heading to continue his investigation. As he walked down the street, his thoughts turned to the investigation at hand. He had decided to handle this part of it himself, for now.

Due to his obvious physical superiority, Mungo was on duty back at the house. His role would best be served by keeping a close watch on Prudence and the girls, in case the villain made an appearance at the townhouse.

The danger to Prudence and her students was still very real. And whoever was behind such villainy would strike again, Alfred was certain.

Prudence was a threat to someone. But who? Was it some fanatic who thought all prostitutes were consigned to Hell, and shouldn't be allowed a chance to start again? Was it someone else with a connection to the prostitutes themselves? Or could the villain hold an old grudge against her late father, and be taking his revenge against the daughter? Whoever he was, the villain was dangerous, and couldn't be underestimated.

Alfred had made some discreet inquiries through his Bow Street Runner, a man named Devlin, asking around about brothels and who exactly owned them. Mr. Devlin had obtained a few leads, names and addresses of some of the most exclusive and closely-guarded underground brothels in London. Finding out who owned them, however, was going to be much more difficult.

But somehow, Alfred would find the link between the attacks against Prudence and the prostitutes she was trying to help. He had to, before the villain succeeded in stopping Prudence's crusade once and for all.

Alfred crossed onto another street, this one running one street over from the theater. Though it was early, some of the streetwalkers would be out. Their business never seemed to stop, no matter what time of day.

A few strolled near the corner. Their faces looked hard and worn. He thought of chipped and dirty porcelain dolls that had once been beautiful. But, like discarded dolls, carelessness and overuse had destroyed their beauty. These were the girls that Prudence was willing to trade her own future for—possibly her child's future as well.

Did these jaded streetwalkers know about the woman who fought for them so gallantly? Did they care what it might cost her to help them?

Looking at these poor creatures, he could understand why Prudence felt compelled to help them. Their eyes held the wariness of a beaten animal, the hopelessness of one beyond hope.

He could imagine the thrill Prudence felt at putting the sparkle back in those eyes, of bringing a smile to the hard, pinched mouth, of bringing warmth to a heart that had been deadened by a cold, uncaring world.

Prudence had sworn to help these girls. But now, he needed *their* help to protect her.

He neared their group, and noticed their conversation suddenly come to a halt. Two of them turned toward him, pasting on smiles that didn't come close to reaching their eyes. The other one remained expressionless, staring at the ground.

He touched the brim of his hat. "Good morning, ladies."

"Mornin', Guvna," the tallest one said. Her friend nodded and echoed the same. The third one remained silent, though the tall one poked her arm. "Say hallo to the nice gentleman, Minnie."

Still, the girl remained silent, seemingly oblivious to what was going on around her.

The tall one snorted in disgust. "Don't mind 'er, milord. She don't say much."

"Not at all, ladies," Alfred said, inclining his head. Here he was, trying to pour on the charm for a trio of streetwalkers. The absurdity of it made him want to chuckle, if not for the grave purpose behind his mission. "I wonder if I may engage you ladies, for a few moments of your time."

The tall one smiled, like a cat spotting its prey. "'Course, sir," she replied. "Would ye like all three of us at once, then? Or one after the other? Though Minnie 'ere don't look like much now, she can warm yer bed as well as any 'ore in London. Can't ye, Minnie?" She gave the girl a shake, but there was no response.

Alfred cleared his throat. "I had something entirely different in mind."

The tall woman looked skeptical, but clearly didn't want to lose a customer. "'Ow different?"

"Actually, I would simply like to talk with you," he explained.

"Talk? Oh, ye want some dirty stories, ye mean?"

"Sadly, no," he replied. "I simply have a few questions I should like to ask you. And I would be quite willing to pay your usual rates for a few moments of your precious time, Miss...?"

"Jones—Hildie Jones."

"And I'm Bess Flannery, Guv," the other one said.

"What kind o' questions did ye 'ave in mind?" Hildie asked. "'Cuz ye know, we charge extra fer talkin'. Don't we, girls?"

"Yeah—we charge extra!" Bess said enthusiastically.

Alfred nodded. "Of course. An extra charge would be expected for something of this sort. Quite understandable. I would be happy to pay your fee, Miss Jones. What is it?" He reached inside his breast pocket for his for his bill-fold.

Miss Jones looked slightly unprepared to give an exact number. "Uh, well with the three of us, it would be...*twenty pounds*." She seemed pleased with herself for coming up with such an astronomical sum.

"Twenty pounds it is." Alfred took the notes from his wallet and handed them to her.

"Uh.... plus five pounds," she added hastily, as if this would really put it over the top.

"Twenty-five pounds altogether then. Agreed?" He retrieved a five-pound note and handed that to her as well. She stared at the money as if it were a thousand pounds, and to these girls, it probably was.

"Agreed." She stuffed the notes into the low bodice of her threadbare dress.

It had started to drizzle. He motioned for his waiting carriage to come alongside, and ushered the women inside. Along with keeping them dry, it would also keep the girls safe from prying eyes. They might be more inclined to talk within the safety of a coach. And it was probably quite common for their normal services to be engaged thus and carried out along the side of the road.

Alfred closed the door. "I thought we might have more privacy in here, ladies, as well as keeping us out of the rain."

"Very kind of ye," Hildie said. "Now, what d'ye want to talk about, Guv?"

"I wonder if you might be acquainted with a friend of mine. Miss Prudence Atwater?"

At Prudence's name, Hildie and Bess exchanged glances, but said nothing.

Alfred continued. "Miss Atwater runs a school for young ladies, and sometimes comes down here in an effort to recruit new students. She often dresses in the same style as you, to more easily blend in."

"I know who ye mean. We 'aven't seen 'er," Hildie said firmly.

"I know, you probably haven't seen her lately," Alfred replied. "Unfortunately, her school recently burnt to the ground, and she and her students have been staying at my residence in Mayfair until we can find a new home for the school."

"Yeah? What's that got to do with us?" Hildie demanded. "We don't know nothin' about no fire."

"I'm not insinuating that you do, dear lady," he said. "Not at all. But I am gravely concerned for Miss Atwater's welfare. I have reason to believe the fire was deliberately set, and that her life, and the lives of her students could be in jeopardy. Miss Atwater has committed herself to this cause, of offering an education to girls like yourselves, who may not have the opportunities that other young women do. Because of her dedication to helping others, her life is in danger."

He leaned forward, saying, "I'm asking for your help with some information. That is all. It will be strictly confidential, I assure you. I would not want to put any of you in danger for having talked to me, certainly not. And all of you would be welcome to come back with me and join the school directly, if you so choose."

Hildie and Bess exchanged looks.

"I don't know, Guvna," Hildie said. "Could get us in some lot o' trouble."

"I understand," he replied. "And I would not want you to compromise your own safety in any way. But I am simply trying to protect Miss Atwater's safety and the safety of her students by getting to the bottom of these threats."

The girls regarded each other uncertainly.

Alfred continued, "I think that whoever is trying to harm Miss Atwater may be connected to this business in some way. She would do anything for you girls, anything at all to help you. I only ask that you might do the same for her."

Hildie and Bess looked even more uncomfortable.

"The man did pay us, Hildie," Bess said. "And it ain't askin' much, really."

Hildie gave her a look.

Alfred pulled a piece of paper which Mr. Devlin, the Bow Street Runner, had given him. "I have a list of names, here. I'm going to read them out, and you let me know if any of them sounds familiar, alright? You don't have to tell me anything specific, unless you want to. Just tell me if you recognize any of the names. I will take it from there."

He went down the list. "Walters... Tanner... Vogel?"

"I know a Mr. Vogel," Bess offered tentatively, glancing at Hildie, who seemed clearly unhappy at her friend's willingness to talk. "'E's one o' me regulars. Come on, Hildie. 'E paid us, now we got to do what 'e says, just like for everyone else."

"Can you describe Mr. Vogel, Miss Flannery?" Alfred began making notes.

She pursed her lips. "Hmm...short, balding, and with a very small—well, *you* know."

"Uh—that's not important," Alfred said quickly. "How old is Mr. Vogel?"

"About eighty, I think. Wouldn't ye say, Hildie?"

After a moment, Hildie gave a reluctant nod.

A man of eighty on a crusade to stop Prudence? Didn't sound very plausible, but things weren't always what they seemed. He would have Vogel's affairs looked into.

"Had Mr. Vogel ever expressed any anger or prejudices against ladies in your line of work?" Alfred asked.

Bess laughed. "Oh, no! In fact 'e keeps asking me to marry 'im! Doesn't 'e, Hil?"

"Why don't you accept?" he said.

"Don't think 'is wife would approve!"

"I should say not," he answered, chuckling. "Alright, moving on. Beaufort. Napier."

"Uh, Napier...didn't 'e just croak in Red Sal's bed, Hil?" Bess said. "Last week, I think. Right on top of 'er, 'e did."

Alfred crossed off the name. "Well, at least Mr. Napier died happy. Alright, only a few more here. Humphries."

Hildie frowned. "Yeah, I know 'im. The bastard."

Alfred raised his eyebrows. "A vile fellow?"

"No, a rich fella. Used to be a regular. But he threw me over fer Red Sal. 'E's 'er regular now."

"Age? Description?" he asked.

"Ye can't miss 'im," she said. "Six foot four with hair as orange as a carrot. And lots o' freckles. *Everywhere*. And 'e laughs like a donkey."

"Alright. Humphries—freckles everywhere, donkey laugh," Alfred said, writing down the description. "Any reason to suspect him of threatening Miss Atwater?"

"Not really. Bit of a twit. But 'e likes to settle on one girl and stick with 'er for awhile."

"So," Alfred postulated, "he might be upset if one of his favorites was taken off the streets by a crusading school-marm like Miss Atwater?"

Hildie shrugged. "I suppose. But 'e's with Red Sal, now, like I told ye. And before that, 'e was with me."

Alfred circled the name. "I'll look into it just the same. Just a few more names, ladies, and we'll be done. Granville. Cage."

At that the girls went still.

"Cage?" He asked again. "Do any of you know that name?"

"Yes."

Everyone turned to gape at Minnie. Her eyes lifted and she met Alfred's eyes with a clear, direct gaze. "I know that name."

"Minnie!" Hildie grabbed her arm and gave her a shake. "Don't say another word!"

Minnie shook her off. "I know Mr. Cage, sir. He's a brothel-owner."

"Shhhh!" Hildie hissed.

Minnie ignored her, saying, "That's where I came from. A brothel called The Silver Rose. But there are other brothels. Mr. Cage owns a lot of them, and many of us out here as well."

"That's it!" Hildie opened the carriage door and grabbed Bess.

Alfred followed them out onto the street.

Hildie started walking away, then turned back to the carriage and stuffed some of the notes into Minnie's hand. Minnie threw them back at her.

Hildie shook her head, then crouched down to retrieve the money that had fallen to the ground. She stood and stuffed it back into her bodice, then pointed a finger at Minnie. "Don't say I didn't warn ye, my girl. Come on, Bess, we're out of 'ere!"

They walked hastily down the street.

"You'll tell me more of Mr. Cage, Minnie?" Alfred asked, climbing back into the carriage.

"Yes, sir."

"It's very brave of you, my dear. Would you like to tell me more on the way to my home in Mayfair? I'm sure Miss Atwater would very much like to make your acquaintance there."

"Yes, indeed, sir." Minnie regarded him with a heartfelt expression. "And I would very much like to make hers."

CHAPTER SEVENTEEN

Minnie did not have a cockney accent at all, but a very cultured voice that spoke of being well-reared. Alfred was curious to hear how she had come to such dire circumstances.

On the way to Mayfair, Miss Minnie Danvers related the tragic tale of how she had come to a life on the streets of London. The daughter of merchants, she had grown up in a loving home in Surrey. But when her parents were killed in a carriage accident, she had been left in the care of distant relations, Mr. and Mrs. Macklin, of London. The Macklins were anything but pleased to have another mouth to feed, and that combined with Mr. Macklin's propensity for gambling would lead to tragedy for Minnie.

After losing a great deal of money playing at cards with a man named Cage, Macklin found himself unable to pay his debts. So, he offered Minnie as payment. She had been fourteen at the time.

She'd been taken to a posh brothel called The Silver Rose and had spent almost a year, for all intents and purposes, enslaved there. But after another girl, one of Cage's favorites, had accused her of thievery, Minne had been 'demoted' to streetwalker. She'd been on the streets for six months and was now approaching her sixteenth birthday.

It was a chilling tale. And one that Alfred knew would be all too common.

Minnie told him all she knew about Cage, which unfortunately wasn't much. She had never actually seen him. Apparently, he kept a low profile. But there had been talk among the girls. Some of them had come from other brothels that Cage owned. Minnie remembered a few names: The Black Swan, La Violette, The Zephyr, and The Red Room.

Alfred had heard of some of these establishments—had even, he was ashamed to admit—visited a few. But some he had never heard of before. He would have Devlin find out if there were any others connected to Cage.

Minnie explained that most of the girls in these places came from good families. That was what made them so valuable to Cage. He ran exclusive establishments and charged top dollar for his girls' services. Many of them had been suddenly orphaned and had nowhere to go, others were used as payment for gambling debts as Minnie had been. Whatever their reasons, life in a brothel had become their only means of survival.

Cage held his streetwalkers under his thumb as easily as he did the girls in the brothels. He provided cheap housing for them, and had a network of pimps, henchmen and other undesirables constantly watching them and collecting Cage's share of their earnings. Up until today, Minnie had lived with Bess and Hildie in one room in a crumbling boarding house on Scollard Street.

It was a sobering tale, one that left Alfred feeling angry—perhaps exactly the way Prudence had felt the first time she'd listened to one of these girls tell their story. But instead of accepting the futility of their situation, Prudence had taken a stand. She had committed herself to helping as many girls as she could. And she had been successful, to date changing more than a dozen lives.

Like the Crusaders of old, Prudence had chosen a difficult but valiant path, at great personal cost. But would the choice between a family of her own and her continued work on the streets be too much to bear? If Prudence did indeed carry Alfred's child, she may not have a choice. Would she resent a child that took her away from her work with the school? The thought unsettled him.

After arriving at his house in Mayfair, Alfred left Minnie in Dolly's care.

He left again almost immediately, setting out for Bow Street. He was anxious to speak with his runner, Mr. Devlin, and share the new information he'd obtained from Hildie and Bess.

Time was of the essence, and he'd be damned if he was going to wait around for another attempt on Prudence's life.

She could be carrying his child, and whether Prudence liked it or not, he was going to protect them both.

Later that evening, Alfred's carriage arrived at La Violette. The exclusive brothel was located in a fashionable house on Fairbourne Lane, and was a favorite spot for influential men of the *ton*. The interior was decorated in a luxurious Rococo style, with plush purple velvet, gilt mirrors and Italian marble. Alfred knew the decor of the place quite well because he had been inside it before.

In fact, it was where he had lost his virginity.

It had been his fifteenth birthday, and his father had brought him here after the family dinner for a cigar and a game of billiards. And a bit more as well, Alfred had soon found out.

As a randy lad of fifteen, he had been quite tall and filled-out for his age, appearing closer to eighteen or so. Despite his inexperience, Alfred had been thrilled at the idea of visiting the brothel, and in fact thought it the best birthday gift a boy his age could receive.

But later, in the room with young, blond little Josette, he had become over-excited and embarrassed himself by spilling at her first touch. She had only smiled and cleaned him up, and when he'd sufficiently recovered, started again slowly.

Later, Alfred completed the sexual act properly, but had felt strangely unsatisfied by the experience. Somehow, his victory at crossing into manhood had felt artificial and meaningless. He never told that to his father, of course. He had never told that to anyone at all.

He rapped the shiny brass doorknocker and soon the huge door slowly opened. A large man—they were all large in their line of work—stared down at him and seemed unimpressed.

Alfred introduced himself. "Lord Alfred Weston."

The man looked him up and down, then stood back to admit him. Another man—not so large—but who seemed quite capable of rearranging anyone's face, took Alfred's hat and coat. He motioned him into the main room on the right.

Alfred walked into the salon, breathing in the familiar scent of cigars mixed with exotic perfume. Scantily-clad women laughed and giggled, draping themselves over some of the richest men in London.

The shipping magnate, Sir Titus Pickford, stood with a

beautiful girl on each arm, smiling down at them like a red-faced youth. Nearby, the Marquess of Pellam lounged on a sofa, as a young nymph dressed in diaphanous robes fed him grapes. The Earl of Dibney stood next to a marble fireplace, kissing the hand of a young girl dressed as the goddess Aphrodite.

As Alfred looked about the room at the tableau before him, he was struck not by the eroticism, but by the artifice, the brittle fragility and utter emptiness of the scene.

For he knew who these girls were, now. They were not beautiful little dolls, existing solely for a man's pleasure. They were someone's daughters, someone's sisters—all trapped here like birds in a cage.

"Weston!" A loud voice boomed from across the room.Alfred looked over to see a familiar face. Sir Robert Beattie disentangled himself from the girl hanging off him, and made his way over to Alfred. Chomping heartily on a thick cigar, Sir

Robert extended a hand and pumped Alfred's own.

"Sir Robert." Alfred shook the man's hand. "You're looking well."

"Sir Robert? Such formality, what?" He slapped Alfred on the back with gusto. "You know my friends all call me Bobby! Haven't seen you about in a dog's age, Weston. Come over and have a drink with me and Stan."

Sir Robert pulled him toward a group in the corner, saying, "Poor chap's having a devil of a time now that Beatrice is increasing, what? So I treated him to a night with a hot little piece, name of 'Mignon'." He leaned closer and whispered, "You know all the girls in here are imported direct from Paris, Weston? And damned if they don't know a few tricks our English girls would never dream of!"

Alfred tried to stifle a chuckle at the man's mistaken

ideas. "From Paris? You don't say?" In actuality these girls were most likely from Suffolk, and Hertfordshire, and London itself, all well-coached in French accents.

"I do say, old man!" Sir Robert replied. "But you will have one for yourself this evening, what? Or why else would you be here?"

"Why else indeed?" Alfred said, giving a confident grin.

Sir Robert pulled the amply-endowed Mignon close beside him as they joined the group, saying, "These girls really know how to get a man's blood racing, don't they?"

Alfred made his bows as he was introduced. Lord Hollis, Sir Abelard de Burgh, Viscount Thane, and Sir Stanley Northrop all shook hands with him, and welcomed him to their exclusive gathering. Sir Robert offered him a cigar, and Lord Hollis, whom Alfred knew from his days at Eton, procured him a glass of port.

Eventually Sir Stanley decided to take Mignon up to a private room. Alfred was sorry to see her go, but there was nothing to be done. At least Sir Stanley looked to be an amiable chap, who would treat the girl decently.

Soon the proprietress, Madame du Charmes appeared with another girl to entertain them.

The mature but attractive madam introduced a beautiful girl, Fleurette. With large, pale blue eyes and flowing flaxen hair, Fleurette resembled an angel. Her gown was transparent white, and clung to round, milky breasts and curvaceous hips. The gown, what there was of it, had obviously been designed to tempt and tease, and yet still maintain an aura of virginal purity about the wearer.

It was very effective.

Before, Alfred would have felt a stab of arousal at such an erotic sight. But now he refused to be baited by such carefully orchestrated sexuality. And he refused to act like the other boorish men who blindly kept these women prisoners here.

Sir Robert said, "She is lovely, Madame." He lifted a tendril of the girl's hair and brought it to his nose, inhaling the perfumed tresses. "And she is aptly-named, for she smells as sweet as a rose garden."

Alfred rolled his eyes. The girl's real name was probably something like Philberta or Winifred. And it probably wasn't happenstance that 'Fleurette' smelled like roses, either.

This entire establishment was theater, complete with actors, costumes, and of course, the audience. However, it seemed that everyone was enjoying the show except for himself.

Fleurette smiled up at Sir Robert sweetly, and said in a thick French accent, "Do you like flowers, Monsieur?"

Sir Robert pulled her closer. "Only when they look like you, *ma chere.*" He kissed her possessively, and glanced at Madame du Charmes. "A room for the young Mademoiselle and I."

"Of course, Monsieur. Please follow me," Madame du Charmes said, leading the way toward the opulent staircase.

The group seemed to be breaking up. The viscount was busy with a beautiful redhead, and Sir Abelard had two girls fluttering over him.

That left only him and Lord Hollis. "Fancy a game of billiards, Hollis?"

Lord Hollis smiled, leading the way to the billiard room. "Most men come here for the women, but I come for the billiards. It's a little known secret that La Violette has one of the best billiard rooms in London. The tables are all made of Italian slate."

They entered the billiard room, a dark, mahogany-paneled room which was full of smoke and men. A few girls lounged about the room, but in here, the men were all too intent on the game at hand to pay them much mind.

He and Hollis made their way over to one of the tables and Hollis placed his marker on the side, reserving the next match.

Soon, Alfred and Hollis were chalking their cues, getting ready to play the winners of the previous match.

"I say, Weston," Lord Hollis said, lining up his shot, "isn't that your father over there playing against Lord Walmsley and Viscount Linton?"

Alfred looked up to see his father taking a shot. His partner, a man he recognized as Lord Godfrey, pointed Alfred out to his father. For a moment, they locked eyes, and Alfred saw displeasure there.

He turned his attention back to the game, playing with confidence, enjoying each stroke. They were evenly matched, but their opponents had luck on their side, and soon the game was over. Alfred turned to see his father waiting at the side of the table. He glanced at Hollis, who gave a nod of understanding. He passed his cue to the next player, then went to join his father.

The earl looked at him with an unreadable stare, saying, "Alfred, my boy. Out for an evening's entertainment, are you?"

"Of course," Alfred replied. "A game of billiards, a good cigar...."

His father laughed, but it was a hollow sound. "Come, come. That is not why you've come to La Violette, surely. You've come for other pleasures, have you not?"

"Yes. That must be it."

"It's good to see you here, Alfred," Lord Harrington said. "A father and son should be able to enjoy the same pastimes, should they not? Why, Lord Godfrey and his son come here very Saturday evening after dinner." He pointed to Godfrey and his son puffing away on cigars in two corner wing chairs. "Soon they'll be upstairs in adjoining rooms, each with a little French tart under them. What sport, eh?"

His father passed him another glass of port and motioned to a pair of empty chairs near the fireplace.

Alfred sat across from his father, and tasted the port.

"It seems like only yesterday that I brought you here for the first time." The earl smiled, but it didn't quite reach his eyes. "Made a man of you that day. Shall I hire you a sweet little whore tonight as well, Alfred? A father's gift to a dutiful son?"

Alfred replied, "No thank you, Father. I haven't the time, nor the inclination at the moment. I shall be leaving soon."

"Leaving?" his father asked. "Without sampling the girls' charms? Why did you bother coming out then?"

"To see Hollis," Alfred lied. "He says these are the best billiard tables in London."

"He's right," the earl said, nodding. "Made of Italian slate. And cost a pretty penny, too." He puffed on his cigar, and sat forward, lowering his voice. "Alfred, I must say, I am worried about you. Seeing you here tonight only confirms my fears."

"What about?" Alfred asked. His father's words didn't ring true. It was unlike the earl to worry about anyone save himself.

"I have heard rumors, my boy," Lord Harrington explained. "About you getting in over your head, poking your nose into things you have no business poking it into."

Alfred sat back, choosing his words carefully. "Where did you hear that?"

The earl shrugged. "That is not important. What is important is that you abandon this fruitless cause you have adopted. You may get hurt, Alfred."

Alfred took another drink and replied, "I'm sure I don't know what you're referring to, Father."

"No? Well then, let me say only this, and then I'll drop the matter," Lord Harrington said. "It is after all, only rumor. But take heed. There are people in this city who could become very upset with do-gooders interfering with their business. These people could be dangerous. I only tell you out of concern for your welfare."

Alfred thought he saw something in his father's eyes then, something that spoke of all the lost opportunities between them, opportunities that could never be recovered. Perhaps this was the earl's way of trying to make amends.

"I do care for you, Alfred," he said, finally. "You are, after all, my son."

Suddenly, Alfred remembered being a lad of ten, his father patting him on the back when Alfred had shot his first pheasant. His father had been a cruel man at times, yet they had shared some happy moments together in Alfred's youth, as well. Though his father was far from perfect, Alfred realized that part of him would always remember those times. Perhaps the earl had done the best he could, had given all he could. Perhaps he was giving all he could to his son right now.

"Thank you, Father," Alfred said. "I shall take great care...in all things."

"See that you do, son," Lord Harrington said.

Alfred stood. "I must be going, Father. Great-Aunt Withypoll has a yen to go to the National Gallery tomorrow. And, as you know, she likes to set out early for these things."

"Yes, I do." The earl stood and accompanied Alfred back toward the salon. "Well, I shall be staying for a bit I expect. I have another match with Viscount Linton against Lord Claridge and Sir Abelard de Burgh."

Soon they were at the door and Alfred was donning his coat and hat.

"Good night, my boy, and remember what I said," Lord Harrington advised, following him outside for a moment.

"I will, Father," Alfred said, shaking his hand. His father stepped back inside the house and the door closed behind him.

Alfred descended the stone steps and looked about for his carriage.

There it was—his carriage was stuck between two others down the street. Instead of waiting, he walked to it.

His driver, Tomkins looked down apologetically. "Sorry, milord. We'll be underway soon enough." He pointed to the carriage in front. "One of the brakes seized up. Ronnie's workin' on it."

Just then, the other driver waved and called out, "All clear, Tommy."

"Ye see? I knew he'd fix it. We'll be off in a jif, sir." Tomkins hopped down and opened the door of the carriage for his master.

Alfred made to go inside, but stopped when he saw a figure emerge from La Violette. In the lamplight he saw the familiar profile of his father. Alfred watched, surprised to see the earl step into a nearby carriage. Didn't his father have an important billiard match with the viscount?

Before he could think, he said, "Tomkins, you see that coach that's pulling away there? I want you to follow it. But at a safe distance. Don't let yourself be seen. Follow wherever it goes. Quickly, now!"

"Yes, sir," Tomkins said, closing the door once Alfred was inside. Soon they were off. But to where?

He tried to ignore the gnawing feeling in the pit of his stomach. His father's warnings had seemed heartfelt enough. But questions remained. How had the earl found out about Alfred's investigation? And why had he left the brothel so suddenly after bidding Alfred adieu?

One thing was certain—Alfred was determined to find out.

Chapter Eighteen

Prudence couldn't help but smile as she watched her students admire another Renaissance masterpiece. She stood back as they fluttered about a dramatic sculpture by an unnamed student of Michaelangelo, remarking on the lifelike muscle tone in the arms, the height and strength of the body that seemed ready to move at any moment, and the angelic beauty of the masculine face.

As she watched the girls' animated expressions and listened to their excited chatter, she felt a swell of pride. They had come a long way from the rough streets of London.

Thankfully, the fire at the school had not impeded their studies. They were only slightly behind schedule in their lessons, and though this trip to the National Gallery had not been originally planned, the educational value of such a visit was immeasurable. In one day alone, they had seen the works of over a dozen Italian Masters.

The tour was being led by Alfred's mother, herself a devotee of the arts.

As Lady Harrington discussed a particular piece with

the students, Prudence couldn't help but notice that the woman was a natural born teacher. The girls adored her. So did Prudence. Yet the subtle tension between Alfred and his mother endured. Prudence couldn't help but wonder if they would ever be able to put their differences behind them.

Her own heart sank miserably at the thought. If only she and Alfred could do the same. The question of marriage still stood like a barrier between them. Yet neither one of them seemed able to give up their position on either side of it.

To make matters worse, she had hardly seen Alfred in the past week at all. Except for breakfast and sometimes at supper, there would be whole days where she wouldn't see him at all, even as she lived in his own house.

But she had realized rather painfully that she missed him. More than she wanted to admit.

She missed his smile, the roguish twinkle in his eye, the warmth and texture of his skin and most of all, the feel of his body moving over hers and bringing her to the brink of heaven. Just the thought of that sent a wicked thrill through her veins.

She even missed arguing with him. To be honest, she most especially missed arguing with him, as he was such a worthy opponent.

She felt a twinge in her heart just then, and turned to see Alfred, leaning languidly against a wall, studying her with his dark, charismatic gaze. For a moment, she could have sworn he knew exactly what she was thinking about.

He pushed away from the wall and walked slowly toward her, like a panther calmly stalking its prey. She felt as helpless as a gazelle caught in the cat's sights.

Then he was beside her, looking down at her with the knowing gaze of a lover. She felt naked then, and knew that it was worse than that, for he could strip her to her very soul with just a look.

He paused for a moment, then took her hand. His touch sent a jolt of heat to her core.

How quickly, how effortlessly he could turn her world upside down.

"I've been watching you." He pressed his lips to her hand, and she thrilled at the sensation. "I am no expert on art, Miss Atwater, but in my humble opinion, none of these works could ever compete with what I am beholding now. And I should know, having seen you at your most beautiful." He moved his face closer, and whispered, "Do you know what I'm talking about, Prudence?"

She nodded, trying vainly to rid her mind of the image that swirled there, of his powerful body, naked and warm, loving hers and making her weak with passion.

"I am thinking about how you looked when I was making love to you. I think of you like that every moment."

Prudence gulped. She must be a weak woman, for she was very close to throwing herself before him and begging him to do exactly that to her again at the earliest possible convenience. She eyed a large antique cabinet in the corner and wondered if they would both fit inside.

He smiled down at her wickedly, saying, "I must say, looking at all the statues of nymphs and gods frolicking with each other has done nothing but make me think of *you* traipsing through a garden bower, naked and sweet, and me chasing after you like a randy centaur." He looked pensive for a moment, and said seriously, "Do you think we could play that game in the garden when we return home?"

She laughed then, and gave him a little push. "Not if it is still light out, my lord."

He brightened. "Then, there is hope?"

Prudence shook her head and replied, "You might be waiting quite some time for that, I'm afraid."

"I can wait," he said. "For you, I would wait forever."

His words sobered her. "Forever is a long time, my lord, especially if something can never be."

Sensing her unease, he took her hand again and kissed it chastely. "Never say never, my dear. You may be tempting the gods themselves to prove you wrong."

Alfred led her into the next room, where the girls were already milling about. He gestured to the priceless statues and paintings that filled the vast room.

"Look around you, Prudence," he said. "All of this beauty took time to build, took *sacrifices* to build. These artists made their dreams into reality. A man and a woman together, they're like artists, too. They can create something beautiful—like a child."

She tried to pull away then, but he wouldn't let her escape so easily.

Oh, she didn't want to hear this. Didn't he know how hard this was for her?

He turned her face up to meet his piercing gaze. "What's between us is strong, Prudence. I've never felt this way for another woman. I can see in your eyes that you feel it, too. It's willful, this feeling we have for each other. Bear that in mind when you're alone in your bed, making those logical arguments to yourself, because I'm not going to give up without a fight."

His words shattered her as effortlessly as a hammer would smash an egg. She closed her eyes, and felt him pull her closer.

"You don't fight fairly, my lord."

"Who said life was fair?"

Just then, Emma came rushing over. "Miss Atwater, I've something to show you! Do you remember the painting we studied last week? I've found it over here! Oh...." She looked up at Prudence quizzically, obviously sensing the tension between her and Alfred.

Prudence took a deep breath and replied, "Do you mean, *The Rhapsody of Venus*, Emma?"

Emma nodded, but still looked unsure as to what was going on. "Yes, Miss."

Prudence stepped away from Alfred and took Emma's hand. "Please excuse me, Lord Weston. I must attend to my student."

He nodded silently. As she moved away, she saw the unspoken message in his eyes.

Surrender to me.

It frightened her just how close she had been to doing that. One touch from Lord Weston...a few pretty words were all it had taken to make her melt like ice in the sun.

But if she gave in as he wanted, if she traded her students' happiness for her own, she would never forgive herself.

She mentally shook herself and put an arm about Emma's shoulder. "I would be delighted to see the painting. Will you show me, Emma? And, as you are an artist as well, I should like to hear your detailed observations on seeing the original, firsthand."

Emma beamed. "Oh, yes, Miss! I should like that, very much indeed."

As they reached the doorway to the next room, Prudence turned back to see Alfred gazing at her with a penetrating stare. But before he could cast another of his spells upon her, Prudence took Emma and hurried from the room.

Alfred leaned back against the wall.

He was coming close to breaking her resolve—he could feel it. Prudence had all but melted in his arms earlier, and all but said yes to his marriage proposal.

But if he was so close to success, why did he feel so empty inside? He was sure that he could woo her, could break down her defenses and make her surrender to him completely. He'd seen it in her eyes, seen her valiantly struggling against her own heart. All he had to do was keep charming her into his arms, keep describing the happiness she could experience if she but agreed to be his wife.

Then he would be victorious. He would win the battle of wills that raged between them.

And that was what he wanted, wasn't it?

To win?

Yet, the thought of winning Prudence like that made him feel like a cad. Just as she'd said, he wasn't fighting fair. He was using her own responses, her own passion as a weapon against her. But was it not warranted to secure the future of his unborn child?

If there was a child. He found himself hoping more and more that there was.

"What are you brooding about, m'boy?" Great-Aunt Withypoll said from beside him. Somehow, the diminutive woman had managed to sneak up on him. Which hadn't been an easy feat, considering Alfred had left her in Mungo's charge.

He kissed her hand and then placed it in the crook of his arm. "What did you do with Mungo, Auntie? Or shall I say, what did you do *to* him? I left you in his care."

Lady Weston waved a gnarled hand dismissively. "Oh, it wasn't hard to escape him, my dear. The big burly man was too busy mooning over Miss Simms to notice my departure. And I didn't have the heart to break up their *tete-a-tete*."

"Really?" Alfred led her into the next room. "I didn't know that Mungo had a *penchant* for Dolly."

Lady Weston whacked his arm.

"Ow!" he said. "What in God's name is it about my arm that invites whacking from females? Good Lord, between you and Prudence, I should wonder that I have an arm left at all."

"Don't try to change the subject," Great-Aunt Withypoll said. "Speaking of *penchants*, I am glad to be proven right, yet again, as you have developed one for Miss Atwater and she for you."

Alfred opened his mouth to speak but Lady Weston cut him off.

"Oh, don't bother trying to fool me, m'boy," she said. "I have eyes.

And contrary to what you might think, they still work quite well."

Alfred huffed. "That was why your maid found you wandering about the kitchen looking for your bed, then?"

"Hmph. I told all of you, I wanted a cup of tea. But let us return to the subject of you and Miss Atwater. Even a blind man would be able to see the way you look at each other. Like two lovesick puppies. But this is a very serious business, Alfred. Now, as you have observed on more than one occasion, I am not getting any younger. I long to see you settled with a wife. I long to hold your children in my arms and dote upon them in my final years."

"Auntie, please," Alfred said, "you'll upset yourself."

Lady Weston reached up to touch his face. "I have always loved you like a son, my dear. Bertram and I—" her eyes filled with tears then, and Alfred thought his jaded heart would break. "You know that I was unable to give him children as he so dearly wished. But when your mother went away to Italy, we were blessed with looking after you and your brother. And you were my favorite. I should have tried to hide it better, I know. But I couldn't, I suppose. After I lost Bertram, you were such a consolation to me."

Lady Weston wiped at her eyes with a delicate lace handkerchief. "Now that you have shown an interest in Miss Atwater, I suppose I fear I might lose you."

Alfred rained kisses on her hand, and noticed that the papery skin was as cold as ice. He pressed his hands around hers to warm them. "No, Auntie. You could never lose me. I'm your Alfred, always."

She gave him a weak smile, and patted his hand. "That's what I admire about you, Alfred—your devotion. And perhaps I have been stingy in my old age, refusing to share you with anyone else. Now Miss Atwater has come along, and stolen your heart—just as I wanted her to do. Yet, I am afraid of life without you. I've had you by my side for years now, and I must say, you're a hard habit to break."

"I'm not going anywhere, Auntie," he said, trying to reassure her, "no matter what happens with me and Miss Atwater. I haven't said anything to you, because I didn't want to get your hopes up. At the moment, Miss Atwater is resistant to the idea of marriage—with me or anyone else. I am trying to convince her otherwise, but as you know, she has an independent mind. She is afraid of losing her freedom, and I can't argue against that. She's right—if she marries, she will lose some of the freedoms she has come to know. But she would be gaining a new life—one full of love, devotion and happiness. In my mind it is a worthy trade, but in hers, the price is much too dear."

Great-Aunt Withypoll smiled sadly. "Miss Atwater has

a point, of course. But so do you, Alfred. You must fight for what you want in life, for *whom* you want. I fought for what I wanted, and I have no regrets. You have fulfilled the role of a favorite son for many years. But now it is time for me to let go, I think. Of many things...."

Her eyes fluttered and she crumpled in Alfred's arms.

"*Auntie?*" He patted her face, trying vainly to revive her as he held her limp body in one arm. He shouted over his shoulder to some other patrons. "*Get a doctor!*"

A shocked couple hurried off to fetch help as Alfred sank to the floor, cradling his aunt in his arms.

Chapter Nineteen

"Where is that bloody, damned doctor?" Alfred said, checking his great-aunt's pulse.

She wasn't dying.

She *couldn't* be dying. Not yet. Not when he had so much left to say to her.

Great-Aunt Withypoll had been a mother to him for over twenty years. She had been the one to kiss the scraped knee, to soothe the cuts and bruises of childhood. And she had been the one to comfort him when he cried for his mother in the night. He owed so much to this woman.

She had asked for a grandchild to hold; even though it would actually be a third cousin once removed, or something of the sort. But it didn't matter. His child *would* be her grandchild. If only she could live long enough to see such a child with her own eyes. He vowed to see it come true.

Her eyes fluttered open weakly. Her voice was barely audible. "Alfred...."

A thrill of hope arose in his veins. He stroked her cool cheek and replied, "I'm here. You fainted, that's all. You'll be right as rain again, soon. You just need to catch your breath."

Her eyelids fluttered as she once again lost consciousness.

Dammit! *Where was the bloody doctor?*

Hearing voices above him, Alfred looked up the staircase as a large group of people passed by in the upper gallery. He thought he glimpsed Prudence's distinctive red hair.

"Prudence!" he shouted. "Prudence, are you up there?"

He heard a muffled reply. "*Alfred?*"

"Down here!"

The crowd quickly moved to see what all the fuss was about. They all jostled each other in order to get close to the marble balustrade.

Then some idiot screamed, "She's dead!"

The crowd erupted in panic.

"For God's sake," Alfred shouted above the din, "she's not dead, I tell you. She's fainted!"

But no one listened to him. Blasted idiots. They were all running about in circles, some coming downstairs to get a closer look, some hanging over the marble balustrade with mouths agape, and all of them blocking the stairway and hall.

Alfred looked up to see where Prudence had gone to, and he saw her valiantly trying to make her way toward the staircase. She pushed through the crowd, slowly making progress.

A man followed closely behind her, obviously taking advantage of the path she was clearing. He was tall, and wore a cap that obscured his face.

Why a man of his height would need a young woman like Prudence to clear a path for him, Alfred couldn't fathom. For some reason, Alfred couldn't take his eyes off him.

The man shadowed her every move. He seemed to be staring after Prudence with an unsettling intensity. Yet, something about the man, about his movements, seemed vaguely familiar. Was Alfred imagining things?

Prudence neared the top of the staircase.

The man came close to her, and Alfred got a better look at his face.

Alfred felt his heart slam into his ribs like a fist.

It was the man who had tried to abduct Prudence into the carriage that night in Drury Lane. The one who had gotten away from he and Mungo, along with the other villain who'd been helping him.

Dammit—he thought, he had to warn Prudence, had to get her away from there!

But everything had changed somehow, time twisted and tangled itself into a slow, agonizing torture.

The man raised his arms and reached for the back of Prudence's shoulders, as the staircase loomed below her like the jaws of a great gaping beast.

Though it was fruitless, Alfred thrust out a hand toward her. He yelled the only thing he could think of that would make her run forward, without looking back.

"Prudence, *help me!*"

He saw the look of shock pass over her face as she lifted her skirts in a most unladylike fashion, and made a brilliant dash forward, just out of the man's reach. She didn't see the man behind her grab at the air as he lost his balance.

The crowd watched in horror as the man tumbled down the stairs to the bottom.

He landed with a thud and lay inert on the cold floor, his neck obviously snapped. One leg was twisted grotesquely and blood stained his mouth as his eyes stared up sightlessly at the vaulted ceiling.

Alfred, still holding Great-Aunt Withypoll in one arm, saw the terror in Prudence's eyes as she flew toward him. In a moment she was in his arms, her face buried against his neck. Alfred squeezed her tightly as she trembled, and he felt the dampness of hot tears against his skin.

Around them, utter chaos had broken out. The crowd spilled down the staircase, and people shouted in alarm. A whistle sounded.

Thankfully, some level-headed person had called the constables.

Prudence pulled away from his hold and looked down at Lady Weston. Tears moistened her ocean-blue eyes. "Oh Alfred, will she be alright? She must be alright—she simply *must* be!"

"She will," he replied. "But are you alright, Prudence?"

Glancing at the dead man, she nodded silently.

"We'll find out who was behind this, I promise you." Alfred felt the anger rising in his gut. He ground the words out. "We will put an end to it. *I* will put an end to it."

In moments, Alfred's mother was beside them, tears dampening her eyes, as well. The girls huddled behind her, having been rounded up by Dolly and Mungo.

Mungo looked on with a sober expression as Dolly tried to console the girls.

Alfred watched the newest girl, Minnie, slowly make her way over to the corpse. She stared down at the body, even though Dolly and Mungo were calling at her to come away. Finally Mungo went to remove her, but she shook him off, then met Alfred's gaze.

"I know him," she said, finally. "The man who fell. I know his face!"

Alfred gave a nod. "So do I. Who is he, Minnie—what's his name?"

"Grimes," she answered. "He works for Mr. Cage. I used to see him at The Silver Rose. He was Mr. Cage's righthand man."

Alfred's jaw set as he fought against the rage that boiled in his gut.

So, Cage had set his dog on Prudence yet again. He'd tried to have her killed—very conveniently, too. A fall in a public place, on a crowded afternoon at the National Gallery would be easily explained away. Except the henchman had fallen into his own trap.

Alfred had obviously hit a nerve with his recent investigations. Now Prudence's life was in even greater danger than it was before. Until Alfred could expose Cage, the mysterious villain was still a threat to her.

The constables had arrived, and were quickly followed by not one but three doctors. One was Lady Weston's personal physician.

The Gallery closed early as the constables conducted their investigation. Alfred gave them his card, and told them to come by the house if they had more questions.

They were now ready to move Great-Aunt Withypoll to the waiting carriage. She was still in and out of consciousness. The doctor couldn't say yet what was wrong with the aged lady. He prescribed bedrest, quiet, and a tonic that would improve her strength.

Alfred thanked him for his assistance.

After Mungo assisted with Lady Weston, he assured Alfred that he'd get Lady Harrington, the girls and Prudence home safely. There were other carriages waiting for the party. Dr. Trask would accompany Alfred and Lady Weston back to the townhouse.

As Alfred's carriage pulled away from the curb, his mind spun. Great-Aunt Withypoll was gravely ill, and possibly would die. A madman was on the loose in

London, with his sights set on killing Prudence. And not only Prudence—but possibly Alfred's unborn child, as well.

Just the thought made him want to put his fist through the glass of the carriage window.

But little good that would do.

It was time to take account.

It was time to acknowledge debts.

Some to be paid.... and some to be collected.

Mr. Cage poured himself a brandy, though he knew it would do nothing to quell his foul mood.

Only a moment ago, Mr. Higgins had informed him that Grimes was dead. The idiot had failed once again in his mission. And what made Cage even more angry was that now he wouldn't be able to kill Grimes himself.

It wasn't the first time one of his lieutenants had died in service to Cage. And it wouldn't be the last. But precautions were always taken to protect Cage if one of his men were killed on the job. No one would be able to link Grimes to Cage's shady business dealings.

Hell—Grimes wasn't even his real name. There was no record of him ever having received money from Cage or any of Cage's establishments. Which was as it should be.

Still, there remained the problem of Miss Atwater. She would have to be taken care of. Sometimes, he thought as he downed the last of the brandy, one had to deal with stubborn problems of this nature oneself. Perhaps there was a better way to do this....

A thought struck him, then.

Perhaps he had been approaching this the wrong way.

Perhaps it was time to use Miss Atwater's weaknesses against her.

Instead of being on the offensive, which had so far gotten him nowhere, he would sit back and wait. Then he would set a trap for the little do-gooder.

It was so simple, he wanted to laugh.

Chapter Twenty

"Are ye sure we should be doin' this, Miss?" Mungo's voice whispered from somewhere behind the tree. His face was barely visible in the shadows as Prudence stepped closer, straining to see him in the dark. "Lord Weston will skin me alive, so 'e will."

"Considering that you outweigh Lord Weston by at least three stone, I find that difficult to imagine," Prudence replied.

He peeked out from behind the massive tree trunk. "Well, 'e could do it if I sat there and let 'im clobber me, which I plan to do out o' guilt, anyway. Ye know, my problem is, I just can't refuse ye anything, Miss Atwater. I've got to learn to start sayin' 'no'. There. 'Miss Atwater, *no*, we are *not* going out prowling about the streets o' London lookin' fer Mr. Cage.' There, 'ow did that sound?"

Prudence rolled her eyes. "Mungo, we're *here* already. Saying 'no' now is beside the point."

"It doesn't hurt to practice fer next time," he said.

Prudence gingerly made her way behind the tree trunk, and stood next to Mungo. "I'm glad to know you're thinking ahead."

"We should've told Lord Weston, Miss," Mungo grumbled. "Imagine 'ow vexed 'e'll be if 'e finds you've gone off galivantin' again. Like 'e doesn't 'ave enough to worry about these days, with Lady Weston takin' ill, an' you almost gettin' killed."

Prudence looked up at him. "Whose side are you on? That is precisely why I *didn't* inform Lord Weston about my plans for this evening. He has been at Lady Weston's side constantly, and has barely slept for two days. We are helping him by taking over the investigation, trust me. Now, give me a leg up, so I can look in the window."

Prudence pointed up at the golden-lit windows of the fashionable townhouse.

Mungo bent down and made a stirrup with his hands. Prudence placed her foot in his strong grip. She held onto Mungo's head for balance as he effortlessly lifted her up. The burly man didn't even grunt as he supported her full weight in his hands.

"What are we lookin' fer, Miss?" he asked.

"I don't know, exactly," she said. "But we may be able to glean some important information that will lead us to Mr. Cage's identity."

"Oh, ye mean, like a man walkin' about sayin', 'Hello, world! I am Mr. Cage. Please arrest me and take me to the magistrate'?"

Prudence huffed. "Are you patronizing me, Mungo?"

"Patronizing?" he said. "No, Miss, not me. I'm just tryin' to bring yer attention to the gaping holes in yer plan. Basically, that ye *'aven't got one.*"

Prudence squirmed to pull herself up higher, hooking her fingers around the upper ledge. She could see into the room, now. Through the ivory shears, she saw an ornate parlor, filled with men dressed in their evening finery, and women wearing next to nothing at all.

One thing was for certain—they were at the right address. This was indeed 'The Silver Rose', just as Minnie had described.

Prudence watched and waited, while sounds filtered through the window—the rumble of male laughter, the soft giggling of the young prostitutes who strove to entertain them, the clinking of glasses as two men toasted each other nearby.

A new group of men strolled into the parlor, and Prudence made a little gasp.

"What is it, Miss? Ye see somethin'?" Mungo asked.

Prudence watched the silver-haired man walk grandly through the room, shaking hands and smoking a thick cigar.

It was the Earl of Harrington.

Well, she supposed she shouldn't be surprised. Alfred's father and those of his station often visited such establishments.

"What d'ye see, Miss?" Mungo said, again.

"Just someone who looks familiar, that's all," she answered.

She couldn't help but wonder if the earl had ever met any of her students here before, like Minnie. But as she watched Lord Harrington take a girl into his arms, she couldn't rid herself of the strange knot in her gut.

It was unsettling.

She watched quietly for awhile. Mungo moved slightly, as he adjusted the weight of her in his hands.

Out of the blue, he said, "I've asked Dolly to marry me."

Prudence lost her grip on the ledge and swayed precariously as Mungo fought to keep her up.

"What?" Prudence asked, shocked.

"I said, I've asked Dolly to be me wife, Miss."

"Oh, I heard what you said, Mungo," she replied. "Put me down."

Mungo obeyed, and when she was standing on the ground before him again, he said, "Well, if ye heard me, Miss, why d'ye say, 'What'?"

Prudence felt a strange heaviness gripping her heart, like a thick fist squeezing it. "Well, I was simply surprised, that's all. Are you sure, Mungo?"

"Sure that I asked her? Yeah...."

"That's not what I meant," she said. "But how...why?"

He gave a silly grin. "Because we're in love, miss. And Dolly's goin' to 'ave a baby."

"A *baby*?"

"Yeah," he said, beaming. "Ain't that grand? And we want to 'ave lots o' babies, but just one to start."

Prudence was stunned. "Oh my soul, Mungo. I must say, this is quite a shock. You and Dolly and babies?"

"That's right," he replied, proudly. "It's usually 'ow it works—a man and a woman, in this case me and Dolly, and then—*babies*! It's like those mathematical equations ye teach the girls. Only this time, one plus one equals three."

Prudence tried to quell the pain in her heart. Everything was happening so fast! Of course she was happy for them, how could she not be? But there was also a terrible fear that they would no longer need her.

Dolly and Mungo were her family. Now they were to make a family of their own, of which she could never be a part. And though she knew it was horrible of her to think, she realized that underneath it all, she was a little jealous of them.

A baby.

A family.

These were things she had decided to sacrifice for

herself, all the things she would never experience with Alfred. And now, Dolly and Mungo were going to explore all of that together.

They would most likely want to go their own way, now. That thought was like a punch in the gut, and Prudence closed her eyes against it.

"Are ye alright, Miss?" Mungo asked, looking down at her with concern. "'Ave I upset ye?"

"No. I'm not upset, Mungo. Truly." She looked up into the big round face of the ex-pirate whom she had taken off the streets. He had become her loyal protector, and her dear, dear friend.

Now he was about to make a good husband for another dear friend she had taken off the streets—Dolly.

Mungo looked at her very seriously, and said, "We've been wantin' to ask ye, Miss, if ye would consider keepin' us on for a bit. We'll 'ave another mouth to feed soon, but if ye lowered our wages, it might work out. The baby would be with us in our room, o' course. We wouldn't be much trouble to keep on, and I can start lookin' for another job."

Prudence shook her head. "Oh, I don't think so, Mungo. I cannot agree to that, at all."

He looked crestfallen.

She smiled and shook his arm. "I will not lower your wages one shilling, you buffoon! But I shall increase *both* of them. With another mouth to feed, you'll have more expenses, and besides, I would have to find some way of keeping both of you in my employ by offering a competitive wage."

Mungo grinned, and hope shone in his eyes. "Ye mean, ye want to keep us? All of us? Even the baby when it comes?"

"Oh, yes, Mungo, yes!" she said. "I would be honored if

you could see to staying. Of course, if you wanted to try your fortunes elsewhere, I could never stand in your way. You and Dolly have both been so wonderful to me. And you're my dearest, closest friends."

She thought she saw his eyes glisten as he pulled her to him for a bone-crushing hug. "Oh, thank ye, Miss. From the both of us, thank ye. Dolly was frettin' somethin' awful about how ye'd take the news."

He released her gently, and they both wiped tears from their eyes.

"There was no need to worry," Prudence said. "I am happy for you both. You're truly perfect for each other." Then she laughed.

"What's so funny?" he asked, chuckling too.

"Me!" she replied. "Here I am, busy teaching the girls about science and the importance of observation, and I can't even see two feet in front of my own face. I had no idea you and Dolly had feelings for each other. That's how observant I am. Tell me, how long have you and Dolly been courting, then?"

Mungo looked sheepish. "A few months. It took me some time to bring 'er round. Ye see, I've been in love with Dolly since the first day I set eyes on 'er."

Prudence gulped. "That's beautiful, Mungo."

"I'm not a religious man, Miss," he said, "but d'ye ever think, no matter who ye are, or what ye've done, maybe the Good Lord has someone in mind fer each and every one of us. It's like a little bit of heaven, here on earth. I mean, look at me, an old pirate who couldn't so much as read until a year ago—an' I get to have Dolly fer me wife. When someone loves ye like that, the way Dolly loves me, well, it changes yer whole world. Ye know what I'm talkin' about, don't ye, Miss?"

She couldn't lie. "Yes, I do, Mungo."

"Like ye said, sometimes a body can't see two feet in front of their own face," he said. "'E loves ye, Miss. Whatever else 'appens, be sure of that."

Prudence's heart ached painfully in her breast. All of a sudden, she felt very tired. So much had happened lately, her mind was still trying to come to terms with it all—from Lady Weston's illness to the attempt on her own life. Now, Mungo and Dolly were in love, and it stirred difficult questions for both her and Alfred.

Mungo patted her shoulder. "It'll all work out, Miss. You'll see—Ol' Mungo never tells a lie."

She smiled up at him and followed him around the side of the townhouse toward the street.

Suddenly, they heard footsteps approaching. Mungo stepped in front of Prudence, and she heard the scrape of his blade as he unsheathed it. Mungo's training had taught her to remain perfectly still and silent as she waited for him to make his move.

"It's alright, it's me!" a voice whispered.

"Me, *who*?" Mungo whispered back.

Prudence heard a heavy sigh. "Lord Weston, Mungo."

Mungo cursed softly, "*Oh, Bugger.*"

"Oh, Bloody Hell!" Prudence whispered, panicking. "What do we do?"

Alfred's voice rose a notch as he commanded, "You both come out of there at once, that's what you do! Bloody idiots, the both of you."

Mungo reached back and took Prudence's arm, fairly dragging her toward the street. "We're both in fer it now, Miss. Thanks a lot!"

"Oh!" Prudence exclaimed, shocked.

As they drew closer to the street, Prudence could just make out Alfred's face in the dim lamplight.

He looked like he was ready to tear them both limb

from limb. "And just what do you two think you're doing here, skulking about like thieves?"

Mungo cleared his throat. "Uh, well...."

"Do either of you know how much danger you could have been in tonight?"

"Uh, no, not exactly," Mungo replied.

"I don't know why I'm the least bit surprised," Alfred continued.

"Tell the truth," Mungo said wryly, "I don't either. I mean, ye know Miss Atwater, sir. When she gets an idea in 'er head, she makes a mule seem docile and obedient."

"Mungo!" Prudence whacked his arm.

Alfred frowned. "Don't try to blame Mungo. The man works for you. He was obviously following orders. Though I will deal with him later for his role in all of this."

Mungo shrugged and nodded. "Ah, well. What can ye do? I'll take me lumps, as I've earned them. Shall we say tomorrow, 'bout ten o'clock, sir?"

"That will be acceptable, Mungo," Alfred said with a dark stare. "Now, you may leave. I shall see Miss Atwater home safely."

"Excuse me," Prudence said assertively, "but I believe Mr. Church is in *my* employ."

Mungo turned toward the street and gave a wave as he headed for their carriage.

"Mungo!" she said, but evidently, she'd been abandoned.

Alfred approached, and she saw a mixture of anger and heat in his eyes.

She took a step backwards, bumping into a tree.

In a moment, Alfred's body was pressed against her. He pinned her to the tree, his eyes blazing down on her.

Then his mouth covered hers and he kissed her like a man who was starving—for her mouth, her body, her very soul.

Alfred growled in the back of his throat as he kissed her, and the sound sent a shiver through her blood.

Taking her hand, he pulled her along with him toward the darkened, empty street. He ducked down an alleyway, walking quickly as Prudence struggled to keep up with him.

They ventured down a narrow part of the alley, and found that it led to a dead end. On one side, an old rotten gate stood half-off its hinges in the rough stone wall. Beyond lay an abandoned lot of some sort, which now glowed eerily in the moonlight. Across from it, a crumbling stone arch framed a bricked-up doorway.

Alfred spun her around and pressed her into the doorway up against the hard brick.

"Do you have any idea what could have happened out here tonight?" he demanded. "I told you to stay off the streets until we find out who is behind the threats to your life. Why didn't you obey me, Prudence?"

"*Obey?*" Prudence's jaw clenched as the word assaulted her ears. "May I remind you, sir, that we are not married. I am not required to obey you."

"No, you are not," he said, "not at the moment. But I intend to remedy the situation posthaste."

Prudence pushed against the massive wall of his chest. "And how are you going to manage that? Do you intend to take me prisoner, then?"

"And why not?" he asked, wickedly. "Since you have quite mercilessly taken me prisoner. Bloody hell, of all the women in London, why did I have to pick you to fall so *foolishly in love with...?*"

CHAPTER TWENTY-ONE

At his words, her breath caught in her chest. She wanted to cover her ears, to block out the sound of his voice.

Because she was a coward.

She was a coward whose heart was about to betray her.

He pressed his hard body against hers and brushed his lips against her cheek. His breath was warm in the cool night air.

"Yes, you heard me," he said. "I'm in love with you, Prudence. Though it defies all logic and every whit of good sense the Lord gave a man. But somehow, with all your scatterbrained schemes, with all your bravery and wit, and innocent passion, you've captured my heart."

Her head spun, and she stared helplessly into his dark, impassioned eyes.

"Marry me, Prudence." His mouth teased hers softly, and she opened her lips to him, tilting her head back to offer him deeper entry.

His strong hands cradled her face. "Let me love you as I long to do. I'm haunted by dreams of you crying out with pleasure as you did in my arms that night. I wake up reaching for you, but you aren't there. And I want you there beside me, Prudence. Every night. Every morning. For the rest of our lives."

Prudence couldn't keep a whimper from escaping her lips as he trailed demanding kisses down her neck. She felt her cape falling from her shoulders, and then her shoulders and breasts were bare and the cool night air teased her hot, tingling skin. She couldn't think any more, couldn't fight against her own desire which swept violently through her veins.

She needed him like this—rough and insistent, ready to fight for her, to break down the walls that stood between them, if only for this one perfect moment. For this moment she was utterly and completely his.

Prudence kissed him hungrily, grabbing fistfuls of his thick hair as she pulled his head down toward her. She marveled at how easily he could attack her defenses. Alfred could dismantle her carefully constructed battlements with only a kiss.

This man was like the Black Knight and the White Prince all rolled into one—both destroyer and rescuer, enemy and friend.

His mouth captured the tip of her breast, and she gasped as hot pleasure ripped through her. He was merciless, sucking hard and flicking his tongue against her naked skin until she felt herself shaking. She struggled for breath, clutching at him feverishly as she felt his hard hands slide up and under her skirt.

With a rough motion, he hiked her skirt up around her waist. He pressed his palms flat and ran them up her thighs, pushing her back further against the wall. Then he slammed his powerful body against her and covered her mouth with his own as his hand delved between her legs.

His possessive touch sent bolts of molten heat to her

core, threatening to melt her limbs to nothing. She gasped for breath and held onto him tightly as he tortured her with maddening, devilish strokes.

His fingers slipped inside her and she closed her eyes tight, unable to stop herself from moving to the rhythm he set with the strength of his hand.

She felt like a puppet, a slave, dancing to his music, unable to think or move of her own free will.

With deft strokes he brought her to the brink of heaven. When he took his hand away she wanted to cry out, to beg madly for release. She opened her eyes and saw the fire in his as he cupped her bottom and lifted her up.

Instinctively she wrapped her legs about his waist, and he groaned as he entered her. Prudence wanted to laugh and cry all at once, it felt so good, so right.

She wrapped her arms around his neck as he thrust, pinning her against the wall. She felt light, weightless, even, as he held her up effortlessly and drove into her, again and again.

He slowed the pace, then, kissing her neck, taking his time to fire her with his tongue and mouth. His thrusts were slow but deep, and his tongue penetrated her mouth as his sex did her body. She trembled with need.

"Not yet, my beauty," he whispered.

Her eyes fluttered open. "Please..." The passion he stoked was turning to sweet suffering. Surely, she would go mad before this was over.

"Say you love me," he demanded.

Her eyes opened fully and she stared into his.

"Say you love me, Prudence. I need to hear you say it now, like this."

She kissed him, trying to stop his mouth with her own, but he broke the kiss.

"You know it's true," he said, panting. His eyes held her

prisoner as easily as his body did. "Right now, when I'm inside you—this is *honesty*, Prudence. This is truth. No pretense, just you and me as we really are, as we really feel."

He quickened the pace, then, thrusting harder, faster.

She moaned and turned her head away, unable to withstand the piercing intensity of his gaze. She clutched at his muscular arms and shoulders as he thrust into her.

"Say it, damn you," he growled.

She felt dizzy, if she were on the edge of a storm, and the storm would destroy her. There were tears in her eyes, she realized. Hot, helpless tears. It was too much, she would surely die from this sweet torture, and she wanted him to save her, to pick her up and carry her to safety.

Because he was the only man who could.

"I love you," she gasped, and the hot waves crashed over her, and she cried out with pleasure.

She heard him groan as he drove deep, and she clutched him tight as the sweet violence of his release rocked through her.

They stayed there for a moment, holding onto each other, their bodies still joined. Only the sounds of the night surrounded them.

Prudence moved her head so she could look at him. "I feel as though we're the only two people in the world."

He smiled at her, and kissed her nose. "We are. In our little world, Prudence, we are the only ones here. The only ones who can decide our own fate." He slid out of her, and held her close, pulling the sleeves of her dress up over her shoulders.

He tipped her chin up so she would meet his eyes. "Marry me, Prudence. If you love me as you say you do, then you must marry me."

Prudence's heart throbbed. For a moment, words

escaped her. "I'm sorry, Alfred, but I cannot promise that."

He frowned at her. "So you would willingly choose to deny our child a father?"

"There is no child!" she shot back.

"No?" He pulled her closer. "We just made love, albeit standing up. If not from before, you could be with child now."

She struggled to break away from him, her mind reeling. "Is that why you did this? To try to ensure that I would be with child, to force me to marry you?"

"No! Of course not," Alfred said. "I would never engineer such a thing, and you know it. What happened just now was because of our pure, mad lust for each other. And though you're the most stubborn, pig-headed female I've ever known, with the exception of Great-Aunt Withypoll, I do love you." He circled her in his arms and she felt herself going lax, as if she couldn't stand up anymore. She fought against the tears but they burned her eyes again.

He kissed her tenderly, so tenderly that her heart wanted to break. With a gentle hand he wiped away the tears that stained her cheeks. "You said that you love me, too, Prudence."

She nodded silently, for she couldn't deny it.

"Then say yes. Stop fighting this and be my wife."

She shook her head. "I can't."

"Because of the school?" he asked. "I could fund the school, if that would make you happy. Money is no object. I could hire a staff of the best teachers in England."

"But there's so much more to it than just that." She stopped herself, not wanting to explain the thing that held her back. The thing that made her a poor choice as *any* man's wife. "What about *me*," she said, deflecting the truth, "and my dreams for the school? My father left it in my care. It was his dream, and it's my dream, too. It's something that I must do on my own, don't you see?"

Alfred shook his head. "No, I don't see. More money for the school would mean that you could expand, you could help more girls."

"And would I still be in complete control?" she asked.

"For the most part."

"For the most part isn't good enough, Alfred," she argued. "Do you realize what would happen if we married, and you funded the school as you've said? I wouldn't be able to go about at night looking for girls on the streets, would I?"

Alfred paused. "Well...."

"You see? No husband in his right mind would allow his wife to do what I do."

"I'm glad we agree on that point," he replied.

"Alfred, I do love you," Prudence said. "So much so that it frightens me.

And I was so close to saying yes to your proposal a few moments ago—but I simply cannot."

He stared down at her with a dark expression. "You can't go on denying what we have, Prudence."

"I don't deny it. I'm through denying it," she said, brushing a damp curl away from his face. "But Alfred, I am wise enough to know that our marriage would never work."

"I am not so convinced," he replied.

"Why, because we feel lust for each other?" she asked. "It takes more than lust to make a lasting union. Let me paint you a picture of this marriage that you seem to want so badly." She pulled away from him and looked across at the vacant lot, which glowed eerily in the silver moonlight.

"There is a wedding," she began, "a joyous affair with both of us basking in each other's perfect love. Our wedding night is hot with passion, we make love into the night and fall asleep in each other's arms."

She glanced at him, and he gave her a knowing grin.

"Our lives continue like this for a time," Prudence continued. "You make good on your promise of funding the school. Teachers are hired, and soon it seems the school can practically run itself without me. Our first baby is born, a strong, hardy son, or perhaps a beautiful little daughter. The baby takes up most of my time, and I visit the school less and less. I no longer teach there, of course, as a responsible mother, I am certainly not permitted to go about at night dressed as a streetwalker. I resign myself to the fact that those days are over. A year or so after that, there is another baby, and perhaps another a year after that, all darling little cherubs who we dote on hopelessly. To everyone, even me, it appears that I have a happy life. But one day, I realize that the terrible pain that has been growing in my heart year after year is my resentment toward you. For you didn't want me as I was, but instead wanted me to be something I could never be. A proper wife."

She turned to him, taking in his sober expression.

"I know that I have just described most of the marriages in England," she said. "And who am I to want more? But Alfred, can you honestly tell me that our marriage would not turn out as I've described?"

"No, I cannot," he answered. "But you cannot guarantee that it would turn out that way, either."

"No," Prudence said. "But let me ask you this. If we were to marry, would you allow me to continue my role at the school, exactly as it is, now? Recruiting girls off the street? Teaching every day? Would you?"

Alfred dropped his gaze and sighed heavily. "It's not what I would want."

"You see? Our marital differences have already begun, and we aren't even married," she pointed out.

He stepped toward her, and reached out to touch her arm. "You make a fine argument, Prudence. There's no denying that your mind is as sharp as a whip. You are more intelligent than most men I've had the occasion to meet. You're maddening and adorable and stunningly beautiful. And stubborn as a mule. But none of your arguments have convinced me that we should not marry."

"No? Perhaps this next argument will, then." It was time, she knew, to confess. She couldn't hide the truth from him anymore. Not if she was ever going to convince him what was best for both of them.

She looked him directly in the eye. "What would you say if I told you that my mother was a *prostitute*?"

"I beg your pardon?" Alfred said.

"You heard me—a prostitute," Prudence said. "And I don't know who my real father was. He could have been anyone from an aristocrat to the lowest piece of scum on London's streets. Disconcerting, is it not?"

"Somewhat, yes," he answered.

"Indeed. Now do you want to rethink that marriage proposal, my lord?"

He ignored her question. "Who told you this?"

"My parents," Prudence explained. "They were surprisingly honest about it. That was their way. My mother had left her life on the street and joined my father's small school, which he ran out of his modest house. When she arrived there, she was already with child. She had no idea who the father was. She'd been working steadily, so it could have been one of hundreds. My father didn't care. They quickly fell in love, and married. After my mother died some years later, he continued raising me as his own." She couldn't help but smile at the memory of the great man she had loved so dearly. "He was a wonderful father."

She drew her cape close around her shoulders as the night had grown more chilly, and said, "So, now you see why I do what I do. And why I cannot, and *will* not give it up. My mother was one of those girls. If my father hadn't taken her off the street, and offered her a chance at a better life, I would never have lived. We would have died out there on the street, she and I. How many other lives would be altered if I abandon those girls to their fate, thinking only of myself?"

"Yet, I doubt that either of your parents would expect you never to marry because of the school," Alfred said.

Prudence shook her head. "You don't understand, Alfred. If I was your wife, I would have to lie about my family's past. And I couldn't do that. I can't pretend to be something I'm not. Can you imagine the reaction of your friends when they learned of my scandalous pedigree? You'd become an outcast—Lady Weston would, too. Any children we might have would fare the same. So you see, it's impossible. I am not fit to be a nobleman's wife."

For the first time in this battle of wills with Alfred, he made no argument. He only stared at Prudence with a sober, darkened expression. "We should go home," he said, finally.

"Yes," Prudence agreed.

Alfred led her to the street corner and flagged his waiting coach. They waited in uneasy silence as the vehicle approached.

Prudence knew she should have been feeling victorious at finally convincing Alfred that they could never marry.

Wasn't that what she wanted—to be free?

CHAPTER TWENTY-TWO

"'**L**et me not to the marriage of true minds admit *impediments*,'" Prudence read, glancing at the reposed form of Lady Weston beside her in the enormous bed. She had come to visit her benefactress in her well-appointed bed-chamber. Lady Weston had requested that Prudence read some of Mr. Shakespeare's sonnets aloud. She continued:

"'*Love is not love which alters when it alteration finds...*
or bends with the remover to remove.
O no, it is an ever-fixed mark,
That looks on tempests, and is never shaken;
It is the star to every wandering bark,
Whose worth's unknown, although his height be taken.'"

She stopped for a moment, watching the frail woman as her eyes fluttered slightly and her breathing became rhythmic.

Prudence closed the small book and rose from her chair.

"Don't stop now," Lady Weston said, weakly. "You're just getting to the good part."

Returning to her seat. Prudence found the spot where she had left off in Sonnet 116:

"'Love's not Time's fool, though rosy lips and cheeks
Within his bending sickle's compass come;
Love alters not with his brief hours and weeks,
But bears it out even to the edge of doom.
If this be error and upon me proved,
I never writ, nor no man ever loved.'"

Lady Weston opened her eyes and smiled softly. "A very observant man, Mr. Shakespeare. I must say, I agree with him wholeheartedly."

"About what?" Prudence asked, eager to engage the frail woman in diverting conversation.

Lady Weston's health had been very poor since the day at the museum when she'd collapsed. Neither her appetite nor her energy was strong these days. She was sleeping more than usual, too. The doctor said it could be a failing heart. She was, after all, an old woman. Though no one in the house wanted to admit it, even someone as formidable as Lady Weston could not live forever.

"About everything," Lady Weston replied. "I particularly like the part about Time: *'Love alters not within his brief hours and weeks, but bears it out even to the edge of doom.'* A very reassuring thought when you reach my age. And also that *'Love is not Time's fool...'* though our physical bodies grow old and our appearance changes, the heart does not see that. Love burns as brightly in a *'marriage of true minds'* whether the couple be old or young."

Prudence looked upon Alfred's great-aunt with admiration. "You are very wise, Lady Weston."

"I ought to be, after all this time," she replied.

Prudence couldn't help but chuckle.

"I only hope you, too, will be wise, Miss Atwater," Lady Weston continued, "and that when you reach my age, you will have no regrets about the choices you have made."

"What do you mean?" she asked, though she wasn't sure she wanted to hear it.

"You know very well what I mean," Lady Weston said, seriously. "I am referring to my great-nephew, Alfred. He told me he proposed to you, and you refused him. That in itself is not so unusual the first time 'round—it is sometimes best to make a man wait for your hand in marriage. But from what he described, you have refused outright because you are *fearful*...and I had you pegged for a braver girl than that."

Prudence met her benefactress's accusing gaze. "You don't understand, Lady Weston. For me, marriage is quite impossible—with any man."

"My grand-nephew is not just 'any man,' as you put it," Lady Weston said. "Alfred is the *best* of men, Miss Atwater. He is like a son to me, and I am both proud and lucky to say so. My late husband Bertram and I were not blessed with children, but Alfred and his brother, Richard, became our own as we raised them in their parents' stead. And that was no easy task, I assure you. I remember the boys' hijinks—there were days I wanted to raise the white flag in surrender and give up. But more than that, I remember the laughter and joy they brought us through the years. I love them both, of course, but as you know, Alfred has always been devoted to me. As the younger son of an earl, he will get nothing of his father's estate, so my late husband named Alfred heir to the Weston barony by special remainder. It is through him that the Weston family name will carry on, and I long to see him settled with a wife and child before I die."

"You aren't going to die—" Prudence began.

"Yes, I am," Lady Weston replied, calmly. "If not today, perhaps tomorrow...or next week, or even a year hence. But be assured, I will die, Miss Atwater. On that, you may absolutely count. But before I do, it is my greatest wish to see him take a bride. *You*, my dear."

Prudence shook her head. "I told you, my lady, I cannot marry any man—least of all Alfred."

"Why?" Lady Weston asked. "Because your mother came from the streets?"

Swallowing uncomfortably, Prudence answered, "I wasn't sure you knew about that. And I dare say, Lord Weston should have kept that business to himself."

"That is not our way," Lady Weston replied. "Alfred and I are very honest with one another. I wish you would learn to be the same."

Prudence was shocked to hear such bald criticism. "Forgive me, Lady Weston, but are you suggesting that I am in the habit of lying?"

"Not to anyone but yourself," she answered, sagely.

"But—" Prudence began to argue, then found herself unable to form an intelligent response.

"You see?" Lady Weston said. "I speak the truth, my dear. The only person you are being dishonest with is yourself. And that is the last person you should attempt to deceive. If you do, you'll find yourself trapped in a life you were never meant to live, and you may only realize that when it's too late. Look at me, Prudence, I am eighty-seven years old. I had a great love—my darling Bertram—and was lucky enough to become his wife. We journeyed through life together, living each day as an incredible adventure, until his death. But in order to do that, we each had to give up something of ourselves, to *give* a piece of ourselves to the other. That is how two people create a true union. And that is what I think you are afraid to do. Alfred said you are afraid to give up your freedom, afraid of losing control of the school. However, I believe that what you truly fear is *yourself*—the new person you'll become if you are brave enough to share your heart and soul in a marriage."

Prudence swallowed uncomfortably. There was a pain in her chest that she tried desperately to ignore, but it didn't go away. She didn't want to hear this from Lady Weston—she didn't want to hear it from anybody. Yet here she sat, unable to leave the great lady's side.

"Make no mistake, Prudence," Lady Weston continued, "marriage is a daunting thing. For either sex, marriage to someone unsuitable can be a torture all its own. But when two people are well-matched, when they complement each other, challenge each other, and comfort each other, marriage is an adventure like no other on earth. I would hate to see you count yourself out of such fun because you are afraid of what people will say about your origins."

"I'm not afraid of what people will say," Prudence explained, "I'm afraid of what *I'll* say when they make insulting comments about my mother. I told Alfred, I won't lie about her."

"He never asked you to," Lady Weston pointed out.

Prudence took a breath in order to keep going with her argument, then stopped and said, "What?"

"I said, Alfred never asked you to lie," Lady Weston said. "Nor have I."

"But as I explained to Alfred," she said, "as his wife, I would be expected to attend balls and soiree's and other society functions with him. And when his aristocratic friends asked about my parents, I couldn't lie about them. When I met you, Lady Weston, I told you only that my parents were dead. You made no further inquiries about my mother's family, so I offered no more information. But someone will ask the question someday. And I will have to answer them truthfully. Do you really want the *ton* to look at Alfred and I, and even you—with ridicule?"

Lady Weston huffed, saying, "They don't scare me. And they shouldn't scare you, either."

"You're saying that if I was Alfred's wife and someone gave me the cut direct, you'd stand by me?" Prudence asked.

"Not only would I stand by you," Lady Weston replied, "I'd launch a few stinging volleys myself!"

Prudence was at a loss for words.

Lady Weston patted Prudence's hand, looking worn out. "You think about what I've said. I am quite tired just now. I must rest."

"Of course, Lady Weston," Prudence replied, feeling terrible for bothering the frail woman with her problems. "Can I bring you anything...? Lady Weston?"

But she was already asleep.

Prudence quietly exited Lady Weston's bed chamber and headed downstairs. She herself was in need of a cup of tea. After the intense conversation with her benefactress, she needed to take some time and think about things.

Things like Alfred...and his proposal of marriage...and whether or not it could ever work between them.

Just picturing his darkly handsome face sent butterflies to Prudence's stomach. She hadn't seen him this morning. He had departed the house early with Lady Harrington, and they would be gone for most of the day.

Was Lady Weston right? Was Prudence truly more

afraid of herself and the uncharted territory of marriage than anything else?

She sighed as she walked into the salon, finding Dolly at work mending one of the girls' frocks. A tea service sat on an end table. Prudence poured herself a cup of fragrant tea and plunked herself down on the sofa.

"Goodness sakes, you sound like an elephant stomping about," Dolly said, glancing up from her work. "Is everything alright?"

"As alright as it can be, I suppose," Prudence answered, then she frowned. "No...actually, Dolly, things are not alright. Why does everyone say that when it is hardly ever true?"

Dolly looked uncomfortable. "Is it because of Mungo an' me gettin' married, Miss?"

"Oh dear, no," Prudence said, springing up and giving her friend a quick hug. "That's why people say things are alright when they aren't—they don't want to upset anyone unnecessarily. I am happy for you both, Dolly, more than you could ever know. As I told Mungo, I hope you'll stay on with me at the school, wherever that will be. We need to find a new location. We can't stay here in Lord Weston's townhouse forever."

"I'm glad you're not angry with us," Dolly said. "But, ye'd want us to stay even if we 'ave another mouth to feed?"

"Especially then," Prudence replied. "I consider you and Mungo my family, Dolly."

"An' we feel the same," she said, beaming. "Look at what Mungo gave me." Dolly held out her hand, showing off her third finger.

Prudence gazed at a beautiful gold ring with a dazzling oval emerald in the center.

"What an unusual ring," Prudence remarked. "It's very beautiful."

Dolly grinned, saying, "I can't believe such a lovely thing is mine. Said 'e found it on an island very far away from here...a place called Monkey Island. Doesn't that sound exciting? And 'e's been waitin' to give it to the woman he wants to marry. And now, that's me."

Prudence studied the ring again. "Look at these markings on the sides, etched into the gold," she said. "How very intriguing. It looks like some sort of ancient language."

"I wonder if it once belonged to a king or queen of some old civilization?" Dolly asked, wide-eyed.

"Given Mungo's history, I'd say you might be right," Prudence remarked. "At the very least it looks to be quite valuable. Take good care of it, Dolly."

"Oh, I will, Miss—ye can be sure of that," she said proudly. "'Ow is Lady Weston gettin' on? Has she improved any?"

Prudence took her seat as Dolly went back to her sewing. "She seems to have moments of normalcy followed by sudden weakness, and she tires easily. As you know, her appetite is quite diminished. She will take the tonic Dr. Trask prescribed, but doesn't want much else besides tea. I hope and pray that she will yet regain her strength. Lord Weston would be devastated if she were to die. And truthfully, so would I."

"So would we all, miss," Dolly said. "She is a great lady, indeed. Is there anythin' else troublin' ye? Anything' at all ye want to talk about?"

Prudence forced herself to smile. "No, Dolly. Nothing that I can't handle myself. But I thank you for your concern. We shall get through this. After all, there is a wedding to plan."

Prudence raised her teacup, and thought she heard Dolly say, "*Perhaps there will be two.*"

Choking on her tea, Prudence said, "Pardon me?"

"I said, 'there's something in my shoe,'" Dolly replied, wriggling her foot about.

Finishing her tea, Prudence stood and said, "Yes, well, I must go and work on my lesson plan for tomorrow. If you need me, I shall be in the library."

Prudence left the salon and headed to Alfred's library, but was intercepted by Crawford carrying a small silver tray in the hallway.

"This came for you, Miss Atwater," the butler said, lowering the tray.

Prudence took the envelope and thanked him. She opened it and read the message written on the paper inside:

Miss Atwater,

Please attend me forthwith. I must speak to you regarding the recent attacks against the Atwater School.
I have information which we must discuss.
However, tell no one of our meeting.
My carriage awaits outside.

—The Earl of Harrington

She replaced the note in the envelope and went to fetch her cloak. Though the message had warned against it, she said to Crawford, "I must go out to meet an old friend. I shan't be too long."

"Of course, Miss," he replied with a bow. "Will you be back in time for dinner?"

"Oh yes," Prudence answered. "I can't see being later than that. Good day, Crawford."

"Good day, Miss Atwater," he said as she departed.

Prudence descended the stone steps of the townhouse and scanned the street for the earl's carriage. She saw one parked on the street a few houses down and approached it. As she neared, she noticed it didn't bear Lord Harrington's coat of arms, and meant to pass it by. But the door swung open, and she saw Alfred's father beckoning her inside.

"Hurry, Miss Atwater," he said, reaching out a hand. "And do try to keep your head down. I may have been followed here."

Prudence did as the earl bid her, climbing into the carriage and sitting on the plush seat opposite him.

"Your note sounded urgent, my lord," she said.

"It is," he answered. "I have come by some information regarding these threats against you and your school, Miss Atwater. Given the strained relationship I have with my son, I thought it best to bring it to you directly."

"You have made the right decision, Lord Harrington," she replied. "Though I am grateful to Lord Weston for all of his help, this is not his problem to solve. I alone am responsible for the Atwater School and I will deal with these threats myself. What information have you discovered?"

He rapped the tip of his walking stick on the roof and the carriage pulled away. "It's safer if we are on the move. That way no one can listen in on our conversation, as they might if we were sitting in a coffee house." Glancing out the window he said, "This is a dangerous business, Miss Atwater. I only hope we can stop this madness before anyone gets hurt. You and your students were lucky to escape the fire...but you might not be so fortunate next time. And though my son and I have a strained relationship, I know that he holds you in high regard. Which is why I must do what I can."

"What have you found out?" she asked again. "Do you know the identity of the man behind these threats?"

Lord Harrington sat forward. "There is a belief that one of London's brothel owners is a member of the *ton*—a powerful aristocrat who, in essence, leads a double life. By day, he is the picture of propriety, but by night, he runs a virtual empire in London's underworld. Those who get in his way usually end up disappearing, for good."

"How do you know all of this?" Prudence asked.

The next few moments moved so quickly, she realized too late what was happening.

His hand moved toward her face, and Prudence saw a signet ring on his pinky with the letter "C," for Charles...or *Cage*.

She struggled as he covered her mouth with a rag.

"Because," he growled, "*it's me*."

A strange sensation of weakness came over her suddenly, and she tried to fight against it. But moments later, everything went black.

CHAPTER TWENTY-THREE

"I am glad you agreed to accompany me today, Alfred," Lady Harrington said as they strolled in Hyde Park. They had done a little shopping on Oxford Street—his mother had purchased a new shawl for Great-Aunt Withypoll in the hopes of lifting her spirits. Then they stopped for some afternoon refreshment at Abbingdale's Tea House and after, decided to take in some fresh air in the park.

"I was happy to be of service in helping to choose the shawl," he said. "Great-Aunt Withypoll will be pleased."

She glanced up at him. "But that is not why I asked you to join me, and you know it. You've been avoiding me ever since I arrived from Italy. And though I can't blame you for having mixed feelings about my presence here, I *can* blame you for hiding from those feelings. It's no use, Alfred. We must talk this out. We must be honest with each other."

Alfred cleared his throat. "It's a little late for that, Mama."

"It's never too late, Alfred," she countered. "As long as there is breath in our bodies, it is never too late for us to heal old hurts and start again. Now, more than ever, you should know that. A woman whom we both love very much is seriously ill and may die. And if you think I am going to let Great-Aunt Withypoll breathe her last knowing we are still estranged, you have another think coming."

Alfred stopped in his tracks, trying to contain his temper. "Be careful what you wish for, Mama. If we go down this road, it won't be pretty. Be assured of that."

"Sometimes life isn't pretty, Alfred," she answered. "I, of all people, know that only too well. I have wasted too many years away from my children because of things that weren't pretty...things like the truth...things like secrets and betrayal and heartbreak. But I have come back to face those things, and take back what has been stolen from me."

"You abandoned your children," he said, as anger flared in his veins. "You abandoned *me*. And you want me to feel sorry for you now? Sorry about what was stolen from you? How about what was stolen from me, Richard and James? I was eight years old, for bloody sake! You never even said goodbye. I ran after your carriage, begging you to come back, but you didn't. I watched and waited for you, for weeks. Then weeks turned into months, and months into years. All I had of you was a miniature portrait. That's the mother I grew up with, because you were too busy gallivanting around the Continent to care about your own children."

"That's what your father told you, I'm sure," she said, bitterly.

"At least he was here to tell me *something*," Alfred said. "As I grew older, I realized that not all marriages are happy ones. Some couples choose to live apart. But you could have tried to explain that to us at some point. You could have arranged to visit us on a few occasions. When we went to live with Great-Aunt Withypoll and Bertram—when Father was tied up with his business arrangements. But we never saw you. I can only assume you didn't care."

Lady Harrington shook her head. "It is precisely because I *did* care that I stayed away, Alfred."

"That makes no sense," he said, confused.

"It will, when I am through," she answered. "Alfred, you and your brother were—and always will be—the joys of my life. A mother's love knows no bounds. She will do anything to see her children safe and protected. And that is exactly what I did for you boys."

"By leaving us to grow up without a mother?" he demanded.

"Yes," she said, fighting to contain her emotions. "Do you think it was easy for me to leave my babies behind? It would have been easier to rip out my heart! Sometimes I wished he had done that instead, rather than banish me from those I held dear."

"By 'he,' you mean Father?" Alfred said. "Why would your husband send you away? What could you have possibly done to deserve that?"

"I threatened to expose him," Lady Harrington explained. "I discovered your father's heinous secrets, and in the heat of the moment, I threatened to splash the truth across the front page of the *Times*. He became enraged. He said if I didn't keep my mouth shut and leave England, he would harm you and your brothers. I couldn't risk that. Though it destroyed me to leave you, I did what he demanded."

Alfred tried to make sense of what his mother was saying. "What was the secret you discovered about him? What was so horrible?"

"Your father is a brothel-owner, Alfred," she said,

finally. "He buys and sells women as if they are no more than inventory in a shop. He controls their lives, and if they try to leave his employ, bad things happen. I overheard a conversation one evening that he was having with one of his associates, and what I heard chilled my blood. As if making money off prostitution wasn't bad enough..."

"But why would he do that, and risk destroying his reputation?" Alfred asked.

"Money," she said, simply. "Your grandfather, the fifth earl, was a gambler and lost most of the family fortune. When your father inherited the title, it was all that was left of the legacy. Of course, I didn't know that at the time, no one did. But your father was obsessed with increasing the family's wealth. He would stop at nothing until he regained what your grandfather lost, and brought in even more money. I threatened all of that, so he punished me by separating me from my children. It has been a hard sentence to bear."

Alfred tried to take in everything his mother was saying...so many years had passed without her in their lives. He barely knew her anymore. Yet a part of his heart couldn't help but recognize this woman on an elemental level. The little boy in him remembered her, even if the grown man refused.

"But why come back to us now?" he asked. "My brothers want nothing to do with you. Why open up those old wounds?"

"Because of Aunt Withypoll, who has been like a mother to you in my stead," she answered. "I could not let her die without seeing her again, and at least attempting to put this horrible situation to rights. We have lost many years, Alfred—it's true. Your brothers may yet find it in their hearts to forgive me. I hope they do. I want to be part of all of your lives from now on. When you marry and have children, I want to be the doting grandmother. In the end, my son, all we have is each other. Not wealth or power or money can take the place of family. I wish your father could have realized that."

"But wasn't it dangerous for you to return to London?" Alfred asked. "If Father threatened you before, why were you willing to risk his wrath now?"

"I refused to live my life in fear any longer," Lady Harrington said. "Charles had taken so much from me— the best years of my life with my children. I realized there was nothing more he could do to me. I was going to come back here and fight for whatever was left. And that's what I'm doing, Alfred. I'm fighting for you, now—for you and Aunt Withypoll. I am no longer afraid to stand up and face my foe."

"Has Father made any threats against you since your return?" Alfred demanded.

"No," she replied. "But as you witnessed, things are strained between us. He is not happy that I've turned up again, that I can tell you. I plan to tell him that I will keep his secrets buried if he leaves me—and the rest of the family—alone."

Another thought was forming in Alfred's mind, and it was one he wished he didn't have to face. "You said Father was a brothel-owner, but that was twenty years ago. Do you know for certain that he is still involved in that world?"

"I don't know anything for certain," she said. "He may be involved in reputable business dealings now, or he may be up to his elbows in it, still. He would never tell me such things, especially now."

Everything was falling into place for Alfred, but the picture it painted was dark and horrible.

"Did you ever hear Father refer to himself, or anyone else address him as 'Mr. Cage?'" Alfred asked.

Lady Harrington pondered for a moment. "It was many years ago, Alfred. The details of the night I overheard him and his business associate have faded over time. But nothing comes to mind regarding the name 'Cage.' Why?"

"There is a suspicion that the man behind the fire at the Atwater School is a vengeful brothel-owner named Mr. Cage," Alfred explained. "Some of the girls have heard his name before, but no one has ever seen his face. Cage seems to be a powerful figure behind the scenes. He might be the one trying to stop Prudence's work in taking the girls off the streets. Some of the girls could have died in the fire, Mama. I could have died trying to save them. Do you think Father is capable of such devilish acts?"

"I am not certain, anymore," she replied. "Twenty years ago, he banished me to Italy. He never harmed me, but he threatened to harm you and your brothers back then. They could have been idle threats, made out of anger. But I wasn't going to take the chance, so I obeyed him and left England. Truly, I have no idea what Charles is capable of."

"We should return to the house," Alfred said, finally. "You know how agitated Crawford becomes when we are late for dinner."

"Of course," Lady Harrington said. "We have been away from Aunt Withypoll for too long as it is. But I am thankful that you have heard me out. I hope that we are on a better path with each other now. Because this time, I am not going anywhere. That is a promise."

As Alfred escorted his mother back to their waiting carriage, he tried to make sense of all she had just told him. So many years had passed, so many long-held beliefs about his mother's true feelings were now in doubt.

For most of his life he thought she didn't care about

him or his brothers. Was that simply a fiction his father had created for his own ends?

After all these years, why should Alfred believe anything his mother said?

What if this was all part of a plan to manipulate her children, somehow?

Would Alfred's father admit to any of the allegations Lady Harrington had made? He doubted it. One of them was lying, and had been for quite some time. But why? He couldn't see how returning to England would benefit his mother in any way, other than what she'd explained.

However, if she was telling the truth about her husband, the earl would have little reason to admit such a thing to his children, now. It would paint him as the villain. Alfred had never known his father to admit to wrongdoing to anyone about anything.

Yet, if everything happened as his mother described all those years ago, it meant his father was a very cold and dangerous man.

Could Lord Harrington be the mysterious 'Mr. Cage'?

And if so, was he the man responsible for the threats against Prudence and her students?

Alfred wanted to know the answer to that question, and many more.

CHAPTER TWENTY-FOUR

Crawford opened the front door, regarding Alfred and Lady Harrington with a furrowed brow. "I am relieved to see you've returned, my lord," he said. "I sent for Dr. Trask. I am afraid Lady Weston has taken a turn...."

"You did right, Crawford," Alfred said hurriedly, handing Crawford his hat. "Is the doctor here now?"

The butler nodded. "Yes, my lord. He asked that you attend him directly when you and Lady Harrington arrived home."

Alfred would have bounded up the stairs two at a time but he couldn't abandon his mother to follow behind him. As it was, they ascended the staircase as fast as they could and went to Great-Aunt Withypoll's bed chamber. Knocking lightly on the door, he heard Dr. Trask bid them to enter.

"Crawford said he'd sent for you," Alfred said as he and his mother approached Great-Aunt Withypoll's bedside. The elderly woman looked more frail than she ever had. Her skin was pale and her breathing appeared labored.

Dr. Trask regarded them solemnly. "He was right to do

so, though I am not able to do much more than make her comfortable right now."

"Has the time come, Doctor? Is she dying?" Lady Harrington asked, her brow furrowed with emotion.

"Lady Weston's heart is weakening," he explained. "There is nothing I can do to stop that, I'm afraid."

Alfred swallowed painfully, forcing himself to ask, "Will she make it through the night?"

"There are indications that she may not," Dr. Trask said, gravely. "Her pulse has been erratic and her breathing is labored, which is to be expected with her condition, at present. Then again, I have been wrong a handful times before during my career. Indeed, I hope I am wrong, now. All who have been blessed with knowing Lady Weston hope such a great lady will live forever."

Lady Harrington reached out a hand to her son. "Oh, Alfred, I don't want to lose her—not now, when I've finally returned home. Aunt Withypoll is so dear to me. In truth she has been like a mother to us both."

Alfred stared down at the frail woman tucked into the huge bed before them and felt his heart swell with devotion. He couldn't believe his beloved great-aunt might lose this battle, for she could out-maneuver almost anyone or anything. Yet he knew Dr. Trask was right. No one could keep a heart beating when it was ready to stop.

"Where is Miss Atwater?" Alfred asked. "She has become very close to Lady Weston. She should be here, as well."

"That's just it, my lord," Dr. Trask said. "Crawford informed me that Miss Atwater has gone missing. She hasn't been seen for quite some time and no one knows where she is. When I arrived an hour ago, they were searching the premises with no luck, it seems."

Alfred frowned, as a mixture of irritation and fear

flooded his veins. "*Missing*? Why didn't Crawford tell me as soon as we arrived?"

"Most likely his immediate concern was for Aunt Withypoll," his mother said.

"Damnation!" Alfred cursed. "With the current threats against her and the school, one would think Miss Atwater would take care to inform the household of her whereabouts."

Unless she wasn't able to inform them, he thought to himself a moment after.

Alfred and his mother regarded each other, reading each other's minds.

"Does anyone know if Lord Harrington came to call today?" Alfred asked the doctor.

Trask shook his head. "I heard no mention of your father coming to visit. Was he expected?"

"No," Alfred replied. He reached out to take Lady Weston's hand in his, and though it killed him, he said, "Auntie, I cannot stay with you, though now more than ever, I want to be at your side. Miss Atwater has gone missing, and she may be in great danger. I must find her. Will you wait for me until I return?"

Lady Weston's eyes fluttered weakly as she opened them. She focused briefly on Alfred, her voice no more than a whisper as she said, "*Go and find her, Alfred. Bring her back home.*"

Alfred gently patted her hand, saying, "I will, Auntie. That is a promise. Mother will stay with you until I return. Rest, now."

Great-Aunt Withypoll gave a weak nod, closing her eyes again and drifting into unconsciousness.

"Dr. Trask, will you stay here as well, while I'm gone?" Alfred asked.

The doctor nodded. "Hopefully I will not be summoned

to another case. I will look after Lady Weston and make sure she is not in any pain."

"Thank you," Alfred said. "Mother, you'll be alright?"

"Yes," Lady Harrington gave a smile, but wiped at her eyes. "I won't leave her side, Alfred."

Taking one last look at his beloved great-aunt, Alfred exited the room and descended the staircase in search of Crawford.

Reaching the bottom floor, he bellowed, "Crawford! Where are you, man? Crawford?"

The butler appeared at the end of the hallway and walked briskly toward his master, saying, "I am here, my lord. Dr. Trask must have told you about Miss Atwater's disappearance."

"He has," Alfred replied, knowing his anger would have to wait until later. "Have you found her, yet?"

"No, my lord," the butler answered. "Mr. Church and Miss Simms have been searching the grounds, and I have searched the house from top to bottom. She is not here. I told them that I did not see her return from her outing this afternoon. She may indeed have simply lost track of time."

"What outing?" Alfred demanded.

"A note was delivered for Miss Atwater earlier today," Crawford explained. "After reading it, she advised me she had to go and meet a friend, and that she wouldn't be long."

"She didn't say where she was going?" Alfred asked.

"No, my lord. But she seemed to make the decision to leave rather hurriedly," the butler explained.

"The note—did she leave it behind?"

"She did not, my lord," Crawford answered. "I searched the hallway for it, even the front step of the house, hoping she had dropped it there. Alas, I found nothing."

A knock sounded on the front door.

"Perhaps that is Miss Atwater, now," the butler said, going to answer it.

But it was not Miss Awater.

Mungo charged inside with Dolly close behind. "We found somethin' outside," he said, waving a piece of paper in his hand.

"Read it, Lord Weston," Dolly said. "We're not sure what to make of it."

Alfred read the crumpled note aloud: "'*Miss Atwater, Please attend me forthwith. I must speak to you regarding the recent attacks against the Atwater School. I have information which we must discuss. However, tell no one of our meeting. My carriage awaits outside. —The Earl of Harrington.*' Crawford, is this the note which was delivered to Miss Atwater earlier today?"

"It looks to be the same, my lord," Crawford answered.

"But why would Lord Harrington request a secret meeting with Miss Atwater?" Dolly asked. "Why wouldn't 'e ask for yer help in the matter, milord?"

Alfred frowned, trying to quell the dark foreboding in his heart. "That is a good question, Dolly. And one we must quickly answer," he said. "Mungo, go and get every weapon you have which can be easily concealed and meet me here in five minutes. Crawford, go and get my pistols, if you please."

As Mungo and Crawford departed, Dolly said, "Is Miss Atwater in trouble, milord? Surely, if yer father is with her..."

Alfred met Dolly's eyes, saying gravely, "That is precisely why I worry for her safety, Miss Simms. It may be nothing, but the truth may be something worse than we ever thought. I pray that I am wrong."

Dolly blinked away tears. "Oh, please go an' find Miss Atwater, milord! Bring 'er back safe."

"That is my intention, Dolly," he said. "While Mungo and I are gone, I need you to help Lady Harrington in any way you can. I know you must look after the girls, but Lady Weston is quite ill. She may not last the night. Crawford is here, and he will protect the house. He knows how to shoot a pistol and swing a few punches if need be."

"For that matter, so do I," she asserted.

"Good to know, Dolly," he replied. "I have the utmost confidence in you."

Mungo and Crawford reappeared, and Alfred took the pistols from his butler. "Do not be afraid to use your own pistol in our absence, Crawford. I explained to Miss Simms that you will be on guard tonight."

"Of course, my lord," Crawford replied. "I shall protect the house with my last breath."

"Do you have your weapons at the ready, Mungo?" Alfred asked.

Mungo opened his jacket and displayed several dangerous-looking knives. Custom-made sheaths were sewn into the lining, and there was even a holster for his pistol.

The ex-pirate said, "Ready, milord. Let's go an' fetch Miss Atwater, an' bring 'er home."

CHAPTER TWENTY-FIVE

Prudence opened her eyes slowly, fighting against the groggy sensation that seemed to paralyze her body. Her head ached with a dull thud, and her throat was parched with thirst.

Forcing herself to focus her eyes, she blinked repeatedly as she tried to get her bearings.

She tried to move but realized that she was bound. Her wrists were tied behind her back and she was on the floor in an awkward position, secured to the foot of a heavy four-poster bed. A gag had been tied around her mouth.

What had happened? Where was she?

Prudence scanned the room for clues as to her whereabouts, but she didn't recognize it. The bed chamber was decorated in an opulently garish style, with deep red draperies trimmed in black fringe and accessories to match. The room was luxurious, but there was something off about it.

How had she gotten here? Her mind was muddy... She tried to control the fear that pulsed in her veins, for she knew it would not help her situation. She had to think clearly.

Then it all came back—Lord Harrington, the carriage, and the strong smelling rag he'd put over her mouth. He'd knocked her out and brought her to this place. But why would Alfred's father do such a thing?

The door opened, and Lord Harrington entered, holding a brandy snifter in his hand.

"Ah, I see you are awake, Miss Atwater," he said pleasantly.

She struggled and tried to say something—still hoping that this was all a misunderstanding or that Lord Harrington had temporarily lost his mind.

He sat in a wing chair. "Please don't tire yourself with trying to speak or escape your bonds. It is futile and you will only hurt yourself. I am sorry it had to come to this, but there was no other option. I gave you several warnings which you chose to ignore. I don't like this situation any more than you do, but I am a businessman, Miss Atwater. And I must protect the empire I have worked to build."

Prudence stared at Lord Harrington mutely in horror.

He was the one behind the threats to her...the one who burned down her school...the one who sent his henchman after her at the National Gallery.

Alfred's father was Mr. Cage.

Prudence kicked her feet and screamed into the gag, but it was no use.

"I told you not to bother doing that," Lord Harrington said, "but once again, your stubborn nature shows through. It is your choice, my dear. I care not if you dislocate your arm flailing about like a heathen. Soon you will no longer be my problem."

Prudence blinked up at him—this lord of the realm who sat there as if all of this were perfectly normal. Perhaps he was mad....

Lord Harrington smiled at her and said, "In a little

while, some gentlemen will come in to look at you. Not to worry. Nothing untoward will occur. Not here, anyway. There's going to be an auction, Miss Atwater. It would be difficult to keep you on in one of my brothels—word might get out regarding your identity, or you might find a way to escape. I certainly cannot have that. So I am selling you to the highest bidder. Whichever gentleman bids the most will take you away tonight and do with you as he pleases—preferably far away from London. I shall wash my hands of you and you will no longer be a threat to my business."

Prudence's heart beat thunderously in her chest.

This was a like a nightmare, only it was all too real.

How many other girls had this happened to, she wondered? And how many of them had ended up dead when the buyer was finished with them?

Her father had raised her to use her intellect to solve her problems. If only she wasn't gagged! If only she could talk to Lord Harrington, or Mr. Cage, or whatever he called himself. Surely she could get herself out of this before it was too late. She had to find a way to stall him, somehow.

If this dastardly auction took place, Prudence might never see Alfred again—or Dolly, or Mungo, or their unborn child, or the girls, or Lady Weston. They were her family now, and all she wanted was to be with them again.

Though it killed her to think it, perhaps Alfred was right. Perhaps she'd taken too many risks in her efforts to help the streetwalkers that men like Lord Harrington employed. Yet she knew she could never have turned her back on those women, even now, when her own life was in peril.

She had to think...had to figure out a way to escape.

"Well, it has been charming spending this time with you, Miss Atwater," Lord Harrington said, as if they were guests at a soiree. "However, I must go and prepare for my buyers. They will be arriving soon. Then you will finally be taken care of, and I shall make a tidy profit from it. Until then."

With that Lord Harrington exited the room, leaving Prudence alone and still tied to the bedpost. If only she could loosen these bonds! But her wrists were bound very securely. She could scream for help if she could get the gag off her mouth, but it was doubtful anyone in this place would come to her aid. She tried to move the bed post but it was far too heavy. It sat like an immovable stone on the floor.

Think, Prudence, think!

The gag in her mouth seemed to be a strip of muslin... Only one option presented itself to her at the moment. Prudence began slowly chewing at the fabric tied around her mouth. While she did that, she concentrated on how she might untie the bonds at her wrists.

Alfred... I won't let them take me away from you, her heart cried out.

I will find my way back to you, no matter what it takes. And even if you are angry at me for falling into this trap, I don't care. I only want to see you again, to feel your arms around me once more, and your lips on mine.

As Prudence focused on the task at hand, she filled her mind and heart with Alfred—her soul-mate, her lover, her friend.

For there was something very important she had to tell him....

Alfred and Mungo hopped out of the carriage and onto the street.

"Just like before, Matthews," he said to his driver. "Wait for us around the corner. If you see us running, get ready for a quick departure."

"Yes, milord," Matthews replied. "You can count on me."

Alfred had the utmost confidence in Matthews, for the man had served with him in the Peninsula.

"Alright, Mungo," Alfred said as they trotted toward the posh-looking house on the corner of Eddlington Street. "This is The Black Swan, another of Cage's brothels. Prudence may be held somewhere inside. We'll go round to the back door and you keep your pistol trained on whoever answers."

Mungo held up a pistol and a curved knife. "Don't worry milord, we'll soon get 'em talkin.'"

They'd been to one brothel already, The Zephyr, but found nothing. Mungo had snatched a young man working there when he stepped outside for a smoke, dragged him into an alley and roughed him up while Alfred asked the questions. But the shaken footman told them no one matching Prudence's description had been brought in to The Zephyr that night.

They had the names of several brothels thanks to Minnie's information. Of course, there could be more establishments they didn't know about, but at least it was a starting point.

The thought of Prudence out there somewhere with God-knew-what happening to her made Alfred almost mad with fury. But he had to put those feelings aside now, and focus on finding her before it was too late.

Alfred and Mungo climbed over the wrought-iron fence surrounding the property and ran across the dark gardens toward the back of the house. The windows were lit inside and the sounds of men talking and laughing echoed through the night. Light female voices trickled over top.

Approaching the back door, Mungo reached out a meaty fist and knocked upon it. In a few moments it opened and a big, burly man filled the door frame.

"McTavish?" Mungo said, lowering his pistol.

"Mungo Church?" the man said, the hint of a grin on his broad face. He looked around before stepping outside to greet them. "You old sea dog! I thought you was dead."

"I could say the same about you, Tav," Mungo replied, slapping the man on the back. "Will wonders never cease."

"How long you been in London, bucko?" McTavish asked. "Or are ye still sailin' the old briny?"

"I'm retired from that life," Mungo said. "I work for a lady now—Miss Atwater. She's gone missing. That's why we're here. We need your help, Tav."

"You don't have to ask, Mungo," he replied. "You've got it. What can I do?"

"This is Lord Weston," Mungo said. "Miss Atwater is in love with him."

Alfred shot a surprised glance at Mungo, who continued, "Even if she don't know it, milord, she is. And 'e loves her too. Miss Atwater is a strong-willed young lady, but brave as they come. She 'elps girls like what work here, takes them off the street and gives them an education. She found me on the street, I was almost dead. She took me in and nursed me, and taught me to read."

"You can read?" McTavish asked, amazed.

"Yeah, and do numbers and everything," Mungo explained. "But Miss Atwater's generosity has got 'er into hot water. She's made some powerful enemies, and we think one of 'em snatched 'er."

"We think the brothel owner, Mr. Cage, has abducted her," Alfred said. "We know this is one of his establishments. Have there been any new girls brought in tonight?"

McTavish led them a few steps away from the house, saying, "This is one of Mr. Cage's houses. And I could lose my job for tellin' ye so—or worse. But old Mungo saved me life once, so I owe him. There hasn't been any new girls brought here tonight, but I heard tell of somethin' big going on at one of the other houses, one called, The Sapphire. It's not as well-known as the other houses—very exclusive—on Frederick Place. There's to be an auction...a new girl was brought in. I don't know much more than that."

"Was there a description of this girl?" Alfred asked.

McTavish shook his head. "No. But one of the other guards was sent over there for crowd control, in case things get out of 'and. That's all I know."

Alfred exchanged a look with Mungo. "Let's go. We haven't a moment to lose."

"Just wait," McTavish said, pulling out a key ring. He took one off and handed it to Mungo. "The house number is fourteen, and this might come in 'andy when ye get there."

"Much obliged," Mungo said with a grin.

"Our thanks to you, Mr. McTavish," Alfred said as they turned to depart.

If Prudence was indeed to be sold at some diabolical auction, they had to get to The Sapphire fast.

For it wasn't just Prudence who might be sold...it was Alfred's unborn child, as well. His family, dammit!

His father was going to pay for this, very dearly indeed.

Quickly returning to the carriage, Alfred gave Matthews the address. The driver took them to Frederick Place, and soon they were standing on the street, planning a two-pronged attack.

"I'll go up on the roof and shimmy down to one of the upper windows," Alfred said. "You use the key McTavish gave you and enter through the back door. Once inside, tell them he sent you as an extra guard for the auction. Try to discover where Prudence is being held. And don't be afraid to use your weapons."

Mungo gave him a look. "Have I ever been, milord?"

Alfred nodded. "Right. Meet you inside. Good luck, Mungo."

"And good luck to you, milord," Mungo said, then disappeared around the house.

Alfred went to the adjacent alleyway and looked for a way up. Seeing a thick drainpipe against a wall, he tested it for stability. Satisfied, he began slowly climbing up. He grit his teeth as his muscles were tested, but kept going. As an intelligence officer in the war, he'd scaled fortress walls and rock faces—this was nothing new for him.

The only thing new about this rescue scenario was that his emotions were involved. A woman he loved more than life itself was inside. If anything happened to Prudence, he didn't know what he'd do.

Soon he was up and over the edge of the roof, walking quickly across it to the building that housed The Sapphire brothel. Finding another drainpipe, Alfred shimmied down to an upper ledge and stepped onto it. He came to the first window and could see through a gap in the heavy curtains. A man and woman were engaged in sex upon the bed, but the woman was blonde.

He moved to the next window and looked inside. It was empty. He started to move along, but his eye caught sight of something.

A foot.

It pushed out again from behind the end of the big bed. Then Alfred saw a glimpse of wild auburn hair.

Prudence.

Goddammit, she was struggling...of anyone was hurting her, he'd kill them with his bare hands.

He tried to open the window but it was locked from the inside. Using his elbow, he broke one of the glass panes as gently as he could, trying to be quiet. He pushed out the broken pane and reached inside, unlocking the window.

Prudence's head popped up over the side of the bed, and her eyes lit up when she saw him.

"Alfred?" she said in disbelief as he came through the window.

He rushed to her side, checking her for injuries and pulling her in for a heated kiss.

"Are you alright?" he asked, brushing her hair from her face. "Have you been hurt? Dear God, Prudence, I thought I'd lost you."

"I'm alright," she assured. "It's your father, Alfred—he's Mr. Cage."

"I know," he replied, cutting the bonds from her wrists and pulling the chewed gag from where it lay rent around her neck.

"You *know*?" she asked as he helped her to her feet.

"We found the note he sent to you, asking to meet," he said. "Mother told me a chilling story about their marriage, and why she went to Italy. I'll tell you all when we are safely out of here."

"And just where do you think you're going?" a voice asked from the doorway.

Alfred shoved Prudence behind him, faced his father, and cocked his pistol.

CHAPTER TWENTY-SIX

Alfred stared at the man who had taken so much from him—his mother, his childhood—and who wanted to take more from him, still.

Lord Harrington levelled his own pistol at his son. "Put down your gun, boy. We both know you won't shoot me."

"If you truly believe that, you don't know me at all," Alfred replied, darkly. "You took Mother away from me for all those years. You're not taking Prudence, too."

Harrington sneered. "Women are all the same, Alfred. They only weaken a man. Look at you now—willing to die for this little baggage? What a fool you are."

"I have been a fool to believe you my entire life," he said, "as well as my brothers did. We believed your lies. But we aren't children anymore. We can judge for ourselves. You're nothing more than a manipulator, a cheat, and a user of women...and I despise you for it."

The earl gave a snake-like smile. "I have built an empire and I have no regrets. But you soon will if you don't step away and wash your hands of this girl, immediately."

"Never," Alfred replied, still aiming the pistol at his father. "I'll blow your brains out before I let you take Prudence."

"Why should you 'ave all the fun, milord?" It was Mungo, his pistol pressed against the back of Lord Harington's head. "I was hoping I might 'ave a go at it, what with the fact that 'e could 'ave killed one of the girls or Dolly by settin' fire to the school." He stepped closer, growling in Lord Harrington's ear, "Dolly Simms is going to be my wife, sir, and the mother of my children, and I don't take kindly to anyone threatenin' my family—which, by the way, Miss Atwater is, too. *She is my family.* And you are done tormenting 'er."

Lord Harrington glared, saying, "We seem to be at a stalemate."

"No," Mungo said, "no stalemate. There are two pistols pointed at ye, and ye only have the one. That is not a stalemate. That is you being out-gunned, and losing." He pressed his pistol harder into the back of Harrington's head. "Now you just come in here and do what ol' Mungo tells ye."

Alfred yanked the pistol from his father's hand and kept that one trained on him, too.

"Hands behind yer back," Mungo ordered, sheathing his pistol and pulling a length of rope from an inner pocket of his jacket. He tied Lord Harrington's hands behind him and then shoved him to the floor, fastening the man's wrists to the bedpost, as Prudence's had been.

Ripping part of the bedsheet, Mungo tied it around Lord Harrington's mouth, gagging him.

"There," Mungo said. "That ought to hold 'im til the constables arrive. Now, to get us out of 'ere...."

"Are there many guards downstairs, Mungo?" Alfred asked.

"Only two that I saw, one at the front door, and the other one roaming about," he replied. "Most of the patrons are drunk, so we won't find much resistance there."

Alfred opened an armoir and pulled out a black silk cloak. He pulled it over Prudence's shoulders and raised the hood to cover her red hair. "I say we make a break for it, go downstairs out the back door. Escaping through the window is risky. I'd have to climb down the drainpipe with Prudence on my back and that might be difficult to manage. But we must go quickly. The longer we stay here, the harder it will be to get out."

"So right, milord," Mungo agreed. "Give one of the pistols to Miss Atwater. I taught 'er how to shoot. But if we go quickly, there'll be no need to."

Alfred gave a pistol to Prudence. "Are you ready?"

"As I'll ever be," she replied. "Let's get out of here."

Alfred ushered them into the hallway, closing the door on his protesting father. He led the way to the far end of the hall, with Prudence behind him and Mungo taking up the rear. As they passed several rooms they could hear the sounds of copulation from inside a few. At least the patrons inside wouldn't notice their departure.

Now to the back stairway.

Alfred opened the door and scanned for signs of danger. "All clear," he said. "Let's go."

They ran down the stairs as quietly as they could, soon reaching the main floor. In a few steps they would be free.

Alfred turned a corner and saw a big bear of a man standing idly near the back door....one of the guards. There was nothing for it, they were too close, now. Alfred raised his pistol—Prudence and Mungo followed suit.

"Get out of the way," he said to the burly guard. "We've no beef with you, but I'll put a hole in your head of you don't move. Now!"

The man stared at them silently, then moved out of the way with no more pressing.

Alfred opened the door and led the trio out into the back garden, ushering Prudence to safety. He wanted to pull her into his arms right now and crush her to him, but there was no time. They had to get to the carriage and back to the townhouse.

Alfred, Prudence and Mungo ran down the dark street. Alfred looked behind them, but saw that no one chased them. The guard from the brothel obviously didn't get paid enough for that.

Once inside the carriage, Alfred cradled Prudence in his arms as they pulled away and headed home. Mungo sat opposite them, his pistol still drawn and ready as he looked out the window, scanning the street for trouble.

"It's alright," Alfred said as Prudence buried her head in his shoulder. "I've got you, now. I've got you."

But did he really? He and Mungo had rescued Prudence from the brothel. That much was true. But would she choose to remain in Alfred's life as he truly wanted her...as his wife?

It was a question he resolved to have answered, one way or another.

Prudence tied the robe about her waist and ran a comb through her damp hair. It felt so good to be clean again...

Dolly had scooped her away as soon as they'd returned to Alfred's townhouse and ran a soothing bath for her. Prudence had argued, of course, wanting instead to go to Lady Weston's side. But Dolly would have none of it, saying Prudence was in no state to tend to the sick at such a time.

Lady Harrington was at the aged lady's side, and would keep vigil during the night. Everyone agreed that the best thing for Prudence after such an ordeal, was rest.

But she didn't want to rest. There were too many thoughts in her head, too many feelings in her heart, and too many things she needed to say before this night was through.

So, in Prudence-like fashion, she did what she wanted, anyway.

Hastily twisting her hair into a plait, Prudence carried a candle into the hallway. She crept down the hall toward one room in particular, and knocked lightly on the door.

Slowly, the door creaked open.

The sight of Alfred holding a flickering candelabra and standing shirtless in the doorway almost took her breath away.

God, he was beautiful...as beautiful as a man could be.

Strong...dangerous...a seasoned warrior.

Her warrior.

"I thought Dolly told you to get some sleep," he said curtly.

He was angry with her...like a parent angry with an unruly child who had wandered into danger.

She might feel the same about their child if it was as headstrong as she was...

Suddenly, Prudence wanted to laugh. It would be a fair fate for her to have a child as willful as she, and as stubborn as Alfred. For she wanted that child more than anything, now. And she wanted Alfred by her side as they watched it grow.

"I cannot sleep," Prudence said. "May I come in?"

He leaned against the door frame. The sight of his muscular body moving languidly in the candle light nearly did her in.

"Do you think that's wise, considering my state of undress?" he asked.

She tried not to smile, for he was playing with her. "I assure you, Lord Weston, you are perfectly safe with me."

"You're certain?" He stepped aside so she could enter. "I've seen you handle a pistol, madam, and it was quite impressive."

"Thank you for that, my lord," she said, "but I am not here to discuss my weaponry skills, which, as you say, are quite impressive."

Alfred sighed. "Can this not wait until morning? I'm tired. I've spent most of the evening rescuing you. I want to go to bed."

"I want to go to bed, too," Prudence answered. "With you."

"With—*what*?" he said.

"I want to go bed with you, Alfred," she said calmly. "I want to go to bed with you every night, and wake up every morning beside you...*as your wife*."

Alfred stood as if stunned for a moment, shaking his head as if to clear it. "Well, this is certainly a change of tune. You wish to accept my proposal?"

"No," she replied. "Actually, I do not."

He tapped his chin. "You wish to go to bed with me every night as my legally wedded wife, yet you do not accept my proposal of marriage?"

Prudence nodded happily. "That is exactly right."

"I do not understand you," he said, frowning.

"Yes you do," she countered. "That is why I love you, Alfred. You *do* understand me—and all my foibles, my headstrong nature, and my need for independence. That is why I cannot accept your proposal of marriage... I must make one of my own."

He stared down at her, his sensuous mouth curving with just the hint of a smile. "Continue," he said.

"But before I get to that," she said, "let me go back to some of the earlier events of the evening. I feared for my life, tonight. Your father, though he himself did not harm me, was perfectly willing to sell me to the highest bidder. I have no doubt that if that transaction had occurred, I may have suffered serious harm, indeed, perhaps never to be heard from again. It was a sobering thought as I sat there, bound to the foot of that bed, unable to help myself. I thought of you, of Dolly and Mungo, of my students, and of course, Lady Weston—all people who are so dear to me. I wanted only to see you all again...to see my *family* again. For that is who you are. It took me awhile to fully appreciate that fact."

Prudence reached out to place his strong hand on her flat belly, reveling in the primal sensation of it.

"I may be carrying your child, Alfred," she said. "As I sat there, bound and helpless, I thought of the new life that might be growing inside me. The thought that the two of us might die frightened me more than I'd ever been before. Suddenly, everything became clear. I want to bear your child, I want us to be a family together, and I don't care what anyone thinks. All I care about is you."

"Finally, you are seeing reason," Alfred said, then made a big show of checking her forehead for fever. "Gadzooks, are you alright, Prudence? You're actually making sense, for once. You must be ill."

She shooed his hands away. "Perhaps I was before, but I am better now. I know what I want in life, and I am no longer afraid to reach out and take it. I want you, Alfred. I want you and our children, and all the joys and sorrows that marriage brings. And in that regard, I have a question for you."

He looked down at her with a devilish grin, and said, "My heart is all a-flutter, Miss Atwater. Whatever would you want to ask me?"

She ignored him and took a deep breath. "Lord Alfred Weston, will you do me the honor of becoming my husband?"

"This is so sudden, Miss Atwater," he said. "A proposal of marriage has never been put to me before, and that is the truth. But I am so young, so inexperienced, so unprepared. I will have to say...that I will consider it."

Prudence frowned at him. "I beg your pardon?"

Then he pulled her into his arms and replied, "I'd have to consider myself insane if I didn't say 'yes,' though others might consider me so if I did. But, as you pointed out, none of that matters—only our love, and our life together as husband and wife. Truly, Prudence, you certainly took your time. I thought you'd never ask."

"So did I, my lord," she replied, tipping her chin up for a kiss. "So did I."

CHAPTER TWENTY-SEVEN

Prudence snuggled against the warm, masculine body beside her in bed, and knew she was in heaven. Alfred had loved her long into the night, but this time had been different between them. Their passion had kindled slowly together, unhurried and beautifully sweet. It was more than a meeting of physical bodies, but a meeting of hearts, minds and souls.

She had never felt more content or safe than she did at that moment.

This was to be her life with him, and she welcomed it.

As sunlight began to creep through the side of the heavy curtains, Prudence knew they couldn't linger much longer. There were the students to attend to, and she wanted to see Lady Weston, if permitted.

Throwing back the covers, she stood and donned her nightgown and robe. Alfred's valet would be coming to wake him soon. She would have to sneak back to her room quickly to avoid being seen.

Prudence exited Alfred's bedchamber and walked quickly down the hall to the room she shared with Dolly.

As she slipped inside, Dolly lifted her head from the pillow and raised sleepy eyes toward Prudence.

"Not again, Miss!" Dolly said.

"Yes again, Dolly," Prudence replied, unable to hide a grin.

"Well, I s'pose I shouldn't talk, what with my 'istory," her friend said. "I didn't even hear ye sneak away. After such a night, I thought ye'd sleep soundly."

"That's just it," Prudence explained. "I couldn't sleep at all. My mind was full of thoughts and questions. One in particular for Lord Weston."

"What was it?" Dolly asked, sitting up.

"You'll find out in due course," she answered. "Now, we must start the day. The girls will up before long, with hungry bodies and hungry minds which we must fill. But before I begin classes, I should like to visit Lady Weston, if her condition allows. Alfred told me she took a turn for the worse yesterday."

Dolly rose and tied her hair into a knot. "That she did, Miss. I know the doctor was 'ere. Not much 'e can do, I'm afraid."

"We must hope for a miracle, then," Prudence said, thinking that stranger things had happened of late.

Later, when Dolly was downstairs overseeing the students' breakfast, Prudence went to Lady Weston's bed chamber.

She knocked lightly on the door, but heard no response.

Dear God, had Lady Weston passed away during the night?

Prudence opened the door, and what she saw inside the room nearly knocked her over.

Lady Weston sat up in the bed, looking quite perturbed, indeed.

"Ah, finally...someone has come," she said. Her voice was weak and raspy still, but the color of her skin had improved. "I cannot reach the bell pull."

Prudence closed the door behind her, crossing the room and going to the aged lady's bedside. "Lady Weston. How are you feeling?"

"Hungry!" she replied. "I daresay, I am famished. Why has my breakfast tray not been brought up yet? Has the cook left our employ?"

"No, not in the least," Prudence replied, amazed at the improvement in Lady Weston's health. "But where is Lady Harrington?"

"Alicia?" she asked. "I'm sure I do not know. Is she not in her rooms?"

"Lady Harrington has been at your bedside all night, keeping vigil," Prudence said, adding, "Perhaps she had to attend to something."

"Vigil?" Lady Weston demanded. "Whatever for...was I dying?"

"Dr. Trask seemed to think your condition was quite serious," Prudence answered.

Lady Weston huffed. "That quack—what does he know? I am old, that is all. I am bound to have spells from time to time, in fact, I'm entitled to them! Now, if someone doesn't bring me a proper breakfast soon, I shall most certainly die of hunger."

"Of course, Lady Weston," Prudence said, moving to tug on the velvet bell pull.

Soon, the door opened and a maid entered, looking surprised to see her mistress sitting up in bed.

"Lady Weston would like a breakfast tray, Hester," Prudence said. "Something light—tea, toast and marmalade."

"I told you I am *hungry*, Miss Atwater," Lady Weston

asserted. "Hester, tell Cook I shall want eggs, ham and bacon along with it."

Hester looked from Prudence to Lady Weston for direction.

Prudence shook her head and said, "Just the tea and toast, Hester. That will be all."

"No—I want eggs and ham, as well!" Lady Weston called out but the maid had already gone. Then she looked at Prudence with obvious shock. "Miss Atwater, I am fond of you, as you know. But who do you think you are to contradict my express orders to my staff?"

"Forgive me, Lady Weston," Prudence said. "I mean no disrespect, but I must do what is best for you. I owe it to Alfred and Lady Harrington. And to answer your question, I am soon to be your great-niece-in-law."

Lady Weston stared at Prudence for a moment, then said, "You have accepted Alfred's proposal?"

"No," she replied. "He has accepted mine. I have asked Alfred to be my husband."

The aged lady smiled. "Brava, my dear. In that case, you may indeed contradict my orders from time to time. As the new Lady Weston, this shall be your house, and it shall be your right."

Prudence clasped Lady Weston's hand gently. "I would only do so out of care for you, my lady."

The door opened and Lady Harrington came in, stopping suddenly when she saw Lady Weston. She rushed forward. "Auntie! What are you doing sitting up? Are you alright?"

Lady Weston smiled and replied, "I am better than ever, Alicia, my dear. Miss Atwater has just shared some wonderful news with me, which affects you, as well. Would you like to tell her, or may I?"

Prudence gave a nod. "You certainly may, my lady."

"Miss Atwater has asked our dear Alfred to marry her," Lady Weston said, beaming.

Lady Harrington, still in shock over her aunt's dramatic improvement, said, "She asked *him* to marry her?"

"And he accepted," Lady Weston explained.

"I am not sure," Lady Harrington said, "but I think the world may have just turned upside down. Auntie was gravely ill but is on the mend, and now women are proposing marriage." Then, she laughed and pulled Prudence close for a hug. "But all I care about is happiness—yours, Alfred's and Aunt Withypoll's."

"Thank you, Lady Harrington," Prudence said. "Lady Weston understands, and so does Alfred, but I had to do it my way."

The door opened again and Hester walked in carrying a tray. She was followed by Alfred, looking dashing as always, who said, "I just heard the news. Auntie is sitting up and wants something to eat."

The maid placed the tray in front of Lady Weston and exited the room.

Alfred perused the tray, and said with a smile, "Tea, toast and marmalade...exactly what you used to order for me when I was convalescing as a boy, Auntie. You'll soon be right as rain."

"Quite right, Alfred," she said, happily. "Miss Atwater wisely overturned my request for eggs, ham and bacon, as well. A very capable and authoritative young lady."

Alfred raised a brow. "Miss Atwater contradicted your orders, and you allowed it?"

"I most certainly did," Lady Weston replied. "As she is going to be mistress of this house, I thought it best to get the staff used to the idea of taking orders from her."

Alfred glanced at Prudence inquisitively.

"The news of our engagement sort of came out," she said, shrugging.

"My dear, I think it is well past time for any semblance of convention regarding our relationship," he said, calmly. "It is perfectly fine that you made the announcement to Auntie and Mama. After all, we are to be family."

Prudence took his hand, her heart filling with love, pride, and new-found peace. "My dear Lord Weston, I believe we already are...."

Epilogue

One Year Later
Broomley Park, Luton

Prudence shielded her eyes from the bright sunshine as she gazed over the vast grounds of Broomley Park, the Weston family seat. It was still hard for her to believe that she was mistress of such a place, as well as the London townhouse, and all the other Weston property in Norfolk she hadn't even seen yet.

Life was full of surprises, she thought with a smile.

A year ago, if anyone had told her she'd be married to a wonderful man like Alfred, and blessed with a beautiful baby daughter, she'd have thought them mad. Yet, here she was, living a life she'd never expected, but gave thanks for every day.

Her heart swelled with emotion as she watched the figure of a man walk up the hill toward her.

Alfred.

Her husband. Her lover. Her partner in all things.

Thinking back to when she first met him, she'd thought

of herself as the skilled teacher. Little did she know this incredible man would teach her so much about life, love and the essence of family.

He smiled as he neared her, and she felt her heart quicken with desire as she looked up into those dark, devilish eyes.

"We are making good progress on the dormitories," he said. "Mungo expects the men to be finished sooner than planned. The Weston Academy will be ready to house more students in a few weeks' time."

Upon their marriage, Prudence had changed the name of the school to better reflect her new partnership with her husband. She knew her father would have understood.

"But what are you doing out here?" he asked. "Don't you have a class to teach?"

Prudence took his hand as they turned and began walking back to the great house. "Actually, not at the moment. Your mother is teaching a class in art history and Great-Aunt Withypoll is demonstrating table manners and etiquette for a group in the dining room."

"And where is our darling daughter?" he asked.

"Probably having her morning nap," Prudence answered. "Dolly is in the nursery with Emma and Bertie. So you see, I was not needed anywhere."

He pulled her close, saying, "Anywhere but here. What a dutiful wife you are, waiting with bated breath for your husband's return."

She slapped his chest playfully. "Yes, that must be it. I am known for my devotion to marital duty and complete obedience to my husband."

"Have you been sipping the cordial already?" he asked, looking down at her and raising a teasing brow.

Prudence laughed out loud. That was one of the things

she treasured about their marriage. They both made each other laugh.

Since marrying Alfred there had been laughter and tears, and many changes in both of their lives.

Alfred's father had been arrested, tried and imprisoned for his criminal activities. Great-Aunt Withypoll had regained her health and vowed to live until she was one-hundred years old, or even one-hundred and one. Dolly and Mungo had married as well, and Dolly had given birth to their son Albert—whom everyone called Bertie— only a week after Prudence had delivered their daughter, Emma.

Though at one time she feared losing her independence, Prudence had made some concessions in her new life as wife and mother, but strangely, they didn't seem difficult to her now. Perhaps because she was so happy with Alfred and their beautiful baby girl, and with taking her place in this new family they'd created together.

"Have you heard from Mr. McTavish?" she asked as they walked. "Have he and his wife found any new students for us?"

McTavish was an old comrade of Mungo's from his pirate days, Prudence had learned. He'd been working at one of the brothels when Alfred and Mungo had run into him the night she'd been kidnapped, and he'd assisted them in their quest to rescue Prudence.

Now, he and his wife—a woman who had previously worked at the brothel—handled recruitment for the Weston Academy. Though Prudence had once vowed never to give up going into the streets herself to help people in need, she was content to let the McTavish's use their connections to help those trapped in London's dark underworld.

"Mungo and I met with Tav yesterday," Alfred

answered. "He and Rose have taken in two girls who are sisters, and are looking forward to starting a new life here at the Academy. They should be arriving by the end of the week."

"That is wonderful news, Alfred," she said, her heart filling with warmth. "You know, though I would never have believed it a year ago, my little school has grown into something much bigger than my father and I had ever conceived of. And it really is thanks to you, and Great-Aunt Withypoll, and your dear Mama, Dolly and Mungo, and the McTavish's, too. Though you wouldn't think so, even your father deserves some thanks."

Alfred frowned, asking, "How do you figure that? Because of him, I almost lost you—and Emma."

"It was when I was tied to that bedpost, fearing for my life that I realized what was truly important to me," she replied. "You, and our unborn child, and our family. Nothing—not my need for independence or my fear of losing it—was more important than seeing you again. Though it took me awhile to realize it, your father gave me a gift that day, the gift of clarity. Ever since the moment I saw you coming through that window to rescue me, I knew complete happiness. It has never gone away, and it never shall."

Alfred lifted her hand to his lips and kissed it. "Nor shall I, Prudence, my love."

"Thank you for believing in me, Alfred," she said. "You accepted me for who I am, but you changed me, for the better. In my efforts to give my students a new life, I gained a new one for myself, as your wife."

They stopped for a moment, gazing at the manor house of Broomley Park. All the people Prudence loved most in the world were inside it, save for one, and he stood next to her.

She reached up on tiptoe and pulled him close for a kiss—one that expressed all the emotions in her heart—love, desire, devotion and contentment. Then she smiled up at him. "With you at my side, Alfred, I will always be home."

Dear Reader,

Thank you for taking the time to read TAMING THE BRIDE, book two in the *Brides of Mayfair* series. I hope you enjoyed it! If you haven't read book one, I encourage you to try SEDUCING THE BRIDE, where Alfred plays a role as the hero's best friend. That book is available now, and you can read on for more information about that.

Also read on for an excerpt from book three in this series: HIS COURTESAN BRIDE. If you would like to be notified about its release, as well as special events and giveaways, please visit my website at www.michellemcmaster.com and sign up for my mailing list. I would love to send news to you.

I also encourage you to follow me on Bookbub at www.bookbub.com/authors/michelle-mcmaster to learn about temporary 99 cent sales on ebooks from my backlist. Just click the blue follow button, and Bookbub will send you an email to let you know.

Lastly, if you enjoy the thriller genre, please check out my *Watch Me* series, which I write under the pen name of Avery Holt. I have a separate website for my Avery novels, and you can visit Avery's website at www.AveryHolt.com.

Once again, thank you for reading one of my novels.

Until next time!

Michelle McMaster

SEDUCING THE BRIDE

BOOK ONE

Lord Beckett Thornby is in need of a wife. In order to claim his inheritance, the confirmed bachelor must marry. Yet the last place he expects to find a bride is in the backstreets of London, in a rubbish heap.

Isobel Hampton is running from a painful past...and a dangerous man who will stop at nothing until he finds her. A marriage of convenience with a sinfully handsome lord seems like the perfect solution, until Isobel realizes her husband wants much more from her than she is willing to give. Soon, the marriage that was supposed to be "all business" turns into a dangerous dance of seduction that could leave one or both of them with a broken heart.

(Originally published under the title *The Marriage Bargain* in 2000. *Seducing the Bride* is a newly revised and updated edition.)

His Courtesan Bride

Book Three

When Miss Serena Ransom is caught in a scandalous embrace with Lord Kane at a Mayfair ball, her reputation is destroyed and her future looks grim. But when she joins The Courtesan Club, conceived by the famous courtesan, Lady Night, Serena begins a new life and vows to take charge of her own destiny as never before. Serena is a celebrity, and London's most powerful men are competing to become her lover and protector.

Everything is falling into place, except for the one man who threatens everything—Darius Manning, the Earl of Kane.

Serena stirred Darius's passions as no other woman ever had. Even as he kissed her that night at the Mayfair ball, he knew he could never make her his wife, for he was pledged to another. Now, years later, Darius is free at last and cannot forget the passionate, auburn-haired miss that still fires his blood. The wealthy Lord Kane makes Serena an offer she can't refuse, to share his bed as his exclusive courtesan.

But as Darius and Serena begin a journey of unbound pleasure together, they soon learn that the most dangerous emotion of all isn't passion, or desire... but love.

Read on for an excerpt from HIS COURTESAN BRIDE...

Enjoy an excerpt from

ℋis
COURTESAN
BRIDE

Brides of Mayfair series – Book 3

MICHELLE MCMASTER

PROLOGUE

May, 1816
Telford House,
Mayfair, London

"**D**on't you know how dangerous it is for you to be seen with me?" a sinful voice whispered in Serena's ear.

Strong, masculine hands slid around her waist and pulled her flush against him in a dark corner of the dimly lit gardens. The heat of Darius' body penetrated through the delicate fabric of Serena's ivory silk ball gown, a heady contrast to the cool, summer night air that danced around them.

"Of course I do," she managed to whisper. He was right. This was dangerous business, indeed—for both of them.

If they were discovered like this, in such a compromising position, all hell would break loose. Of course, Serena herself stood to lose the most if their forbidden liaison were discovered. But at times like this, that fact seemed dreadfully unimportant.

Warm lips touched Serena's neck just below her ear, making gooseflesh erupt upon her skin.

"Then why did you come?" he demanded.

Serena gasped as his hands slid upward over the bodice of her gown, claiming her breasts as if it was his right. If he had been her husband, it would be his right to touch her so intimately. If he had been her fiancé, even. But Darius, Lord Kane—famous war hero and leading bachelor of the Marriage Mart—was neither of those things to Serena.

Not yet.

She tried to reply, but gasped as deft fingers teased her nipples to achingly hard points.

"You know why," she said, hearing the edge in her voice.

It was a game they played. They both knew the answers to such questions. Yet they asked them, regardless.

"For this?" His warm, wicked mouth burned a trail of hot kisses over her throat and shoulders. Serena leaned her head back against his hard chest, turning her head to give him more access to her tender skin.

"And this?" He quickly loosened the laces at the back of her gown, pulling at the whisper-thin fabric.

Serena shivered helplessly as Darius bared her skin to the night, biting her lip as he slowly palmed her breasts. As her lover pleasured her with his hands, Serena gazed through half-lidded eyes at the opulent manor house in the distance. Golden light spilled out of the tall French windows onto the terrace and courtyard below.

Somewhere inside, mingling with the other guests was Serena's mother, Lady Ransom. Over these past months of the Season, Lady Ransom had coached her daughter well in the tricks and subterfuge necessary to snag a worthy husband. She had taught her to seduce with dancing eyes and a carefree manner. Serena had learned to wield her remarkable beauty as a warrior wields a sword, with purpose and without quarter.

What would Lady Ransom say if she could see her daughter now, engaged in a dangerous dalliance in the sanctuary of the gardens below?

She would admonish her most sternly, Serena knew.

But what her mother didn't know was that Serena had been meeting Lord Kane for clandestine trysts just like this for weeks, now.

Each time, Darius teased and tempted Serena a little further in their wicked game. Such profound pleasure could not be too much of a sin, Serena thought—not when the man in question would be making an offer of marriage before long.

Now she stood in the darkened gardens of Telford House, Serena's fancy gown sliding further down past her shoulders. Lord Kane used his mouth to rain tantalizing kisses down her back. Serena moaned in pleasure, clutching the silk bodice to her chest in an effort to cover herself.

In one smooth movement, Darius spun her to face him. Excitement coursed through her veins at his masterful movement. He was the war hero of Waterloo—strong, capable, and used to getting his way.

This was part of their little game, too. Even in this low light, she could see the unmistakable passion in his eyes. Passion that glowed and burned for her.

Serena still clutched the flimsy fabric to her chest with one hand. The other had reached out and grabbed onto Darius's sleeve for balance as he'd quickly turned her.

"I'll rip that gown to shreds if you don't let go your hold upon it," he warned.

Serena gasped. "You wouldn't."

"I would," he replied with a mischievous grin, and she knew he was toying with her. "Your body is too beautiful to keep covered up. If you were my wife, I would pleasure you night after night in my bed, and you would be quite naked indeed. You'd never want to leave."

Serena felt her knees weaken at the thought. The wicked truth of the matter was that she would like nothing more than to live exactly as Darius described.

A shiver ran over her skin as she imagined all the things Darius would do to her if she were legally bound to him. If she guessed correctly, she would soon find out. Lord Kane wanted her as his wife. He'd all but said so. Theirs would be the most passionate union London had ever seen.

A year from now, she would be the Countess of Kane, wife of the handsome war hero, and her perfect life would be everything she always dreamed....

CHAPTER ONE

*"Becoming a Courtesan is never the first
choice for a woman...which is a pity, for
once they take up the vocation, most women
wonder why they didn't do it sooner."*
—from Memoirs of a Courtesan
by Lady Night

One Year Later

Serena ran her hands over the shimmering gold gown that hugged her trim figure, and felt her pulse quicken at the excitement of the evening. The exquisite silk fabric had been sent from Paris at exceptional cost. Nothing but the best would do for London's newest courtesan.

Lady Devlyn's French maid, Giselle, had spent two hours arranging Serena's thick, auburn hair into an intricate and beguiling design. A strand of pearls wove throughout the tresses, and one bouncing curl dangled enticingly between Serena's shoulder blades. As a final touch, the maid dusted Serena's bare skin with a shimmering powder, fine as fairy dust.

"What is that?" Serena had asked, intrigued.

The maid smiled as she dusted the soft powder puff over Serena's cleavage, which rose above the scandalously low neckline of her gown. "Zis is magic powder," Giselle replied in her thick accent. "Eet gives zee skin a delicious glow, and will make zee men want to touch it, you see. But you will not let zem. Eet will drive zem wild!"

Serena gazed about Lady Devlyn's opulent dressing room and took a deep breath. The walls were covered in pale pink silk, the floor with a rare white Abyssinian carpet. Furnishings of mahogany, cherry-wood and polished brass complimented a pale marble floor. The rest of the house was as luxuriously decorated. Priceless tapestries, paintings and marble busts further adorned one of the most expensive residences in Mayfair.

Serena had come a long way from the terrible scandal of the Telford Ball, and the subsequent loss of her mother.

After those dark days, meeting Lady Devlyn had been one of the most fortuitous events of Serena's life. Lady D— who also used the professional name of Lady Night—had passed on her wisdom to Serena, Felicity and Bliss, and what they had learned from her was much more than simply how to become a skilled courtesan.

Lady Devlyn had taught the girls how to be confident in a man's world, how to pursue pleasure and enjoy decadence without apologies, and most importantly, how to guard your heart against the power of a man's seduction.

"'To thine own self be true,'" Lady Devlyn had said, quoting Shakespeare's Hamlet. "If you follow this adage, my dears, you will never be disappointed. Especially where men are concerned."

Their training had included everything from reading the entire works of Shakespeare and selections from the Classics, to an illuminating book called the Kama Sutra.

Serena smiled as she remembered the look on Bliss' face when she gazed at the illustrations in that ancient text. Not only had it provided instruction on the physical pleasures of their new vocation, it also had an entire chapter dedicated to the life of a courtesan.

Serena had read that particular chapter three times.

Along with advice on managing one's finances, the Kama Sutra provided tips for choosing a suitable man, but warned of becoming too attached to just one. Instead, it encouraged the courtesan to pursue sexual pleasure as a means of spiritual development. And if a man chose to give you expensive gifts along the way, it was most prudent to accept them.

Lady D had also insisted on other, unorthodox training such as fencing, how to shoot a pistol, and even martial arts practiced in the Far East. During one particular lesson, Lady D had entertained them with an exciting story about one of her exploits deep inside Peking's Forbidden City which featured herself, the Emperor of China, and a band of deadly, black-clad warriors. "One can never be too prepared," Lady D had said as she demonstrated how she fought them off, "for whatever situation might arise."

In an effort to better understand the sensual skills they would learn, Serena, Bliss and Felicity also studied human anatomy, which they found wickedly fascinating. But sensuality alone did not a courtesan make. That was only one aspect of their allure.

"A Courtesan is, above all, the epitome of independence," Lady Devlyn explained, "in thought, in passion, as well as in matters of finance. The education I bestow upon you now will cultivate all of these things in your hearts and minds."

The Courtesan Club—as they liked to call themselves—

had arrived at Lady D's Mayfair mansion a few days prior to the exclusive soiree that would mark Serena's debut. In the year that she, Felicity and Bliss had lived at Hargrove Park, Lady D had also taught them how to dress... "so that a man cannot take his eyes off you, how to speak so that a man cannot forget you, and how to indulge in the most wicked pleasures without making the mistake of falling in love."

That last part was probably the most invaluable lesson of all, Serena thought. She had made that mistake before with Darius, and she'd be damned if she did something so foolish again.

Of course, the paradox in all of this was that Serena, soon to be London's newest courtesan, was a virgin. And she had two very well-respected physicians' certificates to prove it.

Instead of being dismayed, Lady D had been delighted at the news of each girl's respective virginity. After a few weeks of studying male anatomy, with both books and a human subject (a strapping, well-endowed young footman who seemed to enjoy the attention) the topic had understandably come up.

Their benefactress had assured the girls that being virgin courtesans would not hinder their careers in the least. In fact, quite the opposite. It would only serve to increase their price when the offers started rolling in.

"You see, my dears," Lady D explained, "men enjoy the fantasy of being the first to deflower a woman, no matter who she may be—courtesan or wife. It only adds to your allure."

At Lady Devlyn's exclusive soiree, Serena would be the first of the Courtesan Club to make her debut. Both Felicity and Bliss would make theirs in a similar way, but at different, exclusive events imaginatively planned for each of them by Lady Devlyn herself. Along with being a font of knowledge on all things carnal, Lady D was an astute business woman. She knew all about the power of supply and demand. Making the other two new courtesans temporarily unavailable would make the most powerful men in London desperate with desire for them.

Lady D had also been leaking titillating tidbits about her new protégés to the underground press for months. Though their identities were a closely guarded secret, thanks to their benefactress's efforts, the Courtesan Club was already famous. All of London was talking about them—albeit behind closed doors. The gossip about Town was that gentlemen were already fighting over them, and the ladies were jealous beyond all. The fact that Lady Devlyn had deigned to pass on her exclusive knowledge and skills to three fresh faced young women was the biggest news to hit London since Wellington's victory at Waterloo.

And though the papers would never believe it, the reason for Lady Night's philanthropy was exactly that—philanthropic. With no children of her own, she wished to pass on her legacy to three independent-minded women whose vivacious spirits could never thrive within society's strict boundaries. Serena, Felicity and Bliss were the mistresses of their own fates and fortunes, now.

"You look absolutely stunning, my dear," Lady D said as she came into Serena's dressing room. "Pierrette was right, this silk is the finest I've ever seen. It makes your green eyes glow like jade, and your skin is as luminous as the golden silk. At first Pierrette refused to part with it, you know. Since I am undoubtedly one of her best customers, she was soon convinced—after I offered a generous price, of course."

Serena replied, "You know the girls and I intend to pay you back for all your expenses—"

"Pish, tosh!" Lady D said, waving a hand dismissively. "You will do no such thing. I told you before, the only recompense I require is that you, Bliss and Felicity use the knowledge I've given you to lead fulfilling lives as independent women, with all the pleasures the world has to offer. And being fabulously wealthy at the end of it all, like me, doesn't hurt, either." She smiled playfully. "Now, what jewels are you going to wear? Ahh...something special, I think."

Lady D opened the ornate cherry-wood jewelry box that stood on a nearby dresser and pulled out the largest diamond Serena had ever seen. "The Maharaja's Diamond? You want me to wear it?"

Lady D smiled, while holding the exquisite canary diamond pendant aloft. "Sitara—it means 'morning star.' The Maharaja and I watched the morning star many times together, after a passion-filled night in his palace. Sitara has always brought me good luck, and it is my hope that the stone will bring you the same good fortune."

Before Serena could protest further, Lady Devlyn was fastening the priceless bauble around Serena's neck. The magnificent jewel hung from a string of smaller white diamonds, which sparkled and winked against Serena's glowing skin. It felt heavenly.

"Ear bobs, of course." Lady D handed Serena a pair of matching tear-drop earrings. "And a bracelet, I think."

With the jewels adorning her, Serena felt an almost magical effect, which had undoubtedly been Lady Devlyn's intention. Serena felt beautiful, she felt powerful and in control. She was ready to become London's newest sensation.

Then why was her heart beating like the wings of a caged bird?

Perhaps it was the reality of what she was about to do.

Playtime was over. The moment she stepped out into the Lady Devlyn's salon, she would announce to the world that she, Serena Ransom, was a courtesan—a woman whose business it was to give a man pleasure.

It seemed a daunting vocation, now.

Lady D lifted Serena's chin with a slim finger, meeting her eyes. It seemed her benefactress could read minds, too. "Remember, my dear—-the men out there will be clamoring for your attention, just as Marc Antony and Caesar begged for Cleopatra's. And that is how you must act. Like a queen—and a queen needs no one. Least of all a man. If you believe that, then so will they. Men will fight duels over you. They will give up everything for you." Lady Devlyn gave a radiant smile. "And isn't that what it's all about?"

Serena took a deep breath. "Yes. That's what it's all about."

"But where are the other girls?" Lady Devlyn asked. "We cannot greet our guests without them."

"We're here!" Bliss called, as she and Felicity bustled into the room, the silk of their gowns swishing across the floor. Bliss' strawberry blonde curls were complimented by flowing sapphire blue silk, while Felicity's dark glossy locks were offset by a gown of emerald green. Felicity and Bliss were to make their debuts at a later date, but the men of the ton would get a peek at them tonight...and talk about them for weeks.

It was all part of Lady Devlyn's plan to make the Courtesan Club a wild success.

"Serena, you look breathtaking!" Felicity enthused, stepping forward to hug her.

Bliss gave her a quick hug as well. "You're a vision. You look like a Greek goddess in that golden gown. The men will go wild."

Lady D gave a languid smile. "Yes, my dear—the men will go wild for it. For her. For all of you. And isn't that what we set out to accomplish with the creation of the Courtesan Club—to bring the richest men in London to their knees?"

The girls regarded each other, their expressions a mixture of excitement, disbelief, and female pride. Now Miss Serena Ransom was about to make her debut as the first member of the Courtesan Club.

A confident smile danced across her lips and her veins hummed with excitement as she and her friends made their way toward the salon.

She hoped London was ready for her.

Darius Manning, Earl of Kane, took another sip from his crystal champagne flute and gazed about the opulent room. In one corner, a string quartet played a Mozart sonata. Footmen milled about serving hors d'eouvres from silver platters. It seemed to all the world like any other high society party. Except that the room was filled with men only, most of whom looked like wolves waiting for the poor little sheep to show up. Darius had to admit, his curiosity was getting the best of him as well.

Where was she?

"What do you think, Dare?" the man beside him asked languidly, popping a grape into his mouth. "Shall you entrap this virgin courtesan in your web tonight? Or will she entrap you?"

Darius flicked a brow at his companion. Major Havelock Price had stood by his side through the bloodiest battles of the Napoleonic Wars and knew him better than any other human being on earth. Still, Darius did not enjoy being thought predictable, especially regarding a woman he hadn't even met yet.

Darius admitted to being many things, a notorious rake and womanizer being chief among them, but predictable? That could sully a man's reputation.

"Gads, let's have a look at the chit before you have me bidding for her, will you? She may not be to my fancy," Darius said coolly.

Havelock tasted a morsel of soft cheese. "Not to your fancy? The only woman I ever knew who didn't strike your fancy was your wife, old friend. And considering what a harpy she was, it was completely understandable—-God rest her soul."

Darius turned and shot a dark look toward Havelock. "It does not become you to speak ill of the dead, my friend."

"Bloody hell— I did say, 'God rest her soul,'" Havelock said. "Forgive me, but Henrietta gave you nothing but grief. Ah, but that is not exactly true. She also gave you her father's immense fortune which saved your family name and estates. But then, that was your plan all along, wasn't it? I shouldn't have skipped over that part. Now you have the wife's fortune, the earldom in good standing, and you're on the market for a courtesan to entertain your nights without any messy complications. I'd say you're on top of the world, old chum."

Darius pondered his friend's words as he studied the other men in the room. Perhaps he should feel that way, considering he could out-bid any man here, even the young, brash duke at the billiard table.

He, the seventh Earl of Kane, was one of the wealthiest men in England. That fact alone had made him many enemies, namely the old families with ancient titles but no money left to run their crumbling estates. Havelock had spoken the truth. Darius had made a fortuitous marriage to Miss Henrietta Barton, heiress to a huge shipping fortune. He had not loved her, though his poor wife had fancied herself in love with him.

That had unfortunately been her undoing.

Darius reached for a succulent strawberry and pushed the unwelcome thoughts away. He'd spent enough time thinking about the women of his past. He was ready to move on.

And the first step in doing that was finding himself a new one to warm his bed.

He took a bite of the tart, luscious berry and decided that whoever this courtesan was, he would have her, for she was exactly what he needed.

Now that he was a widower, Darius was one of London's most sought-after bachelors. The Mad Mamas of the Marriage Mart hounded him at every turn. They all wanted their daughters to be the next Countess of Kane. Well, they could all go to Hades. After Henrietta, he had earned a respite from the shackles of matrimony. As his marriage had left him without an heir, of course he would have to marry again at some point. He had a duty to ensure the family legacy.

But duty could wait.

What he wanted now, was sex.

Pure and simple.

And who better than a courtesan to provide him with imaginative, passionate, uncomplicated sex? Even a mistress was uncomfortably close to being a wife, in his book. But a courtesan was something altogether different. She existed only to beguile and intrigue. Any courtesan trained by the famous Lady Night was bound to be a legend in her own right. The London papers had been talking about her for weeks, speculating on her identity, as well as to the level of her sinful skills. Yes, he would have this "mystery woman" as his own private courtesan. Only she could banish the memories of his past, which haunted him like malevolent ghosts.

A loud gong sounded, echoing throughout the salon and causing the men to murmur amongst themselves when they observed a strange sight indeed. A man appeared at the bottom of the curved, marble staircase. He stood at least six foot five inches tall, dressed in flowing pale orange silk pants and a brilliant gold vest that barely covered his massive bare chest. His skin was the color of bittersweet chocolate, his dark eyes flashed dangerously, and his face was adorned with strange tattoos. On his head sat a turban of darker orange silk, with a brilliant sapphire at the centre of his forehead. A single blue feather stood proudly in the air above the sparkling stone. The man's feet were clad in jeweled leather sandals, and a curved scimitar hung from his waist. His folded arms boasted bulging muscles the size of grapefruits.

Havelock gave Darius a nudge, looking impressed. "I don't know who this bloke is, but I certainly wish we'd had him with us at Waterloo. Boney would have pissed himself."

Some of the other gentlemen in the room appeared to be close to doing that, themselves. They had nervously taken a few steps back from the dangerous-looking man in the turban.

Darius tapped his finger on the armrest of his chair. "What else would you expect from a courtesan as experienced as Lady Night? She's bound to have a bodyguard or two in her employ. And this one looks as if he could take on ten men without breaking a sweat."

"So right," Havelock agreed. "Best not to upset him, I suppose. So when Lady Night and her new protégée appear, try to act like a gentleman."

"Don't I always, when dealing with the fairer sex?" he asked.

"You don't really want me to answer that, do you?" Havelock said wryly.

Darius quirked a brow. Just because he didn't offer to marry any of the women who gave themselves willingly to him for a night of passion, didn't mean he treated them with anything less than respect.

And he always paid for their carriage ride home in the morning.

The bodyguard clapped his massive hands twice. In a booming voice, accented with the inflections of a far-off land, he announced, "Gentlemen, may I present to you, Lady Night."

At that, the lady in question made her entrance, drawing appreciative murmurs and applause from the gentlemen present. She wore a gown of pale lavender silk, her arms clad in white gloves that stretched to the elbow. She fairly dripped in sparkling diamonds and amethysts. Her face was mature, but exquisitely beautiful. It wasn't difficult to imagine emperors and princes falling at her feet, which, apparently, more than a few had done.

"Handsome woman," Havelock said. "Didn't you say you'd met her once before, Dare?"

"Yes, in Bath, just before the war," he answered.

Though Lady Night had been attached to a rich Marquess at the time, the beautiful courtesan had flirted with an impoverished young earl named Darius Manning who was about to go off and fight Napoleon. She had even let him taste a kiss or two, completely free of charge. When he'd left that soiree, he'd felt like a king. The memory of her kiss had sustained him on more than one occasion during his darkest days in the war. For that, he would always thank her.

A mature woman, she was still breathtakingly beautiful. Though a few strands of grey appeared in her chestnut hair, it seemed to compliment the planes of her face—the high cheekbones, the intelligent blue eyes and full mouth. Legend had it she was now one of the richest women in the Kingdom; some of her fortune acquired through the generosity of her benefactors, and some through clever investments. Either way, Lady Night was a woman to remember. If her new protégée was anything like her, Dare mused, the men of London were about to be set into a tailspin from which they would never recover.

Lady Night flashed an entrancing smile at her guests in the packed salon. "Gentlemen, thank you for coming to my little soiree this evening. I am delighted that you have chosen to attend what surely proves to be the most unforgettable night of the Season. Though I have tried to keep news of my protégée under wraps, there has been much speculation about her existence in the press, no doubt which many of you have read. Why, a recent article in *The Sentinel* advised ladies of the *ton* to insist that their husbands remove themselves to the country, so as to protect them from this corrupt creature of Lady Night's creation. One article even suggested a most dreadful course of action: fleeing to the wilds of Scotland for safety!"

At this, robust laughter rolled through the crowd.

One man yelled out in a thick Scottish brogue, "I hail from Scotland, Lady Night, and I can tell ye, a Londoner would nae be safe up there, except for ye and yer bonnie lass we've come ta see!"

More chuckles sounded at this, and Lady Night joined in as well. "Indeed," she said. "A rather drastic scheme. And why? To deny you, the most powerful men in the Kingdom, the chance to make the acquaintance of a beautiful, educated, fascinating young woman—a woman who is unlike any you have met before. Be warned, she is fiercely independent, highly intelligent, and selective. She knows what she wants and will settle for nothing less. On top of all that, she is a virgin...as yet untouched by the passion of a man, but skilled in the knowledge of how to stoke that fire. I know this description will alarm some of the gentlemen here tonight," she said, with a sly look in her eyes, "but to the right man, one who is truly worthy of this exquisite creature's company, these will be attributes that will increase the pleasure—-and yes, gentlemen, there will be much pleasure—of their association."

Lady Night paused a moment, seeming to size up each man in the crowd before she continued.

"Before I introduce you to my new friend," she continued, "I ask that you remember two things: please keep the fisticuffs to a minimum, and duels, if they must be fought tonight, should be conducted on the East Lawn."

"That was quite the sales pitch," Havelock said in a low voice. "I particularly liked the closing remarks. Genius, really."

Darius glanced at his friend, and said, "The thing about it is, if this girl is half as good as her predecessor, there might indeed be a duel on the East Lawn."

"Did you bring your pistol?" Havelock asked casually.

"Of course, but I won't be needing it," Darius said. "I can outbid every man here."

"Even our friend, the Duke of Balfour?"

"Even him, though I should much prefer the excuse of shooting him," Darius answered.

"Balfour hates to lose. You might require that pistol after all," Havelock pronounced.

Darius raised a brow. "Be glad I'm a crack shot. As my

second you will only have to stand there and look pretty. Much as you did at Waterloo."

"Ha, ha." Havelock said, dryly. "If they only knew how many times I saved your sorry arse from Boney's cronies, not to mention Balfour's idiot regiment."

Darius grinned, but didn't reply. He and Havelock had both saved each other's hides during the war; they had lost count who had saved whose more often. By Darius' calculations, they were tied, though Havelock liked to insist he was ahead by one.

"And now, gentlemen, Your Grace," Lady Night nodded at the Duke of Balfour, as he was the highest ranking peer in attendance. The King had promised to come, but his current mistress, Lady Conyngham, has apparently put up quite a fuss at the suggestion. "I give you, the Incomparable Serena...."

A hush descended upon the room as a figure appeared at the top of the wide staircase. Clad in a shimmering golden gown, she stood for a moment, as if she were in no hurry to even acknowledge the throng of salivating men who awaited her on the salon floor. Glittering diamonds adorned her ears and neck, with one magnificent teardrop pendant hanging enticingly between the tops of her creamy, full breasts. Beautiful, thick auburn locks crowned her head in an intricate arrangement, interwoven with gleaming white pearls. Finally, this woman—whom the most powerful men in London had come to see—faced her audience in the salon below.

Darius stared up at her and almost dropped his champagne flute onto the marble the floor.

"Sweet Christ," he growled. "*It's her.*"

Short Story Collections by Michelle McMaster

Summer Passions

Seasons of Love Volume I
Three Delicious Regency Short Stories

"A lady should enjoy those hot summer nights..."

For three lovely ladies in Regency England, the long, hot summer holds the opportunity for decadent pleasures, wicked pursuits, and forbidden passion.

Cupid's Dart

The Marquess of St. Clair has long been a thorn in Daphne Summerville's side. But when she is forced to act as his nursemaid after a bizarre accident, Daphne discovers that the Notorious Marquess has sensual talents she never knew existed.

Lady Ashton Takes a Lover

Lady Ashton's friends finally convince her to take a lover for the summer. At a wicked masquerade ball, she meets a mysterious man who fires her passions and turns her world completely upside down, threatening all she holds dear.

The Wedding Party

Jilted by her intended, Lady Althea Ramsay calls in a favor from her brother's friend, the Duke of Wakefield. He will pose as her fiancé at a society wedding which the odious man will be attending. But Althea soon discovers that playing a part can set real desires burning in the human heart.

Autumn Desires

Seasons of Love Volume II

When autumn leaves start to fall, passions burn like fire...

The second volume in the delightful SEASONS OF LOVE quartet features three unforgettable Regency heroines in three delectable, entertaining short stories.

The Taming Of Miss Carew

Helena "the Hellion" Carew takes pride in speaking her mind, even if it sends most eligible bachelors packing. When her father loses his estate—and Helena—in a card game, she meets the brutish Lord Adrian Rutherford, the one man who has a chance at taming her.

Branded

Abandoned by her husband, Lady Alexandra Trent lives a quiet life in the countryside with her young son, trying desperately to forget the man who left her heart in tatters. But when Brandon returns, he awakens dangerous desires and makes a shocking demand of his wife.

Thief Of Hearts

Olivia and Jack are two of London's most notorious jewel thieves. Skilled and passionate lovers, they take each other to the heights of physical pleasure, yet keep their true feelings secret. As they prepare for their next heist, Olivia discovers something about Jack that could change their lives forever.

ABOUT THE AUTHOR

MICHELLE MCMASTER loves writing about dashing heroes and spunky heroines in her historical romances, and is known for humorous dialogue and memorable characters. Michelle holds a degree in English Literature from Dalhousie University, Nova Scotia. She enjoys traveling, reading, quilting, and gardening. She lives on the east coast of Canada with her husband and their two dogs, a Nova Scotia Duck Tolling Retriever and a Border Collie mix. Please visit her website at www.MichelleMcMaster.com for more information about her novels and to sign up for her email newsletter to stay informed about future new releases.

If you enjoy fast paced thrillers, Michelle McMaster also writes under the pen name Avery Holt. Check out her website at www.AveryHolt.com and look for her exciting *Watch Me* series.

www.ingramcontent.com/pod-product-compliance
Lightning Source LLC
Chambersburg PA
CBHW030319200626
46816CB00006BA/1852